THE HARD STUFF

THE HARD STUFF

Karin Tabke
Bonnie Edwards
Sunny

APHRODISIA

KENSINGTON PUBLISHING CORP.

www.kensingtonbooks.com

APHRODISIA books are published by

Kensington Publishing Corp.
850 Third Avenue
New York, NY 10022

All Kensington titles, imprints, and distributed lines are available at special quantity discounts for bulk purchases for sales promotion, premiums, fund-raising, educational, or institutional use.

Special book excerpts or customized printings can also be created to fit specific needs. For details, write or phone the office of the Kensington Special Sales Manager: Attn. Special Sales Department. Kensington Publishing Corp., 850 Third Avenue, New York, NY 10022. Phone: 1-800-221-2647.

Aphrodisia and the A logo are trademarks of Kensington Publishing Corp. Kensington and the K logo Reg. U.S. Pat. & TM Off.

ISBN 0-7582-1408-1

First Kensington Trade Paperback Printing: January 2006
10 9 8 7 6 5 4 3 2 1

Printed in the United States of America

Contents

Stakeout

Karin Tabke

I want to thank my real life Hot Cop, my husband Gary, for never allowing me to quit, and to my editor Hilary Sares for hanging in there with me.

1

"Who said size doesn't matter?" Stevie asked.

Must have been a little man with a little . . .

She whistled admiringly at the package, grateful for the unexpected perk.

Grinning, she dragged her eyes for a breathless second from the high-powered telescope and looked over her shoulder. The last thing she wanted was for one of the task force guys her lieutenant insisted on saddling her with to think she was some hard-up sexpot.

She laughed out loud. Okay, maybe she was. It had been too long since she last felt the sinful pressure of a man between her legs. And it wasn't because she was a prude. Unfortunately, the most intriguing prospects were the same ones she'd sworn off for years. Cops.

She'd learned the hard way not to be the company inkwell. Too many hassles. Too many knowing grins from her fellow officers, followed by suggestive wolf whistles.

Nope, she made damn sure she wasn't the hot topic of any

lineup. Besides, since her promotion to detective two years ago, she didn't have time for a relationship anyway.

She shrugged and focused back on her subject.

Mario Vincente Spoltori, aka Rocky. Not an original alias, but hell, the man was a walking hard-on. And she bet he gave granite a run for its money.

She'd been surveilling the *escort* for nearly a week, and finally after tedious hours of watching the paint dry, she got her first look at what the privileged ladies of Sacramento couldn't get enough of.

And mamma mia, there was plenty to go around.

She couldn't blame the ladies who waited months to get an hour of this notorious stud's time. No more than she could help that familiar tingle between her legs. Not for Mario. As delightful as she was sure he was in the sack, she was more straight-laced. One-nighters weren't something she actively pursued. She'd only had one in her life, and although it was the best sex she'd ever had, and she would have followed the guy to the ends of the earth, the whole experience left her feeling . . . well, tawdry.

He never called.

No use thinking about a guy she'd never see again.

Prick.

Shaking her head, Stevie gave rock-hard Rocky her full attention, and for a minute put aside the fact he was the reason she'd worked round the clock for the last three months.

She laughed and thought how ironic her current predicament was. Here she was, a perfectly healthy female, and she was considering paying for stud service. Her life was too hectic for anything less than the occasional quickie. And as picky as she was, her options were severely limited.

Strictly as a woman to his man, Stevie considered Rocky's slick muscles and generous endowment. She sighed. Too bad she wasn't into this kind of stuff.

He bent over, flexing his taut ass at her, and continued the slow slide of his underwear down his thighs before he kicked them off.

Well . . . *maybe* . . . nah. Besides, on her cop salary she'd have to give up a lot of somethings for a roll in the hay with the likes of the Italian Stallion across the way.

"Oh, you selfish bastard."

What a waste. Looked like Adonis was sneaking some of the goodies. As big as his cock was, his hand was larger. He stood stark naked facing her in front of his exposed window and stared across the wide boulevard that separated their respective buildings.

He smirked, closed his eyes, tilted his head back, and put on a show. If she didn't know better, she'd swear he knew he had an audience.

Impossible. While his windows were transparent, the small, stuffy office she'd begun to detest had a dark film covering the window, with just a small square cut out for her ever-watchful eyes. No way could he know he was under surveillance.

Stevie dismissed that thought and instead zeroed her attention back on what God had so benevolently given the man. His long dark fingers grasped his rod and in a slow pump he manipulated it to staggering proportions. Stevie licked her dry lips.

Jesus.

His hips ground against an imaginary pussy and he bit at his bottom lip.

Faster and faster and faster he pumped. Stevie's breath held when he splayed himself up against the window, still pumping. Her skin warmed. She didn't want to get sucked in by his erotic display, but she did nonetheless.

She screamed and about jumped out of her skin when the pressure of a large hand squeezed her shoulder.

"Am I interrupting?"

Her shock caused her to lose her balance and fall backward

off her chair. As she was trying to catch herself, two large, very capable hands grabbed her. The touch sent shock waves through her body. She had the undeniable inclination to rub herself up against the hard thigh that supported her back.

"Christ, what the hell?" she yelled, collecting herself and sitting up. Quickly she twisted around and pulled her piece.

She felt the blood drain from her face.

Son of a bitch.

"Jack Thornton."

"It's been a long time, Detective Cavanaugh." His grin rivaled a wide-open barn door. He seemed taller, more muscled. The faint smile lines at the corners of his deep-set hazel eyes accentuated his natural mischievous nature.

She braced herself.

Humiliation and excitement riveted through her, running neck and neck for the finish line. Her skin flushed hot and she resisted the urge to lick her dry lips.

Instead, she did what any woman scorned would do. She stood up and slapped him. Hard. White imprints of her fingers stood boldly out against the tan of his cheek. Before her hand returned home, he grabbed it. He yanked her hard against him, the connection forcing her breath from her chest. Her sensitive nipples stiffened against the hardness of his chest.

"Was that because I didn't call you or because I wouldn't let you get on top?"

Visions of their sweaty, naked bodies writhing in passion amongst the twisted sheets in her academy dorm room sprang to mind. Jack Thornton could give Rocky across the way a few lessons in pleasing a woman. Her chest tightened while other emotions she chose to ignore vied for playtime.

Stevie's breath hitched high in her throat. "That was because you're an egotistical bastard." She pushed hard against him. He released her. She holstered her Sig.

Thorn continued to grin, but the harsh glare of his eyes belied his mirth. "What's so egotistical about making love to a beautiful woman?"

Despite the warmth of the room, her nipples stood at full mast. Stevie pulled on her jacket. The last thing she wanted was to give his inquiring eyes a show.

"More like seducing a virgin."

Thorn moved in closer. "That was your choice, Stevie, not mine." He grinned like an idiot. "By the way, thanks for picking me."

After so many years, the shock of seeing the only man she'd ever had feelings for forced her off balance. The sensation left her angry, and scared.

He backed up at her fist.

"Go ahead, dickhead," she said, "keep the BS coming, I don't need more of an excuse to nail you."

"I need less of one to nail you." He stepped forward, his face a happy place. "Since we're both in agreement, what do you say, my place after we're done here?"

"Pig."

"Pride in Grace, don't I know it."

Stevie couldn't believe it. The only guy she'd dreamed about stood in front of her more than willing to go back down that seductive road with her. If her pride weren't at stake, and her heart unwilling to get squashed again, she'd have her running shoes on.

"What are you doing here?"

Casually he walked past her and looked out the tinted window. He gave the long expanse of buildings quiet contemplation. As if he'd just come back from a coffee break, he righted the tipped-over chair, then sat down and focused in across the way.

"Hmm, looks like the Italian Stallion over there needs clean up on aisle nine."

Regaining her composure, Stevie swung the lens from him,

and squatting level with it, she zeroed in herself. Geez, Rocky had his chum all over the window. "I swear, you guys just love to spread that stuff around, don't you?"

Thorn pulled the lens his way and refocused. "Yeah, it's what we do. Men hunt and propagate the species, women nurture and gather. Basic."

Stevie's eyes narrowed. Neanderthal. She'd been too starry-eyed to see it in the academy seven years ago; at least *she'd* evolved since then.

She pulled the lens back her way and focused on Rocky. "That's it, clean up your mess," she said to the gigolo. Then, as if to herself, she said, "I wonder if there was some kind of statute back then about instructors fraternizing with students?"

Thorn leaned in behind her. "No." His hot breath against her ear stirred up old familiar heat. His clean, woodsy scent engulfed her. Her blood thickened in her veins and whatever hormones she had that induced sex surged through her body. She clenched her muscles before they turned to warm mush.

Stevie remembered how she couldn't wait for her defensive tactics classes. Sergeant Jack Thornton was the instructor, and she repeatedly paid with bruises to be his test dummy.

She almost laughed. She'd had such a crush on him from the get-go. Little did she know she'd end up his parting gift.

"How's the wife and kid?"

He pulled away. "You know my divorce was final before graduation." His eyes clouded. "My stepson is with his father."

Stevie inhaled a deep breath and slowly exhaled. She didn't give a rat's ass about his home life.

"What are you doing here, Thorn?"

He grinned and stood back from the telescope. Casually he pulled back his Italian-cut suit and said, "Special Agent Thornton at your service, ma'am."

She hissed in a long breath, giving him a sideways glare. So the rumors were true. He'd dumped her for Quantico. "You damned feds, why the hell can't you leave us locals alone? Go fight your own crime."

She turned away from him, settled back on the chair he'd vacated, and refocused on Studly. "Now you made me lose him. Get out of here."

"Sorry, detective, your crime has become our crime. We're taking over from here."

"That's a crock, Thornton. Me and my men have been working this case around the clock since the first body showed up. County is coming in to help out, and I'm lead dick." She smiled tightly, keeping her eyes focused on Spoltori. "You've been misinformed."

When there was no response from him, she looked up to find him staring down at her. His eyes narrowed and a slow tic worked his right jawline. "I'm not going to get into a pissing match with you, Cavanaugh. Your chief requested we come in. We're here, I'm heading up the task force."

Stevie sprang out of the chair, throwing her shoulders back. Her antagonism mushroomed when he chuckled and said, "You've been assigned to tag along for the ride." He lowered his voice as if there were others in the room who had no business listening in on their conversation. "And, Stevie, I promise you a helluva ride."

Fury infiltrated every cell she possessed. She worked her fists open and closed. "You've got a hell of a lot of nerve coming in here, telling me you're taking over my case and then propositioning me. Do you think so damned much of yourself or so little of me?"

Thorn's wide-eyed reaction gave her a modicum of satisfaction. He quickly recovered. "I'm sorry if I've given you the impression I have no respect for you, detective." He grinned. "I think I can say with some accuracy you're one of the best cops out there. You should be, I trained you."

"You trained me all right." The words escaped before she

could call them back. He not only mentored her in the classroom and spent countless hours coaching her on the shooting range and defensive tactics, but he taught her how to ride out an orgasm for maximum satisfaction among other sexy little tricks. She squashed the memories and the heat that accompanied them.

Never bashful, she gave her one-night stand a long discriminating look. She would never admit she liked what she saw. He was taller than her five-eight by a good half a foot. His shoulders looked like a linebacker's, built into a rock-hard chest that tapered down to a washboard belly and further to a package that never reclined. The guy had the stamina of a prize bull.

She snorted in contempt. "You taught me my biggest life lesson to date." She traced a finger down his silk tie. "Trust no one." She stepped back and added, "By the way, I don't go for carnie rides."

His full lips slid into a tantalizing smile. His long tanned fingers slid into his trouser pockets. "Anytime you change your mind, detective, let me know."

"Don't hold your breath. You'll suffocate if you do."

She turned back to Rocky. He still wasn't there. Probably in the shower. Their guy had an unhealthy fixation with showerheads.

Thorn pulled up the only other piece of furniture in the empty office. A straight-back chair.

"Look, Stevie, I took this case on to work with you, not against you."

Her gut clenched. "You knew this was my case?"

He nodded. "I always do my homework. Tell you what, you can keep your people, but understand they'll have to get along with mine."

Her anger flashed. This was her case, damn it! She'd be damned if she'd just step aside.

"C'mon, detective, show me yours and I'll show you mine," Thorn offered.

Stevie grunted and, knowing he wanted to trade information, she gave him something else. She pulled her Sig. "Mine's loaded."

He smiled again, his white teeth gleaming in the filtered afternoon light. "Mine's bigger." He pulled a mini assault pistol from his shoulder holster.

Stevie whistled. "Nice piece." Replacing her weapon, she reached out her hand, palm up. "Can I touch it?"

His grin turned lethal. He handed her the weapon, his fingertips brushing her palm. Stevie ignored the warm flush the contact instigated.

"Be careful, it's cocked and will discharge at the slightest provocation."

Stevie ignored him, and ran her fingers along the smooth cold steel. She wanted one.

"The magazine holds twenty-two rounds and can discharge the whole wad in less than two seconds."

Her eyes met his. A flash of heat speared her pussy. "What's the fun in that?"

He reached out his hand and slowly withdrew the pistol, the short barrel sliding against her moist palm. In a quick movement he ejected the magazine and replaced it with another one he pulled from his jacket pocket. "Lots. It's ready for firing in less time than it takes to clean up from the first barrage."

Stevie ignored the warm wetness between her thighs and the way his nostrils flared like a dog sniffing its mate's sex.

She recognized trouble when she met it. She couldn't do this. "I'll pack up and leave you and Studly to get to know each other."

She bent down to pick up her backpack, but he grabbed her arm and pulled her up and against him. The palpable tension jolted them both. "You're not going anywhere, detective. You know this guy better than his mother. You're stuck with me."

She yanked her arm.

"Take it up with your lui if you have a problem."

A rill of frustration swept through her. The last thing she wanted was to spend her days in this stuffy office across the street from a serial killing man–whore, and watch the guy do half of Sacramento's political wives, with her ex-lover breathing down her neck. She glanced at the three photos of the lifeless victims she'd tacked up on the wall, a constant reminder of why she was there. Her gut somersaulted.

She could do this with her own people, she was a proven detective. But now? With Thorn as a constant distraction? She scowled. No way.

"Sorry to burst your bubble, but I'll quit before I'd hole up with you eight hours a day waiting to get a lead on Romeo over there."

His eyes narrowed, their gold-green irises flaring jade. "I thought you were better trained than that, detective. Can't stand a little heat? What the hell kind of cop are you anyway?"

That did it. She went toe to toe with him. In the breath of a second she was in his face, her chin notched high, her eyelids narrowed, her back stiffened. "The kind that has some integrity and doesn't have to put up with a sex-crazed fed."

"Chicken."

"Taunting me won't get you a thing, Thorn. I don't *have to* work with you. I *won't* work with you. I'd rather spend the day with Lothario over there and take my chances. At least with him I won't have to play games."

He laughed deeply. "I don't play games, detective. I play for real." He leaned into her, his face only a few inches from hers. She could see the golden flecks in his eyes and smell the minty warmth of his breath. "That guy is connected to three dead women, and I aim to nab him before he does another one. Take another look at those faces, detective." He pointed at the wall of death.

Dead eyes stared at her, begging to be put to rest.

"*I'd* work with the Wicked Witch of the West if it would bring the victims justice."

Her fists clenched and unclenched. Damn him! "My responsibility is also to the victims. But how the hell am I supposed to do my job with you breathing down my neck like a dog denied?"

"Consider it an adverse condition and deal with it."

Stevie growled. As much as she didn't want to work with Thorn she wanted to nail Spoltori more. She had a responsibility to the families of the victims and to the victims themselves. No one deserved to die the way those women had. She smiled blithely. Not even Jack Thornton.

"I'll work with you, *Jack*. But let's get a few facts straight first. You touch me, I punch you." She grabbed a handful of her breasts. She smiled inwardly at his sharp intake of breath. "These are mine. I only share if I want to. Touch them and I'll geld you."

Thorn laughed, the sound deep and mellow. "Oh, Stevie, I wish I'd had another day to spend with you."

She stepped back, sliding her hands into her jeans pockets. How many times through her haze of anger when she discovered him gone had she wished for the same thing?

"Yeah, me too. It would have taken me no time to skin you alive."

She was spared Thorn's response when another suit walked in. She deduced before Thorn's intro he was another fed.

"Detective Cavanaugh, meet Agent Deavers. He's my communications specialist."

Stevie extended her hand to the tall, handsome agent. "I'd say I'm glad to meet you, Deavers, but under the circumstances I'm feeling a little bit cheated."

He nodded and gave Thorn a knowing look. "We get that a lot."

Stevie gave Thorn a hard look. "We're already set up in my office, what do you say we use that as HQ for our party?"

Both men nodded, and it was a small consolation.

2

She should have known. Jack Thornton was a guy who did what he wanted, when he wanted, and on his own terms.

So, when she entered the gloomy office to begin another day of watching Mario Spoltori, suspected lady killer, shower and rub himself down with assorted oils, she shouldn't have been surprised when she found Jack already there, comfortably leaning into his own high-powered set of binoculars. Selfish bastard. He looked all cozy and dug in.

"Have a problem with sharing, *sir*?"

His gleaming white teeth glowed against the soft wash of morning sunlight that filtered through the—Damn it!

"You cut another hole out of the film? What do you think this is, a peep show?" *What a perv.*

Thorn stood and walked over to a small table that wasn't there yesterday and poured a cup of coffee from a pot that also wasn't there yesterday. He sipped slowly, watching her over his cup. "Did it ever occur to you that two sets of eyes are better than one?"

Yeah, it occurred to her all right. She'd spent a fitful night tossing and turning in her cold bed. The thought of both her and Jack witnessing what was bound to be an x-rated peep show had done a number on her. She didn't know if she'd be able to maintain her composure sitting next to the only man who had satisfied her, repeatedly, while watching Mario satisfy either himself or his lady Johns, repeatedly.

She opened her mouth to protest his presence. She quickly closed it when she noticed an empty cup sitting next to the coffee pot. *Coffee.* She didn't ask, she poured.

"You're welcome."

"Leave me be." Shoving past him, she plopped down on her chair, careful not to slosh coffee all over herself.

Just as she began to focus in on Mario her cell phone rang. "Cavanaugh."

"It's Sloan."

"If you're calling to tell me about my new fed friends, Lieutenant, you're a day late."

"Those bastards don't waste time."

She shot Thorn a heated glare. "Apparently not, sir. What happened to teaming up with County?"

"Chief Jordan happened. He's getting leaned on hard by the governor. So give Thornton your full cooperation. I'm taking enough heat from the chief on this case. I hear this fed is top dog in Nor Cal."

Yeah, he was top dog all right. And she remembered all too vividly him pumping into her from behind, doggy style. Her thighs flinched and her skin flushed warm. "Yes, sir."

Covertly she watched Thorn from beneath her lashes. His scent lingered in the air. He smelled like a walk through a park on a spring day. Clean, masculine. His square jaw glowed smooth from a recent shave. She watched his fingers turn the plastic lens rotors, focusing his scope.

She remembered all too well what those long, thick appendages were capable of.

Abruptly her lui's frustrated voice snapped her out of her

trip down memory lane. "Cavanaugh! You said that too fast and too easy. Give me your word you won't hinder this investigation."

She grimaced. He knew her control-freak nature all too well. "I have no intention of letting a murderer get away because of my personal feelings, sir."

Thorn's body tensed. He looked at her expectantly, and gave her the cut-off signal.

"Gotta go, sir. I'll keep you informed."

"Quick," Thorn said. "Focus in on the living room, our boy has a visitor."

Excitement zipped through her. This would be the first. Over the past week, she'd only had the pleasure of watching Mario indulge himself in himself. Now she'd see what all the hoopla was about.

The visitor surprised her. A man. White and balding. "Turn around," she muttered. While she had a great shot of the back of his head, he managed to keep his face obscured. "Did you get an initial look at him?"

"No, our boy got in the way."

"Maybe the video caught it."

"Maybe. They seem to be having some type of meeting."

"Looks that way." She gave Thorn a quick glance before focusing back on Mario and his guest. "You know our boy is into dominance and submission. According to the D&S chat rooms I've lurked in, he's the master, in more ways than one."

"You learn anything?"

She speared him with a glare, then turned back to watching the two men comfortably chat over a cup of coffee.

"Yeah, people who are into this stuff are either tops or bottoms. Rocky's renowned for being the master of tops." Both men set down their cups and Mario led the man into another room off the living room, the only one with no visibility.

"Damn," she grumbled. "The one place we can't watch. I

have no idea what's in that room. It doesn't show up on the floor plan. For all we know it could be a hidden chamber of horrors."

"Distinct possibility. Considering two of the three vics had contusions around the wrists and ankles consistent with restraints."

"Yeah, and Alderman Keenan's wife had what appeared to be lash marks across her breasts and genitalia. It wasn't play stuff. More like a top out of control. Did you review her autopsy report?"

Standing so close to Stevie that she felt his heat, Thorn continued to focus. "Yeah. The way she was tortured, I got the feeling the guy who did it wasn't a big fan of the alderman's wife."

Somewhere along the way, the play had ended and the fight for her life had begun. Poor woman. Her fingernails were broken and her knuckles bruised from her battle to survive. Unfortunately, no skin or fluid samples were retrieved. The killer had made sure of that by dousing her body with embalming fluid.

"Yeah, she went down fighting. I respect that in a woman," Thorn said.

"Since when do you respect women?"

"I've always respected women. That's why they like me so much."

She heard the grin in his voice and refused to acknowledge it. She'd just keep her mouth shut, her fingers crossed, and say a prayer they'd get enough on Mario to put him away. And if they were real lucky, they'd make a strong enough case ensuring death by lethal injection.

"Whatever you say, sir."

The creak of the chair told her he'd moved away from the lens. She kept her eyes sharply focused on Mario's apartment. Only by concentrating on the case could she totally tune out

Thorn. Or at least try. He sure as hell wasn't making it easy. Neither were the damned recurring memories of his stoking her into orgasmic oblivion.

"You disappoint me, Stevie. What happened to the hellcat I knew in the academy?"

"She turned into a safe, boring kitten."

He laughed. "I doubt that." He leaned toward her, bringing his warm scent with him. "Maybe safe isn't so bad after all. More of a challenge to corrupt into dangerous."

Continuing to look through the lens and disappointed that Rocky and his friend hadn't emerged, she answered, "No danger zones. I've officially blown off men."

"Oh, now that *is* a shame. I was hoping we could blow off some steam together, later on."

She smiled. Couldn't help it. "What did you have in mind?"

"Oh, just your basic, everyday, head-banging sex."

"I don't fraternize."

He leaned closer, his warm breath brushing across her cheek. "Pity. I've missed feeling your nails in my back."

"I don't miss the manicures."

"I didn't forget about you."

Inhaling sharply, Stevie caught her breath. She hadn't expected that, but she didn't buy it either. Damned if she'd be bowled over by his smooth lines again. "I can't say the same. I vaguely remember you weren't bad between the sheets." Or that he could make her smile just by entering the room. Or that he never treated her as anything less than his equal. Man, she'd had it bad for him back then.

He laughed low, the soft percussion of his breath heating her skin. "Really? You don't remember how all I had to do was breathe on you and you came?"

She worked her jaw. A flush of heat streamed across her chest. Shit, her nipples speared the inside of her bra, aching for his mouth to suck them down his throat.

"If you don't shut up and get back to work, I'm gonna smack you."

He chuckled and slowly withdrew. "Promises, promises."

"Yeah," she muttered, "tell me about it."

She felt his gaze on her for a long minute before he focused back on Mario.

"I bet Rocky has an S&M chamber," Thorn said.

"He'd have to, he's a renowned switcher."

"Switcher?"

"He goes both ways, top and bottom. From what I hear though, he demands big bucks to be the bottom. Which, after I finalized my psych profile on him, makes sense." She had Thorn's rapt attention. "The man does not like to submit, he thrives on control. So he'd have to be hugely rewarded to allow himself exposure. I've discovered from the chat rooms that bottoms like to be locked up in dog cages. And that the masters, or toppers, are hard-core control freaks."

Thorn nodded. "That would explain why two of the vics had restraint injuries and Donna Rios didn't. From all accounts, she was the control freak."

"If that's the case, how would an assemblyman's secretary come up with the thousands it would have cost for Spoltori to play bottom to her top?"

"Maybe she didn't pay, maybe she just pissed him off."

Stevie chewed her bottom lip thoughtfully. She hadn't considered that angle. Thorn's statement had merit.

"You may have hit on something, Thorn. Her death seemed to be the catalyst. We found her while she was still warm. He made it easy, spreading her out on the steps to the capitol under the full moon."

"And the other two, same deal, different full moon and different state building."

Stevie rubbed the kink in her neck. The only link to the gigolo that each victim had was an unlisted cell phone number in her PDA that traced back to one Mario Vincente Spoltori. The frustrating part was, while there were several calls from each of the dead women to the cell number, there were no return calls from the cell number or any other numbers connected to Mario. It wasn't much, but it was enough for her to know in her gut that Spoltori was the man.

"We need a warrant for each of the victim's computers," Thorn said.

"Good idea, I also know Spoltori goes by TopMaster in certain chat rooms. I bet both Rios's home and office systems will link her to one of those rooms."

Thorn swiped his hand across his chin. "Obtaining a warrant for Rios's work computer won't be easy. Assemblyman Keller isn't going to be happy about that."

"Too effing bad. Use your fed muscle and get the governor involved."

What they needed more was to get inside Spoltori's apartment. Just for a little look-see.

"Mario seems to be going up the chain of command with his killings. First a capitol secretary. Next the county super's wife, and now Alderman Keenan's wife. At this rate he's going to take out a congressman's wife."

Stevie pulled back from the lens. "Crap!" She pulled her cell and called into the task force secretary requesting a complete list of state assemblymen, congressmen, and representatives.

"I could have saved you the call, detective. That info is on its way over as we speak."

"Show off."

"Hardly. I spent half the night wondering *why* political wives."

"Maybe he's got a thing about power. It's obvious from the sadistic nature of his kills he's into total control."

Stevie poured herself another cup of coffee, contemplating Mario's motives. "Look at the guy. With the exception of his eyebrows, he doesn't have a hair on his body. He spends more time in the shower shaving and scrubbing himself than he does out of the shower. He's a fanatic in the gym. From this vantage point, his apartment is as neat as a pin. If one carpet fiber were moved he'd know about it. I don't think I've ever come across a person so religiously in control of himself and his surroundings."

"The guy is tweaked for sure," Thorn said. "Probably obsessive compulsive. I think something must have snapped, though. Some incident incited him to kill. Maybe he's lost control in some important aspect of his life, something that's connected to these ladies. He's lost enough control that he feels he must wield it over his victims by torturing them, and then present them in such a way for us to know *he has* control."

She nodded vigorously. "Yes, yes. That would explain why, with the exception of the first, he kills them clean. Broken necks don't make a mess." Stevie shivered. He broke more than their necks. He started at their feet, breaking the tiny bones in their toes, then crushing the kneecap. He worked his way up, until the pain must have been so unbearable his victims passed out.

Stevie's blood chilled. She could see it in Rocky. Mr. Anal Compulsive Spoltori. Everything must be neat and orderly, in its place. She almost wanted to laugh. He'd scream a bloody riot if he ever had the occasion to visit her house. He'd kill her for the hell of it when he got a gander at her less than stellar housekeeping techniques.

In all fairness to herself, she wasn't technically a slob. She just never seemed to have time to toss stuff out. So she ended up with strategic piles in her house.

Thorn continued to muse out loud. "Could be he's making a statement. Maybe he's serving notice to someone very powerful on the Hill."

"Yeah, maybe he's got an agenda and he's setting the precedent, letting the players know he's not messing around and to take him seriously."

During the course of the conversation it occurred to Stevie just how much she was enjoying their brainstorming. While she certainly was attracted to Jack Thornton as a man, she was just as intrigued by his brain. She admired the way it worked, the way it processed so efficiently.

Another fact that hit like ice water in the face was how compatible they were. When one of them thought it, the other spoke it. She couldn't remember having enjoyed a discussion with a fellow cop as much as she did just now with Jack.

Thorn pulled his cell phone from his jacket. "I'm going to find out what big bills are looming. I also want a financial on this guy."

"I've got it. It was one of the first things I ran. For charging two grand an hour, the guy doesn't have much of a portfolio." She sighed. "I'd sure like to get a look in his place."

Thorn snorted. "I pulled every string I could to get a search warrant."

"Me too, the judges wouldn't touch it."

Thorn focused back on Mario, and Stevie said, "In the last week, he hasn't gone anywhere but his regular haunts. The tail we have on him has stuck to him like a fly on a turd."

Thorn pulled back from the lens and looked directly at her. "He's due. The next full moon is Sunday night. I suggest we pull in a round the clock team."

Stevie nodded and turned back to the lens. "What we need to do is find his secret room."

"Yeah, well, if one of us could turn invisible we'd have a chance, but that's not going to happen anytime soon."

Stevie smiled. Maybe not invisible, but what about the obvious?

Spoltori and his visitor left together. Knowing her men were tailing him, Stevie told Jack she had some computer work to get out of the way and a few phone calls to make. To her relief, he opted to stay and wait for Spoltori's return.

After a heart-to-heart with her chief and lui, Stevie got to work. She logged into the one chat room where she knew Spoltori frequented, and logged on to her messenger server. She smiled. An icon next to Spoltori's screen name, TopMaster, showed he was accepting text messages. She shot one off.

In the time it took to make a pot of coffee her cell phone beeped. She read the cryptic text message. She had her answer. Stevie popped her head into her lui's office and gave him a thumbs up. He returned the gesture and Stevie grinned. She'd show Agent Thornton who had a better handle on this case.

Striding back into the cramped, stuffy office she gave Thornton's back a long, appreciative look. Heat swelled between her legs and she silently cursed. The guy was a stud, no doubt about it. In the years since her one-nighter with him she hadn't been a nun. But when you started with Grade A Prime it was hard to settle for chopped liver.

"Are you staring holes in my back?"

He turned to face her and Stevie raised her eyes to his. Her lips twisted in a mocking smile. "No, I was just thinking about the pain I would inflict if you were my slave."

He stood.

"You should be watching Romeo," she said after a hard swallow.

"Romeo's still out, the guys are on him."

In a slow saunter he moved closer, stalking her. Her heartbeat accelerated and she wanted to tell him to back off. But the weakness in her knees and the moisture between her thighs wanted something else.

"Stay away from me. I'm not interested."

He stopped several feet from her. "Then why are you envisioning me in handcuffs and you torturing me with that sinful mouth of yours?"

"Hardly what I had in mind."

His lips turned up into a sly smile. "Tell me what you *did* have in mind."

Unexpectedly she decided playing with Jack might be fun. Especially if he was the one left hanging. She smiled seductively. "You got the handcuff part right."

"Am I naked?"

Her heart stuttered. "Oh yeah, not a stitch. Spread-eagle on your back."

"Am I hard?"

"Like a rock."

"Do you touch me?"

She nodded. "Yeah, I touch you. A lot."

"Where?"

"First, your cock. I run my hands up and down the length of you. So slowly you jerk against my fingers begging me to go faster and harder." She stepped closer to him. Her skin warmed to her play. "When I don't, you beg louder. I resist. I just run my palm up and down your cock, up and down, stopping at the head, squeezing it—hard. You moan and thrust against me."

Thorn didn't flinch, but she knew what the sharp glint in his dark eyes meant. Slowly, she took a deep breath and exhaled just as slowly. If he touched her she just might be the one begging.

"Slowly I strip down to just my panties and straddle you. You crane your neck wanting to lick me." She stepped back, and slowly shook her head as her eyes locked with his. "But I don't let you."

Thorn ran his tongue along his bottom lip. A soft sheen of perspiration highlighted the rugged planes of his face. "I let my hair down and run the tips along your belly and down between your legs." Stevie sucked her bottom lip in and moaned softly.

"Oh, Jack, you're begging louder now, pleading with me to suck you." She flicked her long braid over her shoulder and moved closer. "I bend down and lick around your belly button, and follow that sexy line of downy hair down to the base of your cock without touching it. Then I suck and lick the sensitive skin between your thighs. The head of your cock rubs against my cheek. You're crazy now, twisting and bucking against the bed, demanding satisfaction." She stepped back. Thorn's chest rose and fell heavily with his accelerated breathing.

Her eyelids weighed heavy and her chest tightened in an effort to draw more breath. She licked her lips and bit down on the bottom one. She sucked in air, and her breasts reared against her tight cashmere sweater.

Her husky voice continued to seduce. "Because you're so big, I have to use both hands to still your wild thrusts. I bend down, mouth open, my tongue running across my lips. I can't wait to take all of you in my mouth. Beads of your cum glisten on the straining head." She glanced down his belly to the protruding mound beneath his belt.

Her nipples throbbed against her bra. Swallowing hard, Stevie drowned a moan. She didn't know who was more turned on. Her or Jack. *Damn him.* No way was she going to take up with the likes of him again. She needed to steer clear of him.

"Just when I lower my lips to take you into my mouth, I squeeze the hell out of your balls and twist them nearly off, and tell you if you ever fucking touch me again I'll geld you."

As she walked out of the room, it gave her supreme satisfaction to see Jack's tented pants flatten.

3

Thorn choked on his coffee and pushed his face closer to the magnifying lens of his high-powered scope. "Damn it, Stevie!"

Not taking his eyes off the scene playing out before him, he pulled his cell phone from his pocket and called down to the truck surveilling Spoltori's building.

"Deavers."

"Get a plainclothes up to the fifteenth floor and have them stand by. It appears Detective Cavanaugh is Spoltori's twelve o'clock," Jack snapped.

Deavers's deep chuckle did nothing to slow Jack's rapid heartbeat. The little fool. What the hell was she doing? Did she have any idea what her actions could do to the case? His gut told him to pull her ASAP. His brain cautioned him. They needed a look inside the apartment. And *if* she were a paying customer they could use her info. He took a deep breath. He couldn't wait to wrap his hands around her throat.

And while he contemplated ways of punishing her, his eyes locked on Stevie's artful curves. His cock stirred. The fitted black miniskirt and studded leather bustier she wore accentuated every inch of what he remembered. Even after seven years he distinctly remembered the soft silkiness of her skin, and the way it heated up beneath his fingers.

"Son of a bitch," he whispered. She walked right up to the wide glass window, pressed her tits against the glass, and winked.

His teeth grated. The bare-chested Italian Stallion slipped his arm around her waist and pulled her back against him. When his hand splayed across Stevie's bountiful breasts, Jack froze. No way, she wouldn't go that far . . .

Stevie whipped her head around and with a scathing hiss she pushed Mario from her. "Did I give you permission to touch me?"

A shiver skittered across her chest. Mario's dark eyes flashed like a feral dog's. The arrogant flare of his nostrils told her she'd better tread carefully. He quickly recovered, cowering.

"That's better, TopMaster."

"Tell me, Mistress, what is it you want me to do?"

Stevie strode past him to the doorway leading down the hall to the hidden room. "As I explained, *my* Mistress is a prominent lady in Sacramento. She's recently relocated to the area and is looking for a discreet male bottom. Your name came up, so I'm here to see what all the hoopla is about."

She turned to find Spoltori standing only inches from her. He smiled wide, yet the gesture was not one of comfort. More like a wolf sizing up its dinner.

"I don't normally choose to be the bottom, but if the price is right I can assume the position."

Stevie smiled and pulled a short crop from her thigh-high black leather boots. She flicked him on his bare shoulder. "Then, by all means, TopMaster, assume the position."

When he didn't drop fast enough for her, Stevie swatted him hard across his pectorals. He flashed her a lopsided smile and slowly descended to his knees.

"Mistress, please, before we go further, let me tell you my safe word."

She laughed, genuinely amused. "I have no use for safe words." She didn't back down when he didn't reply. Instead she exploited his weakness. "Aren't you man enough to take the ultimate dominance from a woman?"

He swallowed hard, his Adam's apple jumping up and down his throat.

"My Mistress can be gentle when she wishes. But . . ." Stevie ran the tip of the leather crop along his traps. "She also gets off pushing her bottoms to the edge. Are you man enough to give her that ultimate pleasure?"

She watched his face change from frightened to excited to angry, all in the span of a few short seconds before he quickly masked his thoughts. She shivered. While his face remained placid, the flash of malevolence in his eyes gave him away.

Maintaining the upper hand of the twisted little scenario, Stevie shoved a well-heeled combat boot on his shoulder and pushed him down so hard he lay splayed on the floor. "Show me why I should pay you three thousand dollars for the privilege of my Mistress spanking you silly."

He moved to stand up. She pushed him back down, harder. "Crawl."

Stevie felt a sense of revenge for his victims as she watched his muscles clench and his body twitch. He hesitated for the briefest of seconds, then quickly crawled like a crab across the smooth hardwood floor to a short hallway. She couldn't help but observe the tight contours of his ass beneath the sheer material of the white loincloth he wore.

She considered Mario. Maybe if he wasn't a killer gigolo and she wasn't a cop, in another life she might take him up on some serious sport fucking.

Jack's handsome face flashed before her, his full lips twisted in a sardonic half smile. *"If it's sport fucking you want, Stevie,*

I'm your man." Growling, she forced the image and the words from her.

"Faster!" she barked at Mario, imagining he was Jack and enjoying the scene twice over.

His crab crawl morphed into a serpent slide. A gait befitting the human snake. He stopped at what she thought was a closet door.

"Mistress, may I stand?"

"Kiss my boots, then rise slowly."

As serious as the situation was, Stevie fought back a smile. Spoltori was experiencing extreme difficulty playing the submissive. His humiliation simmered in his livid gaze. Would it be enough to push him over the edge? Did he have it in for dominant women?

Mario slid toward her leather boots and kissed each one. When he pulled back, she stepped on his hand. She pushed harder. "Tongue them."

When he didn't immediately respond she increased the pressure of her foot on his hand. "I'll break you right now, slave. *Do it!"*

His long, pointed tongue lashed out, and in an angry flick he licked the tip of each boot. "Good boy. Now, let's see what you've got."

He skulked toward the door and opened it. Just a regular closet. Pushing aside several garments, he reached deeper into the closet and turned a knob. A whole new world opened up to them.

Hunching down, like Quasimodo, Mario beckoned her into the sleek black torture chamber. That was the only description befitting it, and knowing what this son of a bitch did to his victims made her sick.

Recessed lighting exposed black lacquered walls sporting a variety of wrist and ankle manacles. Wide, studded leather collars hung from chain leashes attached to the wall. An impressive set of bullwhips hung in a display case dominating one wall. Other, more medieval instruments of pain lay ominously against dark velvet cloth in a display case. Several chrome dog kennels stood side by side against another wall. She looked up and whistled. A set of manacled tethers hung suspended from the ceiling with drawstrings for easy leverage.

"You've done this up real nice, BottomSlave."

Spoltori growled low, causing the hair to spike on her neck. She held her breath, wondering if she'd pushed too far. Their eyes clashed for the briefest of seconds before he looked down at his bare feet and shuffled. "I'm glad you like it, Mistress."

"Yeah, I like it all right. I think my Mistress will like it better."

Stevie glanced at the far wall. Shrouded, dark, and deadly, an ancient iron maiden lay open for inspection. She moved toward it. Her heart rate accelerated, and a sudden burst of perspiration immediately cooled her. Resisting the urge to shudder, Stevie stopped next to the portable torture chamber.

Holy shit! Tracing a finger along one of the shiny six-inch spikes, she could barely contain her excitement. The puncture wounds of the first victim were consistent with the pattern of the deadly spikes protruding from the inside of the casket lid and bed. Enough for a search warrant for sure.

Her breath hissed when Mario stepped within inches of her face. His full lips pulled into a lopsided smile. "Is this what you had in mind, *Mistress*?" She didn't dare show fear. He'd string her out on that iron maiden before her cover could bust down the door.

She flicked him hard with her crop. Welts sprung up against his dark skin. "How dare you speak to me?"

She kneed him hard in the groin, and he dropped to all fours. She smashed him flat with a hard boot to the back. Bending low, she cracked the smooth concrete of the floor in front of his face. "Do you forget your place? One more act of insolence, and my Mistress won't be interested in you. Do you want to give up serving yourself to the top bitch?"

Spittle pooled on the floor beneath his cheek, his body shivered. "*No,* Mistress, *no.* Forgive me, whip me, cage me, I'm your obedient slave."

Giving Mario a shove for good measure, Stevie stood back from him. He lay prone, the perfect submissive. Taking advantage of the moment, Stevie gave the chamber of horrors a quick glance. The black painted walls glowed with a low sheen. Easy to clean. The room oozed cleanliness, the subtle scent of disinfectant lingering in the air. She could eat off the floors. If this was where Mario had killed his victims, she'd bet the state budget there wasn't a shred of evidence for even the most diligent CSI. But they could try. The feds had top-notch people and labs. If any CSI team could obtain evidence, theirs could. It was worth a shot.

She stepped back. As she did, he dragged himself forward, his tongue flicking out toward her boots. "Please, Mistress, please forgive my insolence." Mario's big hands snaked around her boots as he pulled himself against the sleek leather. His whines and wet kisses left her sick to her stomach. Did people really get off on this shit?

What the hell happened to straight, mind-blowing sex? Why did people have to get it all twisted with this weirdo stuff?

"Back off."

His grip tightened for a second before releasing her. She dared him to look up at her, knowing that one slip up in her dominatrix character could blow the whole operation, or worse, be the death of her.

"You might hear from me, slave. I have to decide if you are deserving of my lady."

As she closed the door to Mario's apartment, Stevie let out a long breath. *Shit.* For a second there she thought she'd end up in one of those cages. The guy had serious issues. She felt dirty all of a sudden and longed for a shower. She sprinted to the elevator.

When the elevator door opened, she screamed when a set of very long, very strong arms yanked her into the car, and hit the close button.

"Just what the hell do you think you were doing? You may very well have jeopardized this whole case." Fiery green eyes speared her.

"I—I wanted a peek and knew you'd hassle me about it. My chief gave me permission!"

So much for her guys having her back. She squirmed. Jack's grip tightened.

She'd be damned if she'd let him bully her. Stevie pushed against Thorn's steel grip, trying to ignore the hard heat of his body flush against her nearly naked one. But her body wouldn't obey her mind. Her nipples throbbed responsively. The hard heave of her breasts pushed against the rigid planes of his chest. The action caught them both off guard.

Thorn's eyes narrowed to slits and a low growl rode up from his chest. She could feel the vibration of it against her nipples. Her knees quivered. *What the hell was she doing?*

Twisting out of his grip, Stevie slapped him hard across the cheek. Thorn's stunned look made her laugh. He hit the stop button and the elevator car abruptly halted midfloor. She lurched at the jolt, catching herself against the door.

He grabbed her hand as she went in for another slap. "I deserved the first one yesterday." His face lowered to within inches of hers. "But the second one was uncalled for. Now you owe me."

Jerking her against his chest, he breathed hard. "I'll take my payback now."

His hard lips swooped down on hers before she could tell him where he could take his payback. Stevie's cry of denial was lost under the smothering heat of his assault. And assault was the only word to describe his action. His lips pillaged her mouth, his tongue pushing its way past her teeth. He tasted angry, fiery, and distinctly male.

To her horror, Stevie felt a jab of desire spear her pussy with the velocity of a SWAT team busting in on a drug deal.

She twisted away from him. She needed to get away before she crossed the line she'd sworn never to cross again.

Too late.

He pressed her, chest first, into the cool metal wall of the elevator, his arms bracing the impact just enough not to cause her too much pain. He grabbed her hands and pulled them above her head, preempting another assault. The hard length of his body against her backside left no wiggle room. She was trapped against the wall.

"I didn't know you liked it rough, Cavanaugh." His teeth sank into the exposed skin of her neck.

She cried out, the sound primal, the call of a female in heat. Stevie ground her hips against the hardness of the wall, and wished he would spread her knees, hike her skirt, and take her from behind.

His teeth skimmed the length of her jugular, stopping at the sensitive bend of her shoulder. "I like it rough too."

He pushed harder against her, the rigid length of his cock digging into the small of her back.

"I want you, Stevie. Just like this. Raw and angry."

Releasing her right hand, his long fingers skimmed down the smooth leather of her skirt.

"You want me too."

Feeling as if she were drugged and unable to act, Stevie could only breathe and feel. The slick heat between her legs pulsed. Her skin simmered, the evocative sensation of Thorn's hot, hard body and hotter breath against her back kept refusals silent.

She wanted him.

"Oh, God," she moaned. His hand slid around to her hips and pressed against her mound. Her muscles spasmed. She nearly came when his tongue slid into her ear and his hand pressed a slow, deep rhythm against her.

Her body burned, and like an alcoholic too long without a drink, she craved him. Instinctively her hips undulated against his hand and her deep moans of pleasure filled the sex-charged air of the car. Spreading her legs, she pushed against his cock.

4

Stevie clasped her thighs together. The sublime feel of Thorn's thick finger sliding into her hot wetness nearly pushed her over the edge. Her interior muscles clenched and unclenched, pulling him deeper into her. She rode his undulating finger, grinding hard against it. The sensation consumed her. Delving his tongue into her ear, he pushed deeper into her pussy, tapping into the sweet spot. *Oh, God.* She screamed out as an orgasm ripped through her.

"I want to fuck you, Stevie." Hot breath singed her neck. "Hard." The grinding stiffness of his cock dug into her lower back.

This was insane.

"Thorn," she gasped between ragged breaths, pushing her ass against his cock. "Stop . . ."

Instantly, air separated them.

She screamed out in knife-edged ecstasy only a breath away from pain. His finger, his hard-on, his heat, all of him slipped away from her so fast, it felt as if a vital organ had been ripped from her body.

"Jesus, Stevie. I'm sorry, I—"

She whirled around, took his face into her hands, planting her lips against his. She wasn't done with him, not just yet. She moaned in unison with him. He pulled her hard against him and this time, his cock met her throbbing clit head on. Their tongues battled for dominance. God, she wanted penetration.

But she wanted to preserve her integrity more.

As abruptly as he had, she let go. Thorn looked like he'd just lost his dog. The shocked expression on his face, priceless. They both panted hard, their breaths colliding in the sexually charged air between them. Straightening her short skirt and trying very hard to ignore the way her lips and pussy throbbed, Stevie smiled.

"My terms this time, Thorn. *My terms.*"

She turned from his piercing eyes and pretended his glorious hard-on didn't have her name stamped all over it. She inhaled a long breath through her nose and slowly exhaled, repeating the process until she had control of herself. Neither spoke, and she was glad he kept his silence. After smoothing her hair back to an acceptable style, she punched the button setting the car back into motion. When it settled and the doors opened, she nearly ran into Deavers in her haste to get out.

A different heat swept her from head to toe. There was no way the communications specialist would miss Thorn's raised slacks. Or, she was sure, her flushed face.

Indeed, Deavers's sharp eyes flitted from Thorn's straining trousers to her warming cheeks back to Thorn. Raising her chin, she made the best of an awkward situation.

She gave the fed a quick wink, flicked her head, sending her hair over her shoulder, and stepped past him. Without a word she continued straight for the door to the apartment building.

Once out of sight, Stevie hustled to her car and slid inside. After shutting the door, she flopped back into the leather seat and let out a long breath. Sweet Jesus, what had she done? She'd sworn off cops, which as far as she was concerned included feds. She'd made her stand years ago. She didn't do cops. She knew damned well if she did, her sexual prowess would be the topic of conversation the next morning over coffee and donuts at every local convenience store.

It had taken months for her to live down Thorn's desertion years ago. She'd put on a brave face then, hiding her suffering emotions. As far as her fellow officers were concerned it was just sex, but it went far deeper for her. Jack had touched her like no other person had done since. He encouraged the best of her to come out when normally she would have been too shy to shine. He taught her to rely on her instincts, to go with her gut feelings. To trust.

She rubbed her eyes. And so she had. Her instincts told her Jack felt as deeply for her as she did for him. But he had proved her wrong, and since the morning when she woke alone in bed, after a night of sheet-melting sex, she'd second-guessed her instincts regularly. She trusted no one. Not even herself.

She closed her eyes and grimaced. She'd felt cheated, as if everything he had taught her was a lie. She hadn't been able to get away from it either. Even now, years later, her fellow officers offered up the occasional quip regarding her fling with their instructor. That Thorn was back and she'd obviously allowed him access where no other had been permitted would be the opening topic at the next shift's lineup, and fodder for the next month.

Shit!

She turned the key, expecting the low rumble of her Saleen Mustang to soothe her ruffled feathers. Instead, the vibration from the supercharged engine rumbled against her swollen slit. She cursed, giving the smooth leather of the stick shift a yearning gaze. Visualizing Thorn's long, thick shaft jutting up as rigidly, she would have pounced on it right then and there had he materialized.

Anger surged past her lust. He'd done it to her again. Sucked her right into that sexual warp of his.

Shoving the stick into first gear, Stevie peeled out of the underground parking lot. She grinned. Well, one good thing came of their brief interlude. This time, she was the one who walked away first. And it felt damn good.

By the time Thorn made it back to the observation room, Stevie had cooled considerably. She'd made up her mind that whatever was between her and Thorn would not impact her job. She'd managed to see enough of Rocky's dungeon to hopefully wrangle a search warrant. She made the call, and kept her fingers crossed.

Just as she hit the end button of her cell phone, Thorn strutted into the room—alone. *Thank God.*

Instinctively, her gaze dropped to Thorn's crotch. He grinned like a wolf, and the noticeable bulk flinched.

"Look, Jack, what happened in that elevator was a fluke. We need to watch Rocky and I can't do that if you're mauling me."

He laughed low, the sound throaty and dangerous. "Oh, I won't maul you. Not here anyway." He stopped in front of her. His male scent radiated toward her. It seemed more potent. As if their earlier tryst had enhanced it. She felt her pores open and whatever pheromones had been bouncing around in that elevator reappeared for an encore. She stepped back, the telescope poking her in the ass.

"Did you see the room?" he asked.

She swallowed and wished he wasn't standing so close. "Yes, and it's the poster child for Dungeons R Us."

He scowled down at her for a minute, his eyes smoldering. Her body thrummed. "You may have blown any chance at a warrant."

She doubted it, but had her reasons for not challenging him at the moment. So she steered him away from the subject, and his attention off nipples that poked out at him like heat-seeking missiles. "Sit down. Rocky has some company on the books."

Whirling around before he could read her motives, Stevie sat down and focused on Rocky. Looked like he did have some company. Two in fact. A ripe blonde and a petite brunette.

"Looks like our boy is going for the classic threesome."

Thorn leaned over her back, his warm breath caressing her cheek. His right hand brushed her cheek in a slow backward movement. She smelled her own musky sex scent clinging to his fingers. No doubt his intention.

Jack Thornton was a bad, bad man.

"I've never experienced the pleasure of a threesome, have you?" he asked softly before he pulled away and sat down next to her.

Not taking her eyes off of the blonde being undressed by Spoltori and helped by the brunette, she answered, "No." She wouldn't give him any more than that. Just talking about sex with Jack Thornton made her want to tear her clothes off, and have her way with him.

Damn, he was a distracting male.

"Hey, Stevie?"

"What?"

"Look at me."

"I can't, Rocky's lubing up the blonde."

"If you don't look at me, I'll take the whip to you."

Excitement stabbed her pussy, and her nipples twinged. Grudgingly she looked at him. He smiled a slow, lazy smile. "I knew you'd respond to that." The truth of the statement astounded her, and unexpectedly it was okay with her, because it was okay with Jack. Tracing his middle finger under his nose he slowly inhaled, his eyes half-closing. "Your pussy smells like heaven." Slowly he slid the digit in his mouth and sucked it, making juicy little noises.

Stevie caught her breath, her skin flushed hot. Before she realized she was grinding her twat against the chair, he opened his eyes and pulled the long thickness of his finger from his lips.

"I want to eat you until you scream. *All of you.*" He rubbed the tip of his finger along the bottom curve of his lip. "Then I want you to come all over my face."

He hadn't been shy all those years ago, and he seemed to have gained more ego as a fed. While she wanted to tell him he did nothing for her, it would be a lie. A lie she desperately wished wasn't true. Swallowing hard she mustered up her resolve. First things first.

The little voice in her head reminded her. *You don't do cops. You don't do cops.*

She turned back to the scope. "Keep dreaming."

His low chuckles told her he wasn't buying her coy routine.

"Well, well, well, looks like Rocky has another friend over."

Stevie watched another man enter the room and the surprised look of the two naked women who were currently on all fours vying for a taste of Rocky's limp dick.

Interesting.

Clad from head to toe in black, the newcomer moved with easy familiarity into the room. From her vantage point, Stevie could barely detect eye slits in the mask he wore. She held her breath. Could Rocky have an accomplice? Her eyes darted back to the gigolo. His limp member acknowledged the newcomer with a pulsing salute.

The masked man pushed the two trembling women aside like they were inconsequential sticks of furniture. His mask moved. As he spoke, Rocky's face hardened and the ladies' faces grew concerned.

Despite what was obviously a quarrel, Rocky's erection took on new heights. A nagging thought tugged at her brain. She dismissed it, ignoring her instinct.

"That thing is huge," Stevie whispered.

"Huge hurts."

"That's what I hear." Jack was generously endowed, no doubt about that, but by the looks of Rocky's hard-on . . . Stevie shuddered. No way would she want that thing coming after her.

Rocky gestured to the two ladies, who crouched together, shielding their nakedness with little effect. The man in black leather wedged himself in between them, positioning all three of them nose to ass, nose to ass on all fours while Rocky stood dominantly over them.

Rocky motioned to the blonde behind the masked man to unhook his codpiece. She did so in a slow, loving, subservient manner.

Stevie watched, mesmerized, as the blonde turned the masked one around and took his dick in her hand and slowly began to manipulate it. As it lengthened, she took him into her mouth. Rocky dropped to his knees in front of the brunette, and silently undulated, his dick full and heavy, listing heavy to the right.

"He looks like a damned stud." Stevie swallowed hard and that nagging thought pricked harder at her brain. She went with it. "I think Spoltori's gay."

"I was wondering when you'd figure that out."

She bristled. "If you knew, why didn't you say something?"

Jack's breath was warm against her cheek. "You need to trust your instincts, Cavanaugh. Look at how hard he got when the masked man walked into the room. Look at the way he humiliated the women he killed."

"A misogynist."

"Exactly. Didn't you feel it when you were there?"

Her skin chilled. Yeah, she'd felt it. She closed her eyes for the briefest of seconds, then opened them. This time, instead of chills, her skin warmed. Leave it to Jack to trust her to discover the truth herself instead of just showing her.

The brunette made the mistake of reaching out to touch

Rocky's hard-on. Her reward was a quick spanking on the ass. She cried out and rolled over onto her back, spreading her legs, and offering herself up for punishment. Rocky smiled and stroked her cheek, then her breasts. His fingers trailed lower down her belly to her pussy, she opened wider for him and he spanked her again. When the brunette recoiled he said something to the blonde, who immediately responded by sinking her face between the brunette's thighs.

"If that was me and you disobeyed me," Jack said, "I'd punish you."

Before she thought to keep her images to herself, Stevie blurted, "How?"

"I'd spank you until that heart-shaped ass of yours was hot pink."

Stevie gasped, wiggling her warming tush against the smooth hardness of the chair. She refused to look to her right. Instead she watched Rocky point to the blonde's upturned ass. The masked man thrust his cock deep into her, and when she reared up to protest, Rocky grabbed a handful of her long blond hair. He lowered his face to hers and when she tried to kiss him, he yanked harder on her hair, until she nodded in obedience.

With the blonde otherwise occupied, Rocky turned his attention back to the brunette. She crawled past the little blonde but not so far as to keep her tush out of her face. Rocky spoke to the blonde. Instantly she responded. Spreading the brunette's cheeks, the blonde rubbed a finger up and in between the brunette's folds. Closing her eyes, the brunette undulated, pushing hard against the invading fingers. Stevie watched transfixed as the erotic scene played out before her, not wanting to look away if she could.

Rocky sidled in front of the brunette and directed her gaping mouth to his cock, while the masked man arched backward, spanking and thrusting wildly into the blonde.

Rocky gave another command to the blonde, who obediently slipped a finger deep into the brunette, who jolted against Rocky while her hips undulated against the friction of the hand between her legs.

Jack laughed low. "Oh, no, Stevie, I wouldn't pleasure you that quickly. I'd make you wait until you couldn't stand it for one more second." He sucked in his breath and exhaled with a hiss. "I'd have to tie you up because I know you'd want it all upfront. But I wouldn't give it to you. No way. While you're lying there helpless, I'd dip my fingers into your hot little pussy, then smear your juices all over your mouth." He moaned deep and throaty. "Yeah, I'd smear you everywhere, the sweet smell of your sex everywhere. Then I'd lick every drop off of you."

Thorn scooted his chair and telescope closer to Stevie. She could barely regulate her heartbeat, and didn't trust herself to so much as blink his way. She could imagine his hot, wet tongue lapping her nipples, lapping between her thighs, lapping every last drop of cum off her skin. She squirmed. Oh Lord, it was going to be near to impossible to keep her hands off him.

"I know you'd like that, Stevie. But you'd like my tongue flicking your clit and my fingers buried in your pussy more."

Stevie caught her breath and for a hazy second her vision blurred. Damned if she couldn't feel that intense pressure of his thick fingers inside her. Slowly, deeply, methodically hitting that spot only he knew. *Oh, yes.* Her skin sizzled. The room heated, the air heavy with sexual innuendo.

"I think, Stevie, the minute I licked your clit you'd scream and come all over my face." His finger brushed against her bare arm, and she jumped. "I think, Stevie, you'd like that."

"Thorn, stop. I can't—I can't concentrate."

His deep laugh did nothing to quell the liquid fire that raced through her veins. Instead it added to the heat of her current state.

Stevie held her breath, squeezing her thighs together so hard it hurt. She should have worn underwear, damn it. The seat was slick with her juices and she felt as if she'd slide right off if he didn't shut up.

"Okay, Stevie, I'll stop."

"I can't believe you'd compromise the investigation like this."

He chuckled. "I never compromise, Stevie. Never."

She bit back a quick retort. Instead the words locked in her throat. She coughed and watched the bizarre sex scene unfolding across the street.

The participants had changed positions. Still on all fours, the blonde moved her ass upward into the air and the brunette found it too tempting. Spreading the blonde's cheeks, the brunette nipped her ass but held them open while Rocky took the liberty of running that leviathan of his up and down her crack. The masked man sank the length of himself into the blonde's mouth and while she attempted to take Rocky from behind, the brunette assisted with her tongue.

Out of the blue, Stevie felt a twinge of guilt. "I know we're doing our job here, Jack. But I really feel like we are majorly invading these people's privacy."

"Get over it. I'm sure the victims and their families have no problem with it."

She chanced a quick look his way. She grinned. While he was glued to the scene playing out in Rocky's apartment, the bulge in his pants had yet to recede.

Glancing back through the lens, Stevie felt her stomach lurch. Now Rocky had the blonde pinned chest first against the window. He stared straight ahead, directly into the lens. If she didn't know any better she'd say he looked as if he were challenging her as he pumped his lady John from behind. She was too far away, and the two cutouts in her window were the size of a box of smokes.

Besides, what the hell was she supposed to do? Arrest him for rape? Based on the woman's heavy-lidded eyes, pouty lips, and active participation, she was enjoying the sex play. Even when Rocky slipped handcuffs on her and his eyes flashed dangerously, Stevie knew there was nothing she would do to interfere with two consenting adults.

"You like watching that, Jack? Two men and two women?"

"I'd rather watch you and me under a mirrored ceiling."

"They have those in Vegas. Big round beds with mirrored ceilings."

"I bet you've seen a few."

Stevie's back tensed. His words stung. "That's none of your damn business, Mr. Hit and Run."

Heat flashed in her cheeks. Her mouth tightened. What nerve. She glanced at her watch before looking to her right. It was time to hit the road. The muscles in Thorn's cheek clenched and unclenched. What the hell? He walked out on her years ago after fucking her brains out for twenty-four hours straight and now acted like a lover scorned? Her gut twisted as a thought popped into her head. Was it possible she'd meant more to Jack than just sex? Had he felt the connection she had? Did he still feel it? If she hadn't felt such deep feelings for Jack she never would have allowed him access to her body. She breathed deeply and something inside her softened.

His eyes simmered in anger.

She bristled. So much for her recent soft spot.

She decided Jack could stay and watch the scene play out. She had paperwork she needed to do for the warrant and the last thing she wanted was the testosterone-driven fed breathing down her back.

"I'm heading back to HQ, Thorn. Enjoy the foursome."

5

"Hey, Stevie," Thorn called. She half-expected him to grab her arm and force her to listen to whatever BS he was about to spew. Instead, he kept his eyes focused on the debauchery going on in Rocky's living room.

She stopped and turned to find herself staring at his back. The play of his muscles beneath his tailored shirt was not lost in the dim light of the room. Or the way his long legs stood braced as if he stood at the bow of a ship gazing over the wide expanse of the ocean.

Shit! Why did she let his male affect her female so?

He cleared his throat. "Not sure what for, but I'm sorry."

Stevie stared speechless at his back. *He was sorry? And he didn't know what for?* Oh, she'd love to make *him* sorry!

Fisting her hands, Stevie wanted to pummel the arrogant lines of his back. Instead she strode up to him, stopping mere inches from his back. His heat, like a palpable force, radiated against her skin. She leaned in and barely touched her breasts to his back. At the contact they flinched in unison. But Stevie steeled herself. She'd prove to herself she could withstand his magnetism.

She had a case to solve, and playing sexual patty-cake with Jack wasn't going to put Rocky behind bars. For self-preservation she needed to move past him. She smiled slyly. That and give him a little of his own payback.

She leaned harder. The sharp hiss of his breath gave her supreme satisfaction.

"Don't be sorry, Thorn. I'm not."

Beginning at the top of his left shoulder she traced a finger along the bulging bicep. Squeezing the hardness she continued, "I wouldn't trade a minute of our time together for the world. I loved fucking you." She breathed against his neck and enjoyed watching the fine hairs spike. "I loved being fucked by you. And hell, after a while, I didn't even mind that you never called."

She laughed softly, and continued her trail to his hand, lightly caressing the white knuckles grasping the binoculars. "You taught me more than defensive tactics and sexual positions, Thorn. You taught me that guys pretend to care to get what they want."

His muscles steeled. "I never pretended with you, Stevie."

He made to turn around but she held him off, ignoring the lurch in her chest. It was too late for apologies. Now it was time for payback. "Ah-ah, Agent Thornton. Keep your eyes on the foursome."

Caressing his knuckles with her fingertips, she slid her right hand, palm open, around to the front of his shirt. The smooth, hard feel of his muscles shook her resolve. Mouth set, she continued her assault. Dipping her hand downward toward what she knew was a rising phoenix, she slowly deflected away from it and with firm pressure slid her hand down his thigh. As she pushed her hips against his ass, she ignored the need to rub herself hard against him, to have him turn in her arms, lift her skirt, and just get it over with.

The pressure between her legs pulsed with a life force of its own. It had become almost unbearable. Payback, she discovered, was a double-edged sword.

Thorn's body tightened. "Stevie, you're playing with fire," he whispered.

"No, I'm not. I'm playing with you, Jack. Just like you played with me." She rubbed the hardened tips of her nipples against the smooth fabric of his shirt. "And you love it."

His arm flinched as if he were going to lower the lens.

"No, no, keep your arms up. That's it." She squeezed his thigh. "I like playing with you, Jack. Do you want to know what I would do if I could play with you for real?"

He growled, the primal timbre highly arousing. And challenging. Something deep inside her wanted more than revenge for his callous desertion of her. While she wanted to set the pace and make the rules, her primordial woman wanted him to take her as one would a mate in the wilds. No care given to comfort or setting, no prelude, no foreplay, just pure, lustful mating.

"I'd slowly strip off your clothes." Beginning with her left hand she trailed it up along his sleeve and over his shoulder as if she was actually undressing him. She did the same with her right hand. Admiringly she ran both hands up his back, imagining it bare, manipulating the suppleness of him. "Such smooth, taut skin." She touched her nose between his shoulder blades. "You smell good, Jack, like warm, sunny sex."

Wrapping her hands around his waist she moved upward, caressing his pecs. "Your nipples are hard. I want to suck them."

He hissed in a breath. She manipulated them with her fingertips, making them harder. "Oh, Jack, you like that, don't you?"

Her hand made a slow, purposeful slide down his chest to his waist, traveling lower over the smooth plane of his abdomen. She pantomimed the action of undoing his belt, then the deliberate action of sliding his trousers down his thighs to his knees, then his calves. "Oh, Jack. Look how hard you are. I just want to lick you until you can't stand it."

His hips flinched. "Stay still, Jack." She felt the rise in his body temperature and the quick bursts of his breath against her arms.

"What's Rocky doing to his little blonde?"

"Gone."

She stiffened. "How about the brunette? What are she and the masked man doing?"

"Gone."

Her body tingled. How long had she been seducing him while he stood as if he was still surveilling?

Stevie swallowed hard. "Well then, I guess you can call it a day. The relief squad should be walking in any minute." Stepping back to cool off, Stevie glanced at her watch. They were ten minutes late.

She moved away from Thorn and turned to make a quick exit. She gasped and stopped dead in her tracks. One of her dicks and one of Thorn's feds stood in the open doorway with shit-eating grins the size of a football stadium plastered across their faces.

Shit! Shit! Shit!

She blinked, wanting to close her eyes and walk past them like an ostrich, pretending they weren't there. That wasn't going to happen. So she contemplated her choices. She could play the indifferent card or the guilty card.

She made her decision. A slow, sexy smile spread across her face. She sauntered toward them, stopping just out of arm's reach. "Boys." She nodded her head and glided past them like the queen of the realm.

Once the elevator door opened she couldn't get into it fast enough, curse loud enough, and wish hard enough that she'd never, ever set eyes on Jack Thornton.

Shit!

Stevie ran to her car, slamming the door closed, grateful for the solitude, she started the engine and headed for the PD. She needed air and space, she needed an ice-cold shower and her wits back. Self-revulsion flooded her system. How could she be so weak? She was a trained officer. Trained to maintain composure, not lose it when a hunk from her past happened to walk into her present and tease her. No, she was Detective Cavanaugh, renowned ice queen. Her cool head and precision control were well known and hard won.

Caught twice in less than twenty-four. There would be absolutely no living down her and Thorn's public lust. She gunned the engine, shooting the 'Stang into the back lot of the PD.

Shit!

Throwing the car into park, Stevie sat for a long minute, collecting her thoughts. Knowing she should change before she went to file the paperwork for the search warrant, she opted not to. She figured what the hell, might as well throw more gas on the fire. Let the guys see what they were missing and what they thought Thorn was getting. So long as she knew what was up she didn't care what the rank and file thought.

As she stepped from the car and felt the moist warmth between her legs, Stevie wondered who she was kidding. She cared all right, she cared a lot. In this male-dominated profession it was hard enough for a chick cop to garner the respect of her male counterparts. But when they stopped looking at you as a valuable partner and started to see you only as someone they wanted to screw, well then, the ladies had to work doubly hard at their job, and put up with all of the flack that came with the jacket of free sex.

She threw her hands up in the air. "Oh, screw it." She pivoted with the aplomb of a seasoned ballerina and marched back to her car and pulled a T-shirt from her gym bag. She stripped off her shoulder holster and badge, yanked the tee over her head, then slung the holster back over her shoulder, hung her badge off the waist of her skirt, and smoothed back her mussed hair. She'd be damned if she'd give the dogs upstairs more fodder for the locker room.

While she cursed Jack Thornton for putting her in such an awkward position she also chided herself. The damned fact of the matter was, if she didn't have feelings for Jack he wouldn't be able to affect her so.

She threw her shoulders back and prepared for the worst. It wasn't long in coming.

The dick squad-room was bumper-to-bumper desks, with only low, flimsy partition walls separating them. The place usually hopped with clerks, uniforms, and detectives tracking down leads on the phone. Today, even this late in the workday, was no exception.

The room pulsed with life and . . . testosterone.

In what seemed like slow motion, Stevie strode into the room, daring any of them to open their egotistical mouths. Phones silenced, conversations came to an abrupt halt, and every eye in the room followed her.

The trek to the task force room at the end of the hall seemed endless.

She glanced at Jamison, one of her own men assigned to the task force. He stood pouring himself a nasty-looking cup of coffee. "Did you to get Judge Harmon's clerk on the phone?" He stood mute, a spark of humor shining in his brown eyes.

"Did I say something funny?"

He shook his head slowly.

"No to a joke or no to the judge's clerk?"

He sipped his coffee and winced, from the heat or the lousy taste she didn't know.

"I, uh—no to both."

She gave him a good-natured smack on the shoulder, sending the coffee sloshing over his hand. "That, my man, is why you'll never make it past detective second grade."

She moved past him and met the stares of the other men. Each one of them suddenly found their shoes more interesting than her leather apparel.

Over her shoulder, she called back to the dick. "I'll make the call myself, Jamison, and consider yourself off the task force."

She entered the small enclosed office that served as the task force HQ and soundly shut the door behind her.

Since it was after five both the task force secretary and the detectives' secretary were gone for the day. She shrugged. Even if those ladies were still in house, she'd make the call herself.

Sometimes you just needed to do the job yourself if you wanted it done right. Finding the clerk's number, Stevie chewed her bottom lip. She really should inform Thorn she was going for a warrant to search Rocky's place.

She shrugged and dialed. He'd find out soon enough. As task force supervisor, she'd need his signature on the paperwork before it went to the judge.

The clerk's voice mail answered.

"This is Detective Cavanaugh, Sac PD. I need a call back ASAP. I have a search warrant for Judge Harmon to sign off." She left her callback number and hung up. It didn't bother her that it was pushing five thirty on a Friday night. Harmon's clerks were notorious for staying late. Besides, if she didn't hear back from one soon, she had no problem going directly to the judge's home for his signature. It wouldn't be the first time she'd dragged the man away from his family time.

Stevie exhaled deeply. Writing out the warrant would take hours. She hated tedious paperwork and avoided it as much as humanly possible. But if the warrant wasn't executed with precision and exact wording, the judge would toss it out the door after her.

After writing the first draft, Stevie realized the squad room had quieted. Popping her head out the door, she breathed out a long sigh of relief. Empty.

She glanced at the round clock on the wall ahead of her and grimaced. Seven thirty. Okay. Make a fresh pot of coffee and write the final draft.

Sitting down with her coffee instead of leaving another message at the judge's office, she tracked down his home phone number. It was Friday night and chances were the man was out.

What the hell. She dialed.

"Harmon residence."

"This is Detective Cavanaugh, Sac PD, calling for the judge. Is he in?"

"No, ma'am, Judge Harmon will not return until Monday morning."

"Is he in town?"

"I'm sorry, detective, but the judge is out of the state until Monday morning. He'll be in chambers by noon."

Stevie hung up. She could try a few other judges. But she knew in her gut that what she had was barely enough to merit a judge's consideration, much less a signed warrant. Judge Harmon was notorious for going out on a limb when he had a hunch and could back it up with statute.

Sitting back in her swivel chair, Stevie put her legs up on her desk, crossing them at the ankle, and contemplated her predicament.

Wait for Judge Harmon, her best chance for a warrant, or hit up another judge? Shopping around was a no-no, so she'd have to take her one and only best shot. Now or Monday?

She bolted upright in her chair, nearly tumbling out of it.

Shit!

Monday would not do. If Rocky ran true to form he was due to strike Sunday night. It was conceivable that she held some faceless victim's life in her hands if she didn't act now. But if she failed there would be more to lose in the end.

Stevie stood and began to pace the worn linoleum floor from one end of the task force room to the other as she mulled over her choices.

In the end there was no choice. She needed to get into Rocky's apartment, now. Even if they pulled him in within the next 24 hours, they could hold him until the full moon passed.

Stevie hustled down to the front desk to the DO. His computer would have a slew of judge's names and numbers.

Lost in thought, Stevie skidded to a halt when she came up to the bulletproof window at the front desk and came eye to eye with none other than Mario Spoltori. They both started. Spoltori's eyes widened, then narrowed dangerously, his thin lips twisting into a sneer.

"Whatcha need, Detective Cavanaugh?" the desk officer asked.

There was no way she could explain away the T-shirt over her leather dominatrix outfit, the badge clipped to her waist, the 9mm Sig in the shoulder holster strapped over her chest, or the fact she was on the law's side of the front desk of her precinct PD.

Spoltori didn't give her the opportunity. He bolted. And she took off after him, shouting over her shoulder to the surprised DO, "Call for backup!"

By the time Stevie made it through the maze of doors and out to the front of the building and into the parking lot, she heard the squeal of tires and knew Spoltori made it out. She hustled back into the PD, grabbed a phone, and dialed Thorn's number.

"Thornton."

"It's me. I've been made."

6

"What the hell happened?"

She told him.

"Damn it, Stevie, our boys lost him before he got there. Now we don't have a tail on him."

"I'm sorry, the guys I got out of here couldn't pick him up either. I've got an APB out with instructions not to approach."

"That'll help, but we need to stay on him. This isn't good, Cavanaugh. We have forty-eight hours, tops, before he kills again."

"I know, sir, and I'm working on a warrant. I need your help with it."

A long pause preceded his next words.

"A warrant?"

"To search Rocky's place."

She heard the shift in his energy across the airwaves. When he spoke, his voice snapped with the ferocity of a snapping turtle. "When were you going to inform me of this?"

"What do you think I'm doing now?"

"Damn it, Stevie. You're single-handedly going to kill this

investigation. Just what makes you think you have enough for a search warrant?"

"Lots. I saw Spoltori's dungeon. Couple that with the fact he has knowledge of each victim and the fact he bolted seems like enough probable cause for me." She jammed her fingers through her hair and winced when they got stuck in the tightly bound strands. "For crying out loud, Thorn. Come over and help me nail this so we can get a judge to sign it off."

Stevie paced angrily in front of Jack, who sat stewing at a vacant desk. His eyes never wavered from her leather-clad body. For once he wished she had more to cover her curves. The skimpy Gold's Gym muscle tee she'd thrown on did more to accentuate her full curves than hide them. He felt like he was going to split the seam in his pants.

"I'm telling you, Jack, the iron maiden tracks will be a perfect match to the puncture marks on Donna Rios."

"We need more than that. Any number of devices or means could have produced those puncture wounds."

"Now who's being thick? How many freakin' iron maidens do you think there are in the State of California? And how many do you think belong to a gigolo who has a tie to a murder victim who happens to look like a pincushion? A pincushion that I guarantee will be a perfect match to Rocky's death toy." She plopped into her chair across from him. He blanched. That movement made her tits look like they were going to pop out of her leather vest. He squirmed in his chair and quickly recovered.

Exasperated with her and his continued physical reaction to her, Thorn swiped a hand across his chin. The fine stubble scuffed his fingers. Stevie was driving him crazy. Aside from the obvious, she refused to listen to reason.

She sat there, so sure of herself in that leather getup. He strongly considered pouncing on her, relieving her of her costume and making her see his way.

He'd long ago rolled up his sleeves. Now he leaned over the desk and met her nose to nose. "First of all, Miss Know-It-All, what judge do you think will allow a search warrant without reasonable PC?"

She rolled her eyes. "We have PC. Besides, I'm not talking about one of your fed judges. They're too much work. We can get a local boy."

He slowly shook his head. She amazed him.

He watched the storm in her eyes and her nose crinkling in defiance. He caught himself before he smiled. He remembered that look, the one that came with her dogged determination, the one he'd witnessed many times in the defensive tactics class he taught at the Sac Academy. "You never should have gone into that apartment." He put a quelling hand over her mouth. "I don't care that you were a paying customer. Illegal entry. The judge won't buy it."

She swatted his hand away. "Judge Harmon would if he was in town. And if *he* would, so would another. We both know Spoltori's our man. He proved it by bolting."

"*If*, and that's a big if, we get a warrant, any second year law student will tear it apart. No PC or maybe even entrapment. Are you willing to risk fruits from the poisonous tree, and have anything we find tossed?"

Vehemently she shook her head and he marveled at the way the fluorescent lights bounced off the blond and brunette highlights in her hair, warming them to molten. She pressed her case. "We have enough right now to pick him up for prostitution."

"And risk blowing the murder charges?"

"If it saves another life? Yes."

Stevie's eyes burned into him. He'd been hard-pressed not to look down the deep cleft between her breasts, or at the long curve of her legs as she continually paced up and down the aisle earlier. He'd exercised extreme control not to embarrass them both and have his less than noble actions caught on the surveillance film for all the rank and file to enjoy.

Jack felt a stab of guilt. Stevie didn't deserve ridicule from her fellow cops. She was good at what she did, and when his SAC told him he'd be partnered up with one of Sacramento's finest he wasn't surprised to discover it was Stevie Cavanaugh.

She'd been a standout in the academy, putting most of the male recruits to shame. She ran faster, fought harder, and studied longer than any of them. The first female to graduate at the top of her class, she did it in spite of the bruised egos that came in behind her.

He wanted to soothe away the angry crease in her brow. He wanted to tell her he was sorry for adding to her uphill battle for respect in this dickhead department.

"I paid for his time on my nickel and my own time off. I asked to see his room and he showed me. I don't see that as inadmissible. Let's make a few calls, and if we can't get what we want, we can pick him up on the prostitution charge."

Thorn swiped his hand across his chin again and finally nodded. "Okay, Detective Cavanaugh. We'll play it your way."

She grinned, showing perfectly straight white teeth. His dick twinged. The vivid memory of her skimming those perfect white teeth down his belly to his cock lingered clear as day seven years later.

For the next hour they spent their time on the phone, calling one judge after another. Each time they hit voice mail or were informed the judge was unavailable.

Stevie rubbed her eyes and pulled the band out of her hair to run her fingers through her long tresses. She caught Thorn's warm gaze. "After awhile, those rubber bands give me a headache."

"Don't ever let me stop you from wearing it down. It's my preferred style." Before Stevie could respond, her stomach growled loud enough for her to be embarrassed and Thorn to smile.

"I'm hungry," he said.

She grinned. "Me too. Let's wrap these calls up, then get some burgers at Val's."

Thorn smiled slowly. He had something else in mind to sate his hunger, but for now, he'd settle for food.

But . . . maybe later . . .

"Mayo is pure fat and cholesterol. It'll kill you."

Stevie nodded, muttered, "Mmm-hmmm," and bit into her hamburger. Thorn watched, fascinated, as mayonnaise mingled with mustard, ketchup, and pickles, oozed from the rare piece of meat barely held together by a bun.

"Bess—burgger—eber," she said, chewing a mouthful.

Squirming uncomfortably in his seat, Thorn couldn't stand it. He was fastidious about what he put in his body, and flame-broiled, 20-percent-fat beef wasn't on his list. She dunked a steak fry into a glob of mayo and ketchup, and he cringed. "You will die a horrible death."

Stevie swallowed and took a long sip of her chocolate malted milkshake. "Ahh, and what a way to go."

She pushed her fries across the table to him and nodded at them. "Go ahead. Take a walk on the wild side."

He looked down at his half-eaten veggie burger and admitted it tasted like cardboard.

One fry wouldn't hurt.

One turned into two and before he knew it, Stevie ordered a basket of beer-battered onion rings.

She dipped one deep into the ranch dressing she'd squirted on her plate and held it out to him. "Now, if you really want to live, or die, in your case, take a bite out of this."

He did.

Her eyes twinkled. "That wasn't so bad, was it? Heart still beating?"

She continued to hold her hand in front of him with the

half-eaten ring. Jack slid his hand up her arm and circled her
wrist with his fingers. He noticed how slender and soft she was.
His fingers almost double-lapped her wrist. "Yeah, my heart's
still beating." He pulled her hand to his lips and took another
bite. This time his lips lingered on her fingers and he softly
sucked them. Her eyes widened and the sky blue color darkened to sapphire. He smiled.

"Mmm, I like the taste of that."

Her hand trembled. His fingers tightened around her sultry
skin. He chewed with her fingertips pressed against his lips.
After he swallowed, savoring the salty taste and the smooth
warmth of her skin, he licked each of her fingers like they were
his own. Settling his tongue in the curve between her index and
middle finger, he flicked the sensitive skin there. "I want more."

She smiled slowly and settled back into the smooth bench
seat of the booth. She shook her head. "Uh-uh, Jack. I'm not
going down that road with you."

He dipped another ring and took a bite, slowly chewing, savoring the badness of it. Just like the onion ring, Thorn knew
Stevie could be detrimental to his health. But like a junk-food
junkie, he didn't care. He wanted her as badly as she wanted
that juicy death burger.

"Come home with me."

Stevie dunked a ring and held it out for him. Just as he bit
down on it, she snatched it away. She laughed at him and
popped it into her mouth. "Oh, so close, yet so far."

He slid out of his booth seat around to her side of the table.
Her warmth emanated from the leather bustier and T-shirt.
Was it him or was she hot?

He picked up another onion ring. "I told you, you're playing with fire."

He traced it against her lips, wanting to lick the glossy fryer
grease off them. "I bet I can make you come with your clothes
on."

The thud of her heart thumped against his hand resting on her chest. He chuckled and whispered against her ear, "Ah, you're intrigued." Slowly he withdrew to a more respectable distance.

Her dark eyes glanced nervously around the diner. At this late hour, they were alone. Muffled noises from the kitchen mingled with the do-wop beat from the jukebox. Jack's instincts took full control of the moment.

"I see it in your eyes." He brushed a long, dark strand of her hair from her eyes. He moved in closer. Sliding his hand down her cheek, he rubbed his thumb against her skin. "Your skin is so soft."

His hand lowered to the bend at her neck and shoulder. He laid his hand, palm open, against the top swell of her breasts. They quivered. He smiled and moved closer still. Her breath puffed in short bursts. Her fiery scent engulfed him, reminding him of forbidden things. Things he wanted, regardless of the cost.

"I feel it in your heartbeat, Stevie. You want me too."

She licked her lips. He kissed her then. Not a hard, demanding kiss, but a kiss that savored. He smiled against the warm pliancy of her lips. "Mmm, you taste like a bad, bad burger." He licked her top lip. "With extra mayo."

"I'm worse than a heart attack on a plate, Jack."

He sucked in her bottom lip, swirling his tongue across it. "I'll take my chances."

"You might regret it."

Sliding his hands up her arms he pulled her hard against him. "My only regret is not following up the last time we were this close."

Stiffening, she pushed away. Her eyes morphed from warm and fuzzy blue to spitfire. "Yeah, me too." She moved to stand up. Gently he pulled her back to him.

"I'm not here by mistake, Stevie."

For the briefest of seconds he watched her eyes moisten before she closed her emotional door.

"I put in for the Sac field office as soon as I was eligible. Three years straight now. I could have gone anywhere, but I wanted to be here, near you."

Her hands trembled.

Softly he ran his fingertips up and down her arm. "I wanted to breathe the same air as you. I told you I missed you. I didn't lie."

Her eyelids fluttered and she licked her lips before she tugged at the bottom one with her teeth. "Don't, Jack."

"Don't what, Stevie? Don't tell you the truth?"

"The truth doesn't matter."

He leaned in and kissed the warm spot at the corner of her shoulder and neck. Gooseflesh erupted across her smooth skin. "Remember what I taught you? About following your instincts?"

Her body lost some of its tension. "Yes," she breathed.

"What do they tell you right now?"

"That you're messing with me."

He laughed low and nipped her bare shoulder. "Liar. A good cop always listens to his instincts. Want to know what mine are saying?"

"No, but you're going to tell me anyway."

"Mine say you want me but you're afraid."

She stiffened. "You don't scare me."

He pulled back and looked her hard in the eye. "I may not, but *we* do."

Her lips parted and she hissed in a breath. He smiled. "See?"

She scooted away from him. "I need some time, Jack. I—this case is stressing me. I want Spoltori put away. Maybe after we put it to bed, we can, um . . ."

He sat silently and watched her shuffle her way through a lousy excuse to say no to him. He wanted to tell her he was not the enemy. But he wanted her to trust her instincts more.

"Stevie, stop lying to yourself."

Her lips tightened. "It doesn't matter, Jack. I promised myself a long time ago, no more cops. And as much as I would love one of your world-famous orgasms, I'm not willing to endure the fallout that comes with it."

She slid off the bench away from him and stood. Then, she turned and walked out the door.

Stunned, Jack felt as if a tornado had picked him up, twirled him, and set him down in the same spot. He sat silently and watched through the wide glass window the taillights of her car disappear into the sultry night.

He'd really blown it all those years ago. He continued to stare out into the black night. If he had to do it all over again he wouldn't change a thing. He'd had his reasons for not calling.

Frustrated, he grabbed her half-downed malt and sucked the cup dry. Slamming it down on the table, he cursed. The smooth chocolate taste of the shake lingered on his tongue. Just like the taste of the woman who drank it before him.

He stood and jerked on his jacket. Stevie's last words rang in his ears. She didn't do cops?

Well, he did.

Besides . . .

He grinned and plucked an onion ring off the tray. He took a bite and laughed, chewing the addictive food. He dipped it into the ranch dressing, smothering it beyond recognition, and smiled before he popped the remaining piece in his mouth. With a jaunt to his step, he grinned and thought, *last time I checked, I wasn't a cop.*

Stevie drove too fast along Highway 50. She felt like an escaping criminal, not sure what crime she had committed, but sure she had transgressed nonetheless. Jack's words rang like church bells through her head. God, she wanted to believe him.

"I hate you, Jack Thornton!"

She pounded a fist against the leather steering wheel and cursed the deadly fed again.

She didn't want to be attracted to him, she didn't want to want him, she didn't want to believe his words, and she didn't want any messy complications in her life. And Jack Thornton was a very messy complication.

"Not if you keep him away, he isn't." Stevie grunted, shook her head, and continued her one-sided conversation with herself. "You don't do cops. Cops are bad, bad men. They love you, then leave you, then they talk about it."

Well, actually, Jack hadn't let the cat out of the bag. She had. Kind of.

So what if I slipped up and talked to my Academy counselor over lunch the next day, and the biggest mouth in Nor Cal overheard the gory details?

"Fine, Jack didn't spread the word, but he didn't call, and that's worse."

Stevie nodded her head vigorously.

"Damn straight that's worse."

Did she look like a moron? Did she have IDIOT stamped across her forehead?

"Hell, no!"

No, she didn't and she'd be damned if she would allow herself to be less than a second thought after months of working so closely with Jack Thornton in the Academy, followed up with a wild session of head-banging sex with him.

"Damned straight!"

Besides, she promised herself and reminded herself repeatedly, she didn't do cops!

Although . . .

"Does a fed count?"

7

Stevie made it home in record time. Her internal engine revved and her anxiety pushed a personal high-water mark. She'd failed to obtain a search warrant, a killer was roaming the streets of Sacramento, and Jack was pursuing her relentlessly. If she didn't get some form of release soon, she'd self-destruct.

Skidding to a halt in the driveway, she slammed the 'Stang into Park and jumped out of the car. She had every unit in Sac proper and surrounding cities on the lookout for Spoltori and his vehicle. Until morning, she couldn't move on the warrant.

She ground her teeth and swiped her fingers through her hair. That left Jack. Tension roiled through her body, lighting up every nerve. Even the faintest touch of a breeze caused her skin to simmer. In a lousy attempt to quell her out-of-control sensations, she leaned against the car door and crossed her arms across her chest. The brush of her skin against her nipples jerked her out of her pose. She needed to do something, anything, to kill the riveting sensations in her body. She cursed Jack Thornton again.

How dare he think she'd fall for his line that he'd come back for her? Did it take him seven years to figure that out? One phone call. That's all it would have taken. *One little phone call.*

She glanced up and down the dark, quiet cul de sac and decided a long run might alleviate the tension in her body. At least the physical drain might help her get to sleep. She put on her jogging shoes from her gym bag.

Her paced jog turned into a mad dash to get away from her demons. After a half hour, she wanted to scream with frustration. The devil was inside her and she couldn't outrun herself.

Realizing she had run miles from her neighborhood, she slowed in the darkness of the starless, humid night. Once again, she blamed Jack. It was so easy. She's been doing it for years and felt no qualms about it.

In her mind, they'd formed a bond all that time ago in the academy. They'd become a team, and teammates were supposed to depend on one another. The old adage "When the going got tough, the tough got going" applied to them. But when it was Jack's turn to dig deep, he caved. He couldn't be bothered to end it like a gentleman.

She leaned against a guardrail on the shoulder of the road to catch her breath. The crickets chirped happily in the darkness and a rare breeze rustled through the poppies in full bloom. Her muscles screamed and she dreaded the jog back to her house. She should have hit the treadmill. The night stood still and breathless and she turned back toward her house, and the fine hair on the back of her neck rose. She didn't have her cell phone or piece. She'd been pissed off and forgotten them. She felt naked and vulnerable, just like after she woke to find Jack gone, and her Academy captain told her Jack had gone home to his wife.

A part of her dried up and died that instant. Stevie shook her head and swept her damp hair out of her eyes. No way was she going to give Jack a second chance.

She started to jog, and wondered why giving him a second

chance was such a bad idea. Honest with herself, she admitted she wanted him. She wanted to feel him inside her again. Her pace picked up as she headed down the long, sweeping road. She wanted more than his dick, and therein lay the problem.

From the distance behind her came the sound of a low rumbling engine. She picked up her pace, and the sense she was not alone bit deep. "Damn it, Stevie, you know better than to go anywhere without your cell and piece." Especially with Spoltori on the loose.

The rumbling grew louder and she shot a glance over her shoulder. The funneled tip of light speared the dark night as the car crested the hill. She jogged across the road to the outside shoulder going against the flow of traffic. Unless the driver was blind, she was in no danger of being hit. The anxiety in her gut abated and she continued her paced jog.

It occurred to her almost instantly that the car had adjusted to her jog pace. She glanced over her shoulder again and caught her breath. The car had not only slowed to her pace, but also moved to her side of the road. The high beams flashed on, spotlighting her.

There was nowhere to go, unless she wanted to go over the guardrail and into the ravine below. The car made the choice for her. Its engine revved, the tires squealed, and a ton of sleek metal hurled down the incline straight for her. Stevie jumped over the guardrail and prayed the tumbleweed on the other side was not so dry it couldn't hold the pull of her weight.

The car scraped against the guardrail, sending sparks shooting off into the darkness. Focused on surviving, Stevie didn't catch any distinguishing marks on the vehicle. Instead, she held on to the prickly, dry limbs of the scrub brush. Her bare knees scraped against the dry dirt. The small prickles of the bush rasped against the inside of her arms.

She didn't dare move until she could no longer hear the rumble of the engine.

Sweat rolled down her forehead and stung her eyes, frustrating her. For the first time in a long time she felt helpless, victimized.

As she held on to the scrub brush, flattened against the incline of the ravine, the heavy silence of the night wrapped around her, gentle in its comfort. When the crickets began to infuse the night with their song, as if the insect's song were a signal that all was well, she dug her tennis shoes into the loose dirt and in a steady, measured pull, hoisted herself up to the edge of the shoulder. She sat up with her back against the guardrail and drew a long, cleansing breath.

Son of a bitch. Knowing the worst of her injuries were her scraped elbows and knees, Stevie dusted herself off and climbed over the guardrail, peering down the long bend of the road.

Empty. She began her measured pace and until she was under the familiar lights of her neighborhood she continued to check her back.

As she rounded the street that would eventually turn into her court, she heard the unmistakable sound of that low rumbling engine. Her hair spiked on her neck and she jumped behind a tall cypress in the front yard nearest her.

Once again the engine slowed to prowl mode. Peeking around the cypress she watched a low slung, blacked-out pickup move slowly out of her court. She had no doubt they were looking for someone.

She swallowed hard. Was that someone her?

Was it Spoltori? She shook her head and ignored the throb of her knees and elbows. Her addy was classified info. She'd made sure her personal info was buried deep. Even on the Internet she came up blank.

That the black pickup was not what Spoltori drove made little difference to her. He was no idiot; he could have easily borrowed or stolen the vehicle. As it drove away, she dared not go out into the street to get the license plate number. The road was well lit and if the driver looked in his rearview mirror, she'd be roadkill.

Instead she committed the truck's identifying info to memory. Once it turned the corner, she darted home and called it in.

Not leaving it to the locals, Stevie jumped into her car and canvassed her neighborhood for almost an hour. When she couldn't stand the smell of herself anymore, she headed back to her house.

The driver was long gone.

She felt no respite, despite her hour jogging, and only frustration from trying to locate the prick who ran her off the road. She sat parked in the driveway for a long minute. One thought collided with another. The dead faces of the victims, Spoltori's sardonic grin, Jack's warm smile, the flash of headlights, and the terror of instant death. She let out a long breath she'd been holding. She had too much left to do in this life before she was ready to check out.

She groaned, rubbing the heels of her hands into her tired eyes. If she could do one thing before she died, what would it be? In answer her pussy constricted and she saw in her mind Jack's hazel eyes so dark with passion they looked burnt emerald.

Stevie started stripping off her clothes the minute she walked through the front door, and headed straight for her bedroom.

Before kicking off her running shoes, she turned the shower on full force. The vision of her tired, tense body beneath the hot, pulsating jets flashed like a neon sign in front of her.

Pulling a white fluffy towel from the linen closet, she paused in the steamy bathroom. On second thought, maybe she should take a cold shower, shock her body back to normal.

For a full minute she stood still, contemplating a way to relieve herself of pent-up lust. Then she turned and hurried to her nightstand. Finding what she needed, she headed back into the shower.

The hot wetness of the water felt like heaven against her tired muscles. She welcomed the sting of it on her knees and elbows. It sluiced across her stiff nipples, reminding her why she felt the way she did. Unconsciously, she slid her hand down to the smooth mound between her thighs. She smiled to herself. Had Thorn noticed her shaved pussy earlier?

Probably not. At that moment, neither of them had been inclined to make conversation.

Her grin deepened. Maybe just for the hell of it, she'd call and ask how he liked it.

Pressing her back against the tile, she gasped at the coolness. Her body flared hot against the cool bastion. Stevie slid her fingers across the smooth skin sheltering her clit. With the tip of her index finger she rubbed the stiffening mound. God, she wished it was Thorn's finger slip-sliding across her, moving faster to the beat of her moans. She flicked her fingertips across the stiff nub, back and forth, back and forth.

Moaning, she pushed her hips hard against the friction of her fingers. Penetration, oh God, she needed penetration. Not slowing her finger's sweltering rip across her clit, she felt for the device she'd taken from her nightstand.

Groaning, she grasped the thick rubber shaft of her dildo and pressed the button beneath the skin-soft covering. It hummed to life. With a flick of her wrist, she could adjust the intensity of the vibration, and she could even make the generous head swirl in a slow or fast pace. It had been a long time since she and her little friend Vinny had a date.

With slow deliberation, she pressed the rotating head against one straining nipple, then the other. With the hot water cascading against her, she guided the quivering device lower. Stevie bit her bottom lip when the rotating head replaced her fingers. A surprised scream escaped her before she could catch it. One ragged wave of pleasure ripped through her after another.

It wasn't enough.

Penetration.

Every thought of Jack and the naughty things he could do to her body left her slick. She needed no lubricant. No, picturing Jack Thornton's cock thrusting between her open legs was lubrication enough. Imagining how he would do it, Stevie thrust the supple, rubber-sheathed dildo into the swollen folds of her sex. The humming revved up and the vibration of it against her swollen lips made her catch her breath. Her thighs quaked, and she wished with every cell she possessed that it was Jack between her legs.

"Oh God, Jack. Fuck me. Hard."

Pressing her back flush against the tile, not feeling the coolness of it anymore, she pretended she was in the elevator car with Jack, and now he could have his way with her. And he wasn't gentle about it either.

Legs spread, her head thrown back, she closed her eyes.

The dildo moved in and out, the vibrations pulsating through her body. She imagined Jack's hot breath against her neck before he bit her. She screamed out as an orgasm tore through her.

She rode it out perfectly, not too much, not too little, completely in tune with her body.

Her legs jellied as the convulsions waned. The hot water turned tepid and all of a sudden, Stevie felt very cold and very alone.

She looked at the flesh-colored dildo in her hand and realized it was a poor substitute for the real thing.

She wanted Jack Thornton, damn it, not a dildo that she used so rarely the batteries wore out from nonuse instead of use.

She dropped it to the shower floor and turned off the cold water. Yanking the towel from the stand, she dried herself in angry strokes. She felt no more sated than she had fifteen minutes before. Whoever said an orgasm with a dildo was as satisfying as one with a real live body never had sex with Jack Thornton.

Running her fingers through her tangled wet hair, Stevie swore under her breath. This was getting out of hand. She needed to stop thinking of Jack.

Problem was, the cure would be worse than the curse. Because the only way to cure her craving was to indulge it. And she knew if she did that, she would pay dearly in the heartbreak department.

She glanced back at the empty shower. Maybe she should have stayed in there and let the icy water cure her cold.

Nah, it would only creep back and kick her in the ass later.

Frustration riddled Jack. He tossed and turned in his lumpy bed, cursing everyone and everything.

The vision of Stevie naked, lithe and sweaty beneath him, invaded his conscious and subconscious.

His less than gentlemanly desertion of her at the Academy ate at his gut like a swarm of army ants on a carcass.

Unable to find comfort, he decided to screw sleep for the night. In the living room of his downtown Sac condo, he turned on the television. After surfing the hundreds of channels he paid dearly for, he threw the remote across the room. It shattered against the wall. Under normal circumstances that would have been the end of his Holy Grail. But these weren't normal circumstances, and he didn't care about the damned remote or what sporting events he'd miss out on. The sport he wanted at the moment was fucking Stevie Cavanaugh.

Teeth clenched, he pressed his hand against the bulge tenting his shorts. He groaned. The incessant throb of his cock had long ago become painful. His hand wasn't helping matters.

He paced the small space of his living room. Like a circus

tiger in a cage, he felt trapped, the frustration and tension mounting, wanting desperately to be freed.

Yeah, freedom to lose himself in Stevie's hot body. He wanted her legs wrapped around him. He wanted to watch the way her eyes got dark and smoky, the way she bit her lip when he slipped deep inside her.

Shit! He grabbed a longneck from the fridge. Maybe he could get stinking drunk and take the edge off the hard-on that refused to subside.

He pressed the cool glass to his forehead. It didn't do a damned thing. He drank it down in one long pull. He grabbed another beer. After he twisted off the cap, he realized he could get shit faced and it still wouldn't quell the heat between his legs or the guilt in his heart. He tossed the full beer into the trash can.

Maybe he could just get her in a quiet place and talk to her. Maybe then he could convince her he wasn't a threat to her. That sex was a good thing, especially when two people really wanted each other. What the hell was wrong with consensual sex?

He swiped his hand across the stubble on his chin. The only one consenting so far was him. How could he convince Stevie he wouldn't disappear into thin air again?

Convince her he hadn't just slam-dunk fucked her and then gone on his merry way. Convince her that the circumstances that unfolded while they both slept off their lust that morning were conspiring against them both.

He wanted Stevie to understand the last thing he'd wanted to do was hurt her. He needed to tell her the truth, and maybe with that would come understanding. His body tightened in re-alization. He wanted Stevie Cavanaugh, and he wanted more than her body.

He grabbed his keys and wallet off the coffee table. Glancing at his watch, he grinned in the low light and decided if he couldn't sleep, she wouldn't either.

The temperature of the Sacramento Valley hadn't dipped more than fifteen degrees from the sweltering one hundred degree mark of the day. With the heat, a balmy thickness infused the air. Instead of continuing to toss and turn in the stuffy bedroom that even the dilapidated air conditioner couldn't cool down, Stevie padded out to the generous backyard of her home. This was the reason she had bought the fifty-year-old house. Privacy. The lot was over a third of an acre with giant cypress trees acting as a huge green sound wall, obliterating the neighbors on either side. To her back was a vacant lot.

But what she loved most was the lagoon style pool and spa the last owners had built. It reminded her of a secluded lagoon in Kauai she had discovered on one of her childhood vacations. Maybe the cool water would take some of the sting from her body. Dropping her robe to the ground, Stevie dove naked into the cool, refreshing water.

Her body heat sizzled against the calm rip of water sluicing against her sensitive skin. Her nipples pebbled into hard little knots, causing her to flinch.

Her body accepted the cool water and within seconds she became acclimated. It wasn't what she wanted. She wanted the chill of the water to cool the heat in her body, to shock it into submission. Instead, the very water in which she swam heated up around her.

What did she have to do, short of tracking Jack down to ease the tension in her body? "I hate you, Jack Thornton."

Determined to put him out of her mind and force her body to listen to her, she began to swim laps.

Jack grinned when he heard her words. It didn't matter in the least to him what she said. He grinned because he knew he was under her skin as much as she was under his. The only way they could cure the itch was to scratch. And scratch hard, fast, and frequently.

He wondered how pissed off she'd be if she knew he watched? He'd knocked several times at the front door. Her car was in the driveway, so he knew she was home. When there was no answer to his knocks or the doorbell, he came around to the side yard. Not wanting to get shot, he'd been quiet about it. The scene playing out before him was the last one he expected. Tiki torches softly illuminated the lagoon pool and the woman frantically swimming laps in it. Soft music played in the background. Steam swirled around the built-in spa.

He grinned. Maybe he should shuck his clothes and wait for her in the spa.

Before he could make that decision, Stevie stepped out of the pool like Venus rising from the surf. Her long, lean body shimmered in the firelight, licks of light playing hide and seek across her curves. Jack swallowed hard. She stood at the beach entrance, smoothing her long wet hair back off her face. Her tits, firm and ripe, jutted out and up into the balmy air, daring him to touch. His cock thickened with an infusion of blood.

Desperation crossed his mind. Last supper, famished, starving. It was all about her and he had no shame in it. In the years that separated the day and a half they had spent devouring each other and even the long grueling hours of tactics training at the Academy, she'd never been far from his thoughts.

Her back to him, she bent down to pick up her robe. Her heart-shaped ass drew taut and the dimple on the outside of her right cheek winked at him.

"No, no," he whispered from the shadows. "Don't put it on."

He blew a sigh of relief when she just blotted her face with the terry-cloth fabric.

He groaned and swallowed hard as he watched her saunter over to a doublewide lounge chair to spread out the robe and sit down. The firelight from one of the torches directly behind her illuminated her smooth, damp skin. Shit! He needed to do something. He couldn't just stand there like a frickin' peeping Tom.

His dick twinged hard when she grabbed a bottle of lotion on the little table next to the chaise. He licked his lips as she began to massage it down her legs, then up her belly to her breasts. Her body flinched and he about came out of his pants when she rubbed the palm of her hands against the straining nipples.

Her moans wafted to him.

He swallowed hard for the umpteenth time.

Being a man of action, he made his move.

8

Stevie screamed. A soft, warm pressure on her big toe yanked her right out of her sexy daydream.

Her eyes popped open with shock. One hand automatically crossed over her heavy breasts while the other shielded her pussy. She jumped out of the lounge, fully expecting to find some varmint at the end of it.

Her eyes narrowed. There was a varmint all right, a six-foot-three, two-hundred-ten-pound one. And this particular species sported a shit-eating grin. And she realized with a giddiness reserved for innocent sixteen-year-old girls, she was elated to find him standing there in the flesh.

"Thorn! What are you doing here?"

He remained crouched at the end of the chaise. His eyes twinkled, and his white teeth glowed fiendishly in the torchlight. "I couldn't sleep."

"So?" she said, reaching down to grab her robe. Tugging at the hem, she demanded, "Let go." The fabric didn't budge.

Jack shook his head. "Uh-uh. I like the view too much."

And what a view, she was sure, standing buck-ass naked and

lathered in lotion. Her breasts suddenly felt heavy, the tips tingling. Her pussy hummed to life. "How long have you been here?"

Like the Big Bad Wolf about to huff and puff and blow her down, his grin turned lethal.

"Long enough to know you were thinking about me."

Embarrassed, heat flooded her body. It didn't matter how glad she was to see him. She had her pride. "I—get out of here!" She bent down and pulled hard on the hem of the robe and almost managed to get it from him. Instead he rose with it and covered the two steps of space separating them.

"C'mon, Stevie. We both want the same thing. Don't play coy."

Yes, damn it, they did.

She yanked harder on the fabric. He gave, only to jerk it back, so that she slammed against his chest. Despite his clothes and her thick robe held in front of her, the long thickness of his cock against her belly could not be denied.

She wasn't made of steel, damn it. How was she supposed to resist the very thing that forced her out here in the first place? The thought of the faces of her fellow officers laughing and scoffing flashed in her mind, making it easier to object.

"Let go of me, Jack."

His hands dropped.

She wanted to punch him. Didn't he know she really meant yes? *Grr.* No, no, she really did mean no. As much as she wanted this, she couldn't. She wouldn't risk her rep, not to mention her heart.

To her surprise and disappointment, Jack held up the collar of her short robe. "C'mon, put this on, I won't bite you."

She eyed him warily, wishing he'd do just that. And she wasn't too picky about the spot either. Cautiously she watched him beneath lowered lids while her brain and libido played a game of ping-pong. Jesus, she was going back and forth—should she, shouldn't she?—like a yo-yo dieter in a Krispy Kreme bakery.

Sliding her arms into the robe, she wished vehemently it would vanish into thin air. Instead, Jack took up the slack of the belt and snugly secured it around her waist.

Only a few inches separated them. She decided she wouldn't be the one to widen the gap. He stood quietly, as if some great burden weighed on his conscience.

"What is it?" she asked.

His face tightened. He rubbed a large hand across the stubble of his chin. The soft sandpaper sound intrigued her. She imagined the rough feel of his cheeks between her thighs.

She caught her breath and took a tentative step backward.

What was it her mother always said during her years of dieting? *Now, Stevie, if you get a hankering for a treat, give your body what it craves so it will stop bothering you. 'Cause it won't leave you alone until you have just a bite.* Well, if her mother, who she trusted with her life, could indulge a time or two while dieting, why couldn't she?

She eyed Thorn. Oh yeah, he was a treat all right, but she wasn't so sure one bite would suffice. Maybe she could try. Just a nibble, a little taste.

Maybe.

She watched emotions flicker across his handsome features. His lips twitched, his eyelids fluttered, and his nostrils flared.

He walked past her and said over his shoulder, "I wasn't kidding when I said I couldn't sleep. The AC in my condo is on the blink."

"If you thought you could cool off here, you're out of luck. My AC is as old as Moses and only cools when it feels like it. Even with the fans going full blast, my house is like a furnace."

He walked over to the sloping beach entrance of her pool. "This is really nice."

She didn't trust herself or him, so she kept her distance. "It's the reason I bought the place. That and the privacy."

He turned. With the torchlight behind him, it was hard to read the expression on his face. His voice, though, was deep and resonated confidence. "Do you have something cold to drink? Maybe a beer?"

She nodded. "I have a pitcher of iced tea on the table."

"Sounds okay, but a beer sounds better."

"Sure." She turned and walked into the house. She should have known he'd be up to his old tricks. When she returned with two chilled longnecks in hand, the only clue to his presence was the heap of clothes on the very spot she had dropped her robe to swim.

He broke at the far end of the pool. "C'mon in, Stevie. The water's great."

She set the bottles at the edge of the pool. Sitting down beside them, she dipped her toes in the water.

He swam to her, his strokes long and powerful. Her body responded. Her blood quickened and her heart rate kicked up several notches.

Chest down, he crawled along the incline of the slope. His wide chest emerged, the play of his muscles glistening in the low light. His shoulders looked powerful enough to hold the weight of the world. His long arm reached for one of the bottles, touching her toes. She didn't flinch. Their eyes locked and he smiled. "Oops, sorry."

Slow lapping waves of water broke against the tight slope of his ass. Stevie swallowed hard. If he turned over she was in trouble.

He held the bottle with his right hand and with his left braced himself against the plaster surface. He took a long swig.

"Ahh, that hit the spot."

Setting the bottle out of the way, he inched his way closer, the buoyancy of the water cradling him. His long fingers wrapped around her foot and he tugged slightly. Stevie's breath lodged in her throat. Even through the coolness of the water his body heat infused her. He pulled her foot to him and nibbled on her toe as if he tasted a delicate dessert. She was grateful she'd had a pedicure earlier that week.

Chills flashed across her skin.

His eyes locked on hers, the thick moistness of his tongue lapped around her toe. "Mmm, you taste good."

She continued to hold her breath, wondering if she'd pass out from asphyxiation. "Jack—"

His lips traveled from her toe to her instep. Unhurriedly he nibbled the sensitive skin there. "Hmmmm?"

"Ah, you need to kind of stop that."

His free hand slid up the back of her calf to just behind her knee. The slow, deep pressure of his fingers stirred her senseless. "Maybe I kind of don't want to. Are you going to stop me?" Once more his tongue slipped between her toes, making her body shudder.

There was nothing wimpy about his appetite. He sucked, nibbled, and tortured her with his tongue.

"Oh, that, that feels—good." She wasn't going to lie. Besides, maybe this was the little taste she needed to fend off her craving.

Beneath the robe her skin simmered and she felt the first wave of moisture between her thighs. *Oh boy.*

He pulled himself closer to her, his body glistening in the light. She resisted the urge to run her hands down his back. She yiped when both of his hands smoothed up each of her legs beneath her skimpy robe, only to stop short of the center of her world. Her body responded on its own with a slow undulation.

More moisture seeped from her. Her nipples spiked, demanding some action.

"Jack, this isn't fair."

His lips trailed from her instep to her ankle where he nipped her. "Life isn't fair."

"But—" she gasped, when the tip of his finger brushed across the skin shielding her clit. "Oh no, Jack, don't do that."

His lips traveled upward, beyond her ankle. "Don't you like it?"

Denial right now was a river in Egypt. "Yes, I—" His fingertip whispered across the swollen lips of her sex. "Oh please . . . don't stop that." A thick sensual haze engulfed her. She stopped fighting him.

"C'mon and tell me you want me, Stevie."

Oh, yes, she wanted him, right now, this minute, and the consequences be damned. His lips nibbled at her knee. She flinched.

"What happened?"

Breathless, she said, "I fell jogging."

"Let me kiss it and make it all better."

"Kiss it all, Jack, make it all better."

"It will be my pleasure."

She wanted to pull her eyes away, but she couldn't stop watching, mesmerized by the scene. He truly resembled a man indulging in a gourmet feast. She wanted to lie back against the concrete and allow him full access to her body.

When he looked up at her from her knee, he smiled. "I like your smooth pussy." He sniffed the air, his nose to the wind, his nostrils flaring, a dog sensing its mate close by. "I like the way you smell, all spicy and hot."

Her thighs trembled, and she felt a gush between her legs. *Oh Jeez.* In tune to her as no other man, he knew what her body craved, and he had no qualms about giving it to her.

He slid a finger along her aching cleft, spreading her juices. Her hips quaked and lifted of their own accord. With sensual invitation, her pussy allowed his finger entry.

"Oh Jesus." Her breath hissed out of her lungs. The sublime

pressure of his finger gliding deeply into her was almost her undoing. Her aching muscles clasped around him, demanding he
fill the throbbing void.

In a slow, in-and-out slide, his finger massaged, tortured,
and teased. The slick sound of his action coupled with her low
moans of pleasure pushed her already speeding body into overdrive. Openmouthed, gasping for air, she dug her fingers into
the terry cloth of her robe, twisting the fabric.

She rocked against the sexual rhythm of his hand, her body
on its own course to satisfaction.

She bit back a cry. Oh, dear God, she was acting like a wanton.

"Let go, Stevie, relax," he said against the sensitive skin of
her thigh.

Helpless, she moaned, lying back against the smooth concrete.

"That's my girl."

His lips traveled slowly toward what she wanted more than
anything she could remember.

"Just a little taste, Stevie."

His tongue became more demanding of her skin. Boldly he
stroked her. She cried out when his finger slid from the moist
heat of her. In an effort to stay his hand, she clasped her thighs
closed. "Don't stop."

He laughed softly. "I haven't started. Open your legs."

On command, her thighs loosened.

"Now tell me what you want."

Shyness engulfed her. She'd never told a man what she
wanted, it just—happened. Leave it to Jack to demand it from
her.

"I want—"

His hot breath singed her sensitive flesh.

"Tell me," he breathed.

She gulped and her earlier coyness vanished. "I want you to

make love to me." She rocked toward him. "I want you to make love to me like I'm the only one for you."

She dared to look at him and what she found surprised her. His eyes burned hard with passion and a small smile teased the corners of his lips.

"You're beautiful, Stevie. All flushed and swollen." He circled her clit with this thumb, her wetness making the glide sinfully delicious.

His finger dabbled with the hard nub, rotating around and around. His whiskers brushed against the soft skin of her inner thigh, the scratching sensation tormenting. Her back arched. She went rigid. The tension mounted furiously and just when she thought she would explode, his finger stopped. She screamed out, demanding he finish what he begun. His answer was the heat of his mouth and his rapid-fire tongue. His main course had arrived, and he sumptuously dug in.

A violent wave of tension ripped out of her. She screamed again. Her hips wildly bucked against the voracious pull of his mouth and tongue.

Orgasms crashed through her body, one wave after the other. His tongue flicked and lapped her clit while his lips sucked the juice right out of her. Wildly she responded, unable to get enough, but at times feeling it was too much. Just when she peaked and needed a second to catch herself, he gave it to her, only to torment her again, and again, pushing her further than she'd ever been pushed.

9

"Baby, I've been craving this for years."

"It's been too long."

His thumbs slid along the succulent flesh of her swollen lips and slowly parted them. When the heat of his breath caressed the heat of her skin, Stevie hiked her breath and held it. Oh God, she wanted all of him.

"We've always had a connection, Stevie."

She let out her breath in a slow, measured pace. "Why didn't you call me?"

His thumb slid around her creamy clit. Her heart stutter-stepped in her chest. That felt so good. "I wanted to, but everything happened so fast. You know my divorce was barely final when we met. My ex had a tough time accepting it. She used her son to get to me. He was a good kid. I had some guilt there so it worked."

Stevie heard the regret in his voice. "Go on," she said softly.

He smoothed his fingers across the inside skin of her thigh. "I woke up to my pager going off. I saw my ex's number with 9-1-1. When I called in she told me my stepson had been abducted." He shook his head. "Stevie, I'm sorry, I couldn't get out of there fast enough. By the time I got to my ex, I knew she was lying. Just a ploy to guilt me into coming back. No sooner did she confess to her scheming when my cell rang. It was Quantico. They had had a last-minute dropout for the Academy starting the next day. If I wanted in, I had to take off then and there."

He shook his head and kissed the inside of her thigh. "By the time I was on my way to the airport, I decided it was better that you thought I was a shit. I figured that way you could move on."

Her heart constricted. It amazed her that she understood his reasoning. At that time there was no future for them together with their careers on opposite sides of the country. So he spared them both the heartache of wanting what they couldn't have. But still . . . she pushed her hips against him. "I still think you're a shit."

He grinned, and blew his hot breath along her sweltering opening. "Yeah, but a shit that can make you come all day long."

Her body tightened. "That's right, it's all about the sex, isn't it?"

"It's a start."

"Well then, let's not disappoint ourselves."

She scooted away, out of Thorn's grasp, but kept her thighs slightly parted in coy invitation. "If you want it, Jack, you're going to have to come and get it."

His eyes gleamed feral in the low light of the torches. "Your pussy looks so sweet and hot right now. I'll come and get it. Let me lick it again."

Stevie fought back a moan. She was done letting him make the moves and control the moment. She wanted this, regardless of the fallout, and by damn she was going to get maximum return. Smiling like a contented kitten, Stevie reclined back on her elbows. When Jack made to move toward her, she put her bare foot on his chest. "Uh-uh, Jack, you waited seven years, you can wait some more."

Like an obedient pet, he pushed back so that the water lapped against his chest, exposing only his wide shoulders and head. He smiled slowly. "Don't make me wait too long, or I might have to have my own private party."

"Oh, I don't think you're going to want to do that."

"Why not?"

"Because." She slid her fingers up her swollen folds. "You won't be able to move."

Ever so slowly she massaged her glistening slit. The heated fullness of her lips throbbed, her juice smoothing the way for entry. "You like looking at me, Jack?"

He swallowed and nodded. Gently she traced little circles around her swollen flesh. "Do you like the taste of me?"

Mutely he nodded, not taking his eyes off her. Dipping her fingers into herself, Stevie hissed. She was primed. "Oh, Jack, I wish that was you right now."

She dropped her head back and her heavy lids hovered halfway down her eyes.

Sliding a moist fingertip across her hard nub, Stevie moaned, her hips responding with a slow undulation. Trailing the finger up her belly to her breast, she plucked at a nipple. Goose bumps spread like wild fire across her skin. Finally she rubbed the finger, still laden with her own fluid, across her bottom lip. She sucked it in. "I like the taste of me too."

A low primal moan emanated from the pool. Slowly opening her eyes, Stevie smiled. "Control yourself, Jack. Patience."

She offered him her fingers. "Want some?"

He grabbed them, clasping his hand around hers and brought the tips to his lips. He licked and sucked, slurping loudly.

"Delicious." He licked her index finger like a melting Popsicle. As if an invisible string connected the play of it to her pussy, she twinged and bucked.

Unable to stop herself, she moaned. She pulled her hand clear, panting, fighting for control. She scooted back on her butt and managed to smile again. She murmured breathily, "Let me see you."

Jack didn't need to be asked twice. Like Poseidon rising from his water world to visit a mere mortal, he rose from the pool. Stevie gasped. His thick arousal jutted arrogantly at her.

Maybe her memory had faded, but if she wasn't mistaken, since she'd last seen him like this, the man had grown in the cock department. He was huge, and ready for any test she might have in mind. The swollen tip of his cock tapped against his belly button.

Blood flooded to the sensitive spot between her legs. She gulped. When he reached out a hand and touched himself, she raised her eyes. Their gazes locked. Reverently, his hand began a slow, up-and-down movement.

"Oh, Jack, now you're being selfish." But she couldn't deny that the sight of his cock in his large hand moved her. There was something profoundly erotic watching him stroke himself and seeing his body respond so ardently.

"No more than you."

"Touché." She wanted to crawl over on all fours and take him in her mouth. She wanted him to go down on all fours and ravish her until she couldn't move.

Her indecision must have shown on her face. "What is it, Stevie? Tell me what you want, and I'll give it to you."

Emotion flooded her. Her immediate response to his question was, she wanted *him*. Not just sex, but everything about him. And not just tonight, she wanted all of him every night.

The revelation stunned her. For God's sake, she was in love with Jack Thornton.

"What's wrong?"

If someone had thrown a tub of ice over her she couldn't have felt more chilled.

The muscles in her thighs tightened, then she closed up. Her heart thudded dully in her chest. She gave his glorious hard-on a long, regretful look.

"I . . . Thorn, I—I don't do cops."

Not to be deterred, he dropped to his knees, and moved toward her. "I'm not a cop, Stevie. Haven't been for seven years."

She crab-crawled backward. Like a wolf stalking its prey, he continued toward her. Her nose twitched and the musky scent of him wafted up, filling her senses. "I never told a soul about us," he whispered huskily. "I have no intention of sharing what happens between us with anyone but you."

She inched backward. He inched forward. Her mouth worked open and closed. Her stomach did somersaults, and the pulse in her throat pounded wildly. She wanted to tell him to get the hell out of her life, to leave her alone. She wanted to hurt him like he hurt her. But she couldn't.

"We're working a case together. I think there's something in the General Orders about having sex with a fed."

His grin widened. "No, there isn't." He nipped at her toe. She yipped. "Even if there was," he continued, "certain rules have no business on the books."

Her belly clenched. "You'd break rank to be with me?"

"I'd break more than rank." He crawled over her, his massive chest inches from her face. "I'd break anyone's neck who stood in my way."

His lips dipped to her nose and he kissed her there. "I want you, and I want you now."

"I want you too . . ."

That was all it took. He swept her up into his arms and in two steps laid her down on the wide chaise. Instead of the triumphant grin she expected, his features forged an edge. The edge of a man who displayed extreme self-control. A man who knew what he wanted and would take only one answer.

She'd given Jack the answer when, unable to deny it another

second, she told him she wanted him too. She'd wanted him all those years ago, she'd wanted him the minute he walked back into her life, and she wanted him now. There was no denying it any longer, and no reason to—not when she walked in with her eyes wide open, and was willing to take the bitter medicine of desertion she knew might come.

She smiled seductively. All the more reason to enjoy every second of their little tryst to the fullest. Her body revved in anticipation. Yeah, she wanted him all right, and at this particular moment she wanted him smack dab in the middle of her pussy.

"Take me back seven years, Jack."

He kissed her hard, his lips pushing hers open, his tongue spearing into her mouth, tasting. After that bruising assault he whispered against her ear, "No, Stevie, it's the here and now that's important."

He slid off her robe. Reverently his hot gaze caressed her heavy breasts. Her nipples stood ramrod stiff, and her pussy pulsed, yearning for the penetration it had been denied for so long.

"I love your tits." Like a starved newborn he ravaged one, then the other, his hands scooping them together as he sucked and nipped at each peak. "God, I've missed this body." She arched against him. Reaching past his belly, she ran a hand down his hot thickness. He groaned. Satisfaction rushed through her. "Careful, babe," he said, his voice tough. "I'm about to explode."

The sensitive place between her legs hummed with anticipation. "Explode away. We have all weekend."

He didn't wait. Spreading her thighs farther apart with his knees, he pressed the head of his cock against her aching spot, the back-and-forth motion driving them both mad. Suddenly he stopped.

"Shit, I don't have a condom."

Hanging on to his shoulders, rubbing her clit against the

underside of his cock, she gasped out, "I—oh Christ, Jack, what happened to the fed motto of always being prepared?"

He nudged her with the tip of his cock. "I—sorry, I didn't think."

Stevie clung to his shoulders, finding it difficult to breathe. She'd dreamt of this for years and she couldn't believe he was here, in her arms, hot and ready for her—and they had no condom!

She slid out from underneath him and her mind raced for a solution. "Okay, I have a condom, I know I do, I have to!" Her voice rose several octaves. *This was not happening!*

She darted naked into her house and destroyed her medicine cabinet in her search of that elusive piece of latex.

Pouncing on the little red-and-black box of Trojans, she screamed with joy. "Thank you, God, thank you, thank you, thank you." Her mother had found them in her younger brother's drawer last year and gave them to her, *for safekeeping*.

Like a little girl with a new toy, Stevie raced back to Jack. She was glad to see her impetuous departure and return had done nothing to quell his magnificent erection.

As she rushed up to him she opened the box, and foil-wrapped condoms went flying in every direction.

"Jesus, Stevie, settle down or we'll never get to use one of those."

They both reached for the closest one and Stevie laughed at the absurdity of the situation. Jack's deep chuckles sent shivers through her body. God, she loved this man. His fingers slipped against the wrapper. Unable to wait, she grabbed it out of his hand, sank her teeth into the edge of the wrapper and ripped it open. It shot up in the air, and they both gasped. Jack's reflexes were faster. He snatched it out of the air. Immediately he pushed Stevie down onto the chaise and told her in a firm voice. "Don't move, *do not breathe* until I put this on."

"But I wanted to do the honors."

He shook his head and with one hand he slowly slid the latex sheath down his straining cock. "Next time," he whispered against her lips.

The minute he sheathed himself Stevie pushed up against him. "I can't wait another second, Jack, please."

She screamed when he entered her. She was so wet and so hot, her pussy accommodated his thick girth willingly.

He moved his hips in slow, deliberate thrusts, each one coming closer to shattering her.

"Oh God, Jack, that feels so indescribably delicious." Her hips undulated, wanting more return. The hot thickness of him pulsated inside her, sending spikes of pleasure out to the very core of her being.

He hung suspended over her, his breath hissing as he sucked in air. "Jesus, you're so tight." Stevie pulled him down to her and bit his neck. "Stop. I'm going to come," he gasped. "Give me a minute."

"I can't," she gasped, struggling for breath. "I need you now." She ground her pubis against him. "Make love to me, and don't stop until I tell you to."

He plunged deeply into her, the sensation taking her by surprise. Her hips bucked, the hot heat of his deep thrusts breaking her control. There were no more pretenses for her, her walls crumbled, and she let herself go, exposing all. Her orgasm blindsided her with its ferocious intensity. The experience was so sublime she felt the hot sting of tears in her eyes.

Stevie's raw emotion caught Thorn off guard. She'd opened herself up to him in more ways than sexual. He swallowed hard, feeling unnerved, knowing the cost of her display. His own emotions swelled.

Smoothing her damp hair back from her face, he watched her eyes widen when he increased his tempo. The hot fury of his orgasm shot up and exploded into her. Her thighs tightened around his ass and she clenched hard around him. "Stevie," he

screamed hoarsely, before he buried his face in
warmth of her neck. Even as he rode out the orgasm
geared up to continue the wild ride.

He didn't stop until one orgasm after another ripped through
Stevie. Her thighs quivered, her tits bobbed against the hardness of his chest. Jack felt like a marathon runner who'd hit his
stride. His dick was a piston to her pussy. Pumping, pushing,
producing power. Her hot chasm, tight and slick, sheathed him,
making way for maximum output.

He smiled every time she screamed out his name as another
orgasm ripped through her. He watched, mesmerized, as her
eyes darkened to almost black. He licked the tiny beads of perspiration off her chest and neck. He sank his teeth into her
throat and growled when she whimpered for him to bite harder.

He kept up the incessant pumping of his dick into her until
she extracted every ounce of cum from him.

Whimpering, she eased beneath him and told him he could
stop.

"For a minute," he hoarsely whispered.

As they lay on the chaise, legs and arms entwined, their racing hearts slowed to a more manageable beat. He looked hard
at her moist, parted lips, and the way her creamy breasts still
heaved softly as she fought to control her erratic breathing. He
pulled her closer, and smiled to himself. Not even a call from
the president himself would budge him from Stevie's side.

The thought sobered him. Shit, he was going soft.

He didn't know what time it was, but the air hung thick and
hot around them, cocooning them in muggy warmth.

Glancing sideways he noticed the pitcher of iced tea still had
ice cubes floating in it. He dipped his hand in and pulled one
out, dribbling the cold fluid along her belly.

"Jack," she breathed, her belly quivering. "That feels so
good."

He knew what would feel better.

Sliding his hand down her belly, he covered her smooth mound with his wet hand. Goose bumps popped up beneath the ice trail. Slipping the ice cube in his mouth, he worked his way downward to the swollen folds of her pussy. Her body writhed and she moaned. "Jack, that is so good."

With his tongue, he inserted the fast-melting cube. She shuddered. He scooped another ice cube out of the pitcher and rubbed a trail over each of her taut nipples. Then he sucked on the cube and sucked on the pebbled tip of one breast.

A long leg rubbed against his ass and his cock went stiff. He amazed himself. He looked at Stevie, her eyes half-closed, biting down on her bottom lip in sexual nirvana. She amazed him. The only other time he'd had this kind of stamina with a woman was with Stevie at the academy. She turned him on and inside out, and he couldn't think of anywhere else he'd rather be but here.

"Jack," she whispered. "Let me."

Gently she pushed him on his back, giving his erection a wicked grin. She took her own handful of ice cubes and in a slow, dallying course, worked her way down his belly to the thatch of hair that nested at the base of his cock.

"You are so big and full, Jack. I love your cock. I love the way it comes to life in my hand, and the way it fucks."

Plopping an ice cube in her mouth, she slipped her lips over the throbbing head of his dick. He sucked in his breath, the sublime feel of her hot, wet mouth and the cold slide of the ice cube against him was too much. "Jesus, Stevie."

She smiled against him. With the quick thaw of the ice she sucked heartily at his head while gently cupping his balls in her hands. The juices from her mouth ran down his shaft. She used it as lubrication to begin the age-old manipulation all men craved.

He knew he was too big for her to take completely into her mouth, but she made a good try. Her full lips sucked him while her tongue flicked the tiny opening and the sensitive spot behind the head. Her fingers caressed his balls lovingly. When she slid one of her fingers lower and around to a place where no woman had ever gone, he stiffened, unsure if he would find pleasure there.

Gently, she pressed against his clenched cheeks, urging him to open. "I won't hurt you, Jack. Trust me," she said against the head of his cock. He relaxed. In a soothing fashion she ran her finger between his slick cheeks. When her fingertip touched him, he jutted his cock into her mouth. The erotic charge it provoked startled him.

Instead of pressing farther for entry, she caressed the spot, and like she was chowing down on a corncob, she ate away at his dick. In perfect symmetry, her fingers worked against his anus and her mouth worked his cock. Before he realized where she'd taken him so quickly, he nearly erupted.

While he liked a good blowjob and even better for his partner to swallow his offering, he wanted to spend himself inside her. But she had control of his cock, and it was too late to take it back. He grabbed the edge of the chaise. Grunting and grinding, he let himself go, thrusting into her mouth as she pumped him with her hand.

Sweat coated his body. He looked down, and the sight of her mouth on his dick and her tits bobbing up and down, quickened his thrusting hips. The pressure built to an aching plateau. Just when he thought it couldn't intensify, she slipped her finger into him. He called out her name. In a wild thrash he came in her mouth, his body undulating crazily. She pushed him higher, her finger slowly working its way back and forth as his thighs tightened and he pushed harder and harder.

He felt wild, savage, as if he'd reverted back to the dawn of time.

His breaths careened out of his chest in short, hard puffs when she slipped her finger from him, and her mouth sucked the remaining juice from him.

His fingers slowly unwound from their death grip on the chaise. "Holy Mother of God, Stevie, where did you learn to do that?" The minute he asked, he didn't want to know. The thought of Stevie having sex with any man but himself tore at his gut.

She released him and slid up his belly to his chest. Her body was covered in his sweat. Their scents mingled. It was a scent he would never forget. Sex, in its purest form.

She kissed him full on the mouth. "I just made it up." Grinning, she rubbed her nose against his in an Eskimo kiss. "You like?"

He felt himself blush, his response startled him. "It was— different."

She nuzzled against the crook of his neck, her long hair spilling across his chest. He tangled his fingers in it. The soft, silky strands smelled like him.

"I think once you got past your little homophobic fear, you liked it."

He laughed. "It wasn't bad."

Lifting herself up on an elbow, she traced a finger around his flat nipple. The touch tightened it. "We smell like two whores in a New Orleans whorehouse. What do you say we get a shower?"

When Thorn entered the shower to turn it on, he raised an eyebrow. "What's this?" he asked, picking up Vinny.

Undaunted, Stevie snatched it out of his hand. "That's Vinny and he keeps me company once in a while."

She turned it on and pointed it at him. "I might just introduce you to him later on."

And she did. After they showered, despite Jack's apprehension, Stevie showed him in quick fashion what Vinny was capable of.

10

Thorn slowly woke to the lazy call of a mockingbird outside the window, and the wan rays of dawn filtering through the screen. It was going to be another scorcher. He grinned, thinking of how much hotter he and Stevie would make the day. He stretched his muscles, feeling the burn. He was sore. He'd used muscles in the last few hours he hadn't used in a long time. Well, not to the extent he had with Stevie.

He smiled and rolled over, snuggling against her. His cock thickened against the small of her back. After the last go-around with the vibrator he didn't think he'd be able to get it up until dinnertime. He nuzzled her thick, silky hair, inhaling the scent of her. His chest constricted with emotion. He'd been a fool letting the years slip by. Stevie was special and he'd nearly lost her.

He debated on whether to wake her or not, and decided to let her sleep. One of them needed a clear mind. He slipped from the bed and walked naked to the kitchen in search of food.

He frowned when he opened her fridge. She obviously ate out a lot. A pint of half and half that smelled sour, a jar of mayonnaise—*figures*—and butter. He poked his head in farther. There were a few containers of food he couldn't identify.

His stomach growled. He was hungry and if Stevie expected more out of him when she woke up, he needed to eat. Sure she would be hungry as well, he gathered his clothes from the backyard and quickly dressed. He'd run to the store and be back before she woke.

Stevie stretched and yipped out in pain. Oh Lord, her pussy hurt. She smiled sheepishly. A good hurt. She ran a hand behind her, expecting to feel Jack's hard warmth.

She jackknifed up in the bed. Empty. A swarm of nervous butterflies danced in her gut. She felt sick.

"Jack?"

Silence.

Not again.

She padded to the empty bathroom.

"Jack?"

Maybe he was in the spa. She hurried to the kitchen window. She had a clear view to the backyard and the spot where Jack had shed his clothes earlier that morning. The spot was empty.

Her heart crashed into her stomach and she felt like the biggest fool in the world.

Maybe he was taking a walk. She ran to the front window and pulled back the heavy draperies. Her worse fears were confirmed. The only car in her driveway was hers. She hadn't thought he'd do it again. She'd believed him. Once again, she'd misjudged Jack.

Her heart bottomed out in her gut.

"You bastard!" she screamed at the driveway. "I hate you!"

"They always love you, then leave you, sweetheart."

She gasped and turned around to the deep, familiar voice.

The fact that she was naked didn't occur to her. The fact that the man she suspected of killing three women was in her living room did.

"Spoltori. What are you doing here?" Like she didn't know.

He grinned, the smile of the grim reaper. "I've come to practice my craft, with you as my assistant." He glanced at his watch, and Stevie's training kicked in. She rushed him but he reacted too quickly. He trained a semi directly at her heart. She halted in midstep. The sweltering air turned arctic.

"Please, detective, don't deny me the pleasure of torturing you."

Stevie's mind kicked into survival mode. There wasn't a damn thing in her living room within reach to grab and use to defend herself.

He stalked closer. "I think, Detective Cavanaugh, you just might like what I have in store for you. Especially after what I witnessed these past few hours." His grin widened. "I must say, your man is quite the specimen. I'm going to track his sweet ass down after I'm done with you."

"You watched us?"

He waved the gun at the doorway. "It's no more than what the two you have been doing. How does it feel to know your every private moment is captured on tape?" He patted a bulge in his left pants pocket. Her eyes widened in realization. "Yes, dear, a videotape of you sucking that fed's luscious cock and him going down on you every which way but loose."

"How did you know you were under surveillance?"

He smiled menacingly. "It's all in the pillow talk, sweetheart."

He laughed at her confused expression. "You'd be surprised who I sleep with, and how forthcoming they are when a blowjob is at stake."

"That was you last night on the road."

"Oh, I wanted so badly to play some more with you. I even

drove by your house." He smiled, the gesture twisting his thin, pale lips. "I came back, you know, once I knew you'd be all settled in. But your boyfriend showed up."

"How did you know where I live?"

His smile turned toxic. "I told you, love, it's all in the pillow talk."

Her muscles froze. Jesus, he must have some of the brass in his bed to get have so much detailed information. "What are you going to do with that tape?"

He shrugged his wide shoulders. "I haven't decided yet. But until I do, get that sweet little ass of yours back in your bedroom. I want to see how well my cock fits in your sneaky little cunt."

Unable to stall him further, Stevie turned and slowly walked down the hall. Her hope was he'd get close enough for her to drop and chop block him. He kept his distance.

Then she turned the corner. In the one instant she was out of his view, she pivoted, taking her best shot at survival. Coming around, Spoltori met her fist in his nose and her foot in his right kneecap. He screamed and the gun clattered on the hardwood, skittering down the hall. Stevie leapt after it. So did Spoltori. With him on her back they both crashed to the floor.

Thorn took his time in the 24-hour grocery store. Stevie needed more than a few groceries. He'd have to be on her to keep the kitchen stocked. He liked food after sex and he planned on having both frequently.

He grinned in the frozen-food aisle, the temperature doing nothing to calm his hard-on. *Down, boy, we're in a public place. Save it for Stevie.*

After he placed several pints of ice cream in his cart, Jack made a straight line for the pharmacy. He grabbed the largest box of condoms in the display.

A sudden thought occurred to him. What if Stevie woke up to find him gone? Would she think he'd deserted her again?

He dug for his cell phone and cursed when he realized he'd left it in his car. Quickly he paid for the groceries. Instead of calling her, he drove as fast as he could back to her place.

He was glad to find the house as quiet when he returned as when he left. Good, she was still asleep. To be sure she stayed that way, he tiptoed to the kitchen and set the groceries on the counter.

The soft sound of Stevie's voice stopped him in his tracks. It sounded muffled, far away, but came from her bedroom. So, she was awake. He looked down at the quart of Ben & Jerry's Karmel Sutra in his hand. Grinning, he took off the top. Screw the spoons; they'd eat it off each other. He wouldn't regret the shower that would inevitably follow.

He started down the hallway. A deep voice emanating from her bedroom wiped the smile off his face.

"You pigs think you have more brains than anyone else."

Thorn backtracked quickly to the kitchen where his piece lay in its shoulder holster on the counter. He knew that voice. He'd listened to it on videotape a hundred times. With the stealth of a mountain lion, he worked his way down the hallway.

"Why political wives? What did those ladies ever do to you?"

Spoltori laughed sharply, the sound vicious. "Those simple women had the misfortune to be married to some very unfaithful husbands."

"So? What's it to you? Why kill the ladies? That makes no sense."

Thorn held his breath. The taunting tone in Stevie's voice might push the bastard over the edge quicker than if she kept her mouth shut.

Spoltori laughed again, this time softer. "See what I mean? You're nothing but a stupid she cop. It's not that those women's husbands were unfaithful to them. They were unfaithful to *me*.

By taking out their stupid little bitch wives, I taught them the value of keeping their dicks in their pants."

Thorn hovered outside Stevie's open door, trying to gauge Spoltori's location from his voice.

"They were mine. *Mine*. They promised to be faithful and love me. But when I introduced the bastards to each other they met behind my back." He chuckled. "But I found out."

Thorn heard the scuff of Spoltori's feet to the left of the door, right toward the bed where Stevie's voice had come from. Was she restrained? He needed a peek.

"My little friend Donna Rios happened upon them one night. She was smart, that one." Spoltori's voice lowered an octave. "And greedy. She caught the cheating bastards on video. She put two and two together and told me for a price, I could have the tape." He laughed, the sound ugly. "She didn't know who she was dealing with. By the time my lovely maiden was done with her, little Donna Rios couldn't say a word to save her soul."

Stevie's angry voice shattered Thorn's focus. "You're a bastard, Spoltori, and a dead man walking. Give it up, and I'll see about life without parole."

"You stupid little bitch. No one catches me."

Stevie's soft laughter taunted. "I did."

Thorn's adrenaline spiked. He took a step forward and a loose plank beneath his shoe creaked.

Spoltori whipped around and fired at Jack before he could identify himself. Heat seared his gun arm and he knew he'd been hit.

Another shot rang out, and this time it was Spoltori's eyes that widened in surprise.

The gigolo grabbed his chest, dropping to his knees. Jack switched hands and trained his semi on Spoltori, who released the gun in his hand. It landed on the hardwood with a dull thud. Blood quickly spread through the exit wound. The bullet lodged in the doorjamb near Jack's head.

Jack glanced quickly at Stevie who stood dressed in Smith and Wesson, and sure of herself on the other side of the bedroom.

With the exception of the scratches on her knees and arms she appeared no worse for wear. Jack looked back down at Spoltori, who stared up at him, shock written all over his face. "The bitch," he said, blood gurgling from his lips, "shot me."

Jack flashed the killer a harsh smile as he kicked the gun away from him. Stevie was on the phone dialing 9-1-1. "Be glad she got to you first."

Spoltori coughed and fell flat on his face. Jack knelt down and felt for a pulse. Nothing. "Inform dispatch to call the ME." Jack stepped over him just as Stevie finished giving dispatch her instructions.

In an instant they were in each other's arms. Jack hugged her so tightly to him she squealed in protest. Taking her face into his hands he gazed intensely into her stormy eyes. Something deep inside him shifted. She held his life in the palm of her hands and she didn't even know it. He smiled and kissed her soundly, finding no words at the moment to convey his feelings. She seemed as lost for words as he.

"C'mon, let's get you covered." He stepped into her bathroom and returned with her robe. Helping her on with it, he pulled her past Rocky's body and down the hall into the living room.

"Jack," she said softly, stopping at the end of the hall.

Once more he gathered her up in his arms, holding her tightly to his heart. "Jesus, Stevie, a million thoughts raced through my head when I knew you were in there with him."

She nuzzled his shoulder. "Me too."

He kissed the top of her head, and pushed stray locks of hair behind her ears. "What were you thinking?"

She smiled and hugged him to her tighter. "Age before beauty, Special Agent Thornton."

He returned the smile and his heart stutter-stepped. "I thought how much I'd like to toss out those three dozen condoms I bought at the night mart and start making babies with you."

Stevie's heart thudded in her chest and her throat swelled. She couldn't speak. She opened her mouth to, but nothing came out. The wail of a siren infused the room.

Thorn laughed low. "What do you say, detective? Give me an answer before the cavalry arrives."

Words finally found their way to her. "Jack Thornton, if I ever wake up to find you gone again, I'll geld you so fast you won't need a condom for anything but water balloons."

Throwing his head back he laughed heartily, hugging her close. "You've got a deal."

Body Work

Bonnie Edwards

For my cohorts, dear friends and fellow pen warriors, wonderful women all: the Writers of the Red Door, Edna, Gail and Vanessa.

And for my husband, my love, always.

1

Kicking the Tires

Tyce Branton wiped his hands on a rag and settled against the hood of the Cadillac coupe. She had great lines, long and lean, with headlights that could stall a man's heart. Lines that could make a man's hands itch.

Maybe it wasn't the car that revved him up after all. Maybe it was the woman closing the back kitchen door of her Tudor mansion. Like the Caddy, her color was cream-and-white blonde while the sweep of her long-lined midsection gave her the look of speed, grace, and agility.

She was possessed of a body a man could drive and drive and drive.

Come to Papa.

And she did.

Straight across the courtyard she came. Her long legs eating the ground, hair flying back just enough to show the pink lobes of her ears, the Widow Delaney approached the middle bay of the three-car garage where Tyce stood.

Much younger than even rumor had it, she was a ripe beauty, made for a man to hold on to. Stretch out over. Sink into. As he drank in the sight of her purposeful approach, Tyce recognized a familiar swing to her walk. The set of her shoulders and the light, graceful flow of her hands by her thighs reminded him of someone.

He straightened immediately, alert to an inner rhythm he hadn't felt in years. As her sandals hit the cobblestones, he felt an answering tattoo in his chest and farther south.

It was as if he'd seen her walk toward him thousands of times.

But this woman was no recent acquaintance. He'd never even met the deceased husband. So where? When had he met her?

The sandals she wore had slim straps at the ankles. Thin, elegant ankles. Rhinestones glittered on the toe straps. Her legs were smooth and shiny like those of a pampered mistress. Arms loose, her gait was easy but determined. Her breasts were high, firm, probably fake, while her head was set in a haughty way that said she was very much the lady of the manor.

Tilted in just that way, her chin spoke of determination and pride.

Word was she'd demanded his personal attention. His hands, and no one else's would do. This bit of information came straight from the law firm that had hired him. *No one else's hands but his.* The lawyer had been adamant. Still, if he'd known this woman before, he couldn't place her, didn't know how she'd come to ask for him.

But he was about to find out.

To cover his study he struck a match, held it to the cigarette in his mouth, and kept one eye on the Widow Delaney. From what he'd heard, keeping an eye on the widow was the smartest thing a man could do. The old guy she'd married had been taken for a ride.

He flicked the spent match away, drew on the smoke, and watched as she stuttered to a stall about five feet away.

"Tyce Branton." Her voice, husky and soft, gave him his answer.

His belly dropped, his heart slipped a gear.

"Lisa Brady." He said her name as a bald statement, devoid of the shock he felt.

"It's Lisa Delaney now."

After all these years, Lisa Brady was where she wanted to be: which was as far away from where she started as a woman could get.

"I wasn't sure you'd come," she said. There was warmth in her gaze he didn't care to see.

"I didn't know it was you."

She blinked at that and the warmth cooled to a chill. "I need the best and all reports say that's you."

He held up both hands so she could see the grease for herself. "Yeah. Who'd a guessed."

He watched for the curled lip of disdain he'd replayed for twelve years.

It didn't come.

She clasped her hands in a gesture he remembered. She was nervous. Afraid he wouldn't keep to his contract?

"Everyone says Bodywork by Branton makes a difference at auction." She hesitated, then lifted her chin and went on, "I need all the money I can get. My husband—"

"Oh yeah, Harris Delaney." He cut her off, so she'd know how little he cared. "Real old guy, right? And real rich." He flicked the cigarette to the cobblestone pavement and turned back to focus on the engine. "I've got work to do."

"He was only sixty-seven." She spoke quietly but not defensively as if even she knew their age difference was indefensible.

He snorted.

"How long will this take?" she asked.

Her soft tone made him want to grind at her little-girl-lost routine. She'd never lost her way. Not Lisa, not once.

"Six to eight weeks. Your husband had a helluva collection, but most of these cars have been sitting too long. The fluids should have been drained and the tires—"

"I tried to tell him that, but he always thought he'd drive them someday. Wishful thinking." She bit her lip, swept her too-blue-to-be-believed gaze to his. "They'll be worth more if you can get them going."

Her hesitancy surprised him. She had come all the way from a trailer park near Spokane to horse country just outside Blaine, Washington. Distance was only a small part of the journey. Her path would have taken stamina and determination, not to mention fake tits. Hesitation didn't make sense.

"This money must be important to you," he said, "because you know damn well I can get a car to dance if I want it to." He held up his hands again. "I'm as good as ever."

She studied his hands, let her gaze slide across his shoulders and down to his feet. He stepped behind the Caddy's fender so she wouldn't notice his erection. His cock must have known Lisa before his eyes had. He'd been at attention since she'd stepped out the kitchen door.

"The auction's in six weeks, not eight," she said, with a curt nod. "We'll ship them individually if we have to, but I need as many there as you can have ready."

He knew the auction she meant. It cost five figures just to get in. Only serious buyers allowed. "That's what your lawyer said."

"Oh." She crossed her arms, lifting her breasts. The soft jiggle looked too natural to be silicone. He had an instant memory flash of burying his lips between those smooth mounds. The skin there had tasted like raspberries and cream and smelled like heaven. A heaven she'd defended with every fiber of her being.

His hand tightened on the Cadillac's fender.

"The others are in the warehouse at the far end of the property." She released her arms, setting off another jiggle. With one elegant flick of the wrist she pointed at the crank sticking out from the front of the chassis. "What are you doing with this?"

"All the fluids have been replaced. Now I have to turn the engine over. That's what the crank is for."

"You mean like in old movies?" The ingenuousness in her expression pissed him off, reminded him of the old Lisa. The guileless girl he remembered. The girl he'd been so wrong about.

She'd put on one hell of an act. An act that had got her here, living in a fifteen-room Tudor mansion complete with triple-car garage, pool, and courtyard. The high gates that enclosed the mini-estate required logins and passwords.

The best way to burn pissed-off energy was physical activity. He stepped to the front of the car, grabbed the crank, and shoved it down. The first turn for compression, the second for ignition.

The engine turned over and caught, just the way it should. His spurt of anger was gone. He wiped his palms on his overalls before settling them on the front fender. A beautiful purr rumbled beneath his hands as he listened for any sound out of synch.

"I wouldn't have thought a Cadillac would have a crank." She interrupted his enjoyment of the moment.

"Before 1930 they did."

She moved up beside him and peered at the working motor. Her perfume blended with the sweet scent of oil and other lubricants, giving him a sharp reminder of where each of them lived. He stepped back, pissed off all over again.

"What's next?" she asked.

"I'll let it run for a while, then drain the fluids."

"But you just put them in." She glanced at the sweat on his neck and forehead. He stepped back, out of sniffing range. Damn it! Now he was worrying about honest sweat when what he really wanted was to smear her with it. Slide up and down her pearly, expensive, scented skin and put his sweat all over her.

Some women liked men who worked with their hands. The lawyer's insistence rang through his mind once again. *It had been Lisa who insisted it be his hands and no one else's. Was she slumming?*

"These lubricants will pick up dirt and grit that settled in the moving parts," he explained with less patience than he'd have used with anyone else. "We'll flush that all out and lubricate again."

"Then we can sell the car?"

"You keep asking me questions, this will take longer." He was brusque because he kept catching glimpses of the girl she'd been and he didn't want to. Her curiosity had driven him batty then too. The woman she'd become had no business being this curious. This woman had already learned everything she needed to get by.

"Humor me." Her chin rose and he could have sworn she turned her nose up.

"There are a few other things to do like replace the batteries, check the brakes and electrical systems. Each car should take a day or two."

She frowned at the news. "Do you need help?"

"I've got a helper." He leaned over to watch the engine, accidentally brushing against her arm. She shifted away fast.

"Who?"

"My nephew Jason. He's a good kid."

"Jenny's little boy?" The surprise in her voice showed the passage of time had escaped her notice.

"It's been years, Lisa. Kids grow up."

"Yes, we all do." Her voice went cool again, so haughty he wanted to slide one hand up her thigh while the other scooped her breasts out of her bra. See if she remembered where she came from. See if she was still happy with his hands-on service.

She stepped back suddenly as if she'd read his mind, which

wouldn't surprise him. He'd never been one to hide his thoughts. Getting down and dirty with Lisa Brady again would change the mood of this whole job. This time, he'd keep his head.

"Don't hesitate to ask for anything you need." Her cadence was brisk now: the lady of the manor to the hired help.

He grunted, not wanting to think about need. This close her skin was luminescent, smoother looking than he remembered. Her hair was lighter too. Thin streaks of blond expertly blended with the deeper gold he recalled. Her jaw was straight and sharp, more angular.

"The pool house is through that door on the other side." She indicated the back wall of the garage. "Feel free to use the shower in there if you'd like," she said.

Which told him he stunk up the place. Not that he cared.

He did the only thing he could think of that would make her understand he was the one with the real control here. Fancy houses and large bank balances didn't make a whit of difference when a woman wanted a man's hands.

He slid the tip of his finger along the delicate line of her jaw. She was soft, so damn soft he wanted to trace every inch of her. Scorched by the heat he felt burn up from his gut to his fingertip, he pulled his hand away.

A slight shake of her head told him to keep his distance. He couldn't move away if he wanted to. It was all he could do to let his hand fall to his side. "You're thinner," he said.

She looked him in the eye, not scared, but calculating. Cold. "Better food."

She walked away, not bothering to turn back to speak. "My lawyer will see to your bill."

He watched one fine example of ass stroll across the courtyard and escape through the kitchen door. There was something in the sway of flesh, the jiggly perfection that made him think she was laughing. At him. Keeping his head became the name of the game.

2

Revving the Engine

Heart pounding with sexual frustration and fear Lisa strode into the kitchen after her confrontation with Tyce and nearly knocked a tray out of the cook's hands as she barreled past.

"Sorry," she called back, as she started a full trot through the hall to the sweeping staircase. She slipped off her sandals so they wouldn't slow her down, then took the stairs two at a time to head off the dread in her chest. Dread that threatened to swell and consume her.

Tyce Branton.

She never expected he'd still have the power to make her quake. When she'd arranged for the work to be done on Harris's collection, she knew there was no one else she would trust with the job. She had expected to be able to handle the feelings that seeing him again would dredge up. She was wrong.

Every time Harris had mentioned Tyce Branton's work, success, and skill, she'd come up with excuses not to call him in. She'd been afraid that on sight, she'd want the man.

She'd been right.

Wanting was one thing, but a raging, driving need was another. If she allowed Tyce into her bed, she'd be lost. Just like she nearly was all those years ago. Is that what she wanted? To be taken over by the man? To lose herself in his scent? His arms?

Damn straight it was. She wanted every inch of him, so deep inside she wouldn't be able to raise her hips for more. She wanted to shake for him, scream for him, feel his teeth, his tongue on every quivering inch of her. Her breasts filled, her hands shook, her pussy melted in a stream of desire.

She reached the door of her room out of breath. Why was she running? She was not the girl she used to be. She was a woman. A powerful woman. A wealthy widow.

Wealthy, powerful women did not tear through their kitchens and haul ass up their staircases as if they were being chased by a gang of bikers. At least, none of the wealthy women she knew would do anything as undignified.

Haul ass? Even her thoughts had fallen back to the girl she used to be. A lady would never think *haul ass.* A teenage burger-joint waitress from the La La Land Trailer Park would, though, she thought with a snicker.

"You can take the girl out of the trailer park," she whispered to herself, "and she does everything she can to stay out."

She wasn't that girl anymore. She would not allow her heart to be taken over by Tyce Branton. She would not swoon, not give him more than he gave her. Which, from what she'd seen downstairs, was nothing more than a great ride in the sack. She had to remember that. Great sex did not equal a great love. Not in her world. Not in anyone's.

More collected, she grinned and shook her head, opened her bedroom door. Once inside, she allowed the grin to include a chuckle at her own expense. Tyce Branton couldn't hurt her. Not now.

Not anymore.

She could fire him, but he was the finest mechanic and body

man in the business. If you were selling a Branton vehicle you could expect more money, and money was what she needed.

If the cash was for herself she wouldn't bother selling the collection. Harris's greedy sons could have the cars. She wrapped her arms around her waist and held on, and wished she could move away immediately instead of seeing this through.

But she'd promised Harris she'd get as much as she could for the cars and Lisa always kept her promises. She blew out a breath, gathered her composure, and reminded herself that her last vow to her dying husband was more important than her feelings for Tyce, the cars, or even protecting herself.

So come what may, for the next six weeks she needed Tyce Branton. And she was going to have him.

She walked to her window and peered through the sheer drapes at the French doors that opened onto her bedroom balcony, standing far enough back so Tyce couldn't see her.

He bent over the hood of the car with his hands buried in the engine. From the twisting motion of his right arm he was probably using a wrench. From here she could see the muscles flex in the back of his arms. When he'd forced that crank to move she'd seen huge bulges in his forearms too. His hands had wrapped around the handle and squeezed. His neck had shown the strain, as had the muscles in his back.

How many times had she watched him in this exact pose? Too many times to count. How many times had she yearned for him to focus on her with that same intensity?

He was far more powerfully built today than he was at sixteen, eighteen, and even twenty-two. He was full size everywhere, which she'd noted before he'd hidden behind the car.

The thought of *that* made her elbows sweat.

He had thirty cars to get ready. Everyone said her husband's collection was in good hands. Little did they know Tyce Branton's hands were more talented with women than they'd ever been with cars. Heat climbed up her neck at the memory of what those hands could do to a woman.

Twice he'd held up his hands so she could inspect them. Twice she'd seen them as they'd been twelve years before, sculpting and molding her breasts before he'd set to work on her with his tongue. Thank God she'd had the good sense to stop him there. Her memories were hot enough as they were.

She felt warmth low in her belly and smoothed a hand across herself. It had been years since she'd felt anything close to this kind of heat. She pressed a finger hard against herself, felt the moistness through her skirt and panties.

Tyce Branton had always made her feel this way. Over the years since she'd seen him, he'd become the mainstay of her fantasy life. Many times it had been Tyce who'd walked onstage for her when she needed to remember the feel of a man's hand, or the hard length of a firm body.

Sadly, even that need had fizzled out in recent months. Stress and worry had taken their toll and Lisa had set aside her sexual self in order to be the wife her husband needed.

But Harris was gone now and the first sight of Tyce had brought the sexual Lisa roaring back to life with a force she wouldn't be able to fight, didn't want to fight, if truth be told. She was only thirty, too young to set aside that part of herself.

She settled on the bed, slid out of her panties and prepared to make the roar of sexual need dissipate. She tried to pull up the old Tyce, the version she'd used countless times before, but he'd been swept away the moment she'd heard the Tyce downstairs say her name, Lisa Brady, each syllable a lash of anger.

Her hand worked, her nipples tightened, but still she couldn't find the gentle loving she'd come to expect from her fantasy Tyce. Nothing about Tyce Branton was gentle now. He was rough, ready, and he made her wetter than she'd ever been before.

Still, the roar rose without cresting.

Desperate, Lisa opened the drawer of her nightstand. Inside, cushioned on a bed of lingerie, lay relief. She pulled out the massager Harris had given her two years ago. The gentle sadness in his gaze had officially marked the end of their physical relationship, although it had been dying for over a year.

But it wasn't her husband she thought of now, but the man in the courtyard, the man with strong hands, firm fingers, and a mouth that could kiss a woman senseless.

She set the tip of the personal device to her hottest button, crooning her urgency, and slipped her thumb across the on switch.

Nothing.

She tried again.

No buzz of relief. No hum of satisfaction.

No batteries.

The next morning Lisa found Tyce much as she'd left him, except this time it was the 1948 Jaguar he was working on.

He watched her approach with the same cool, never-wanted-to-see-you-again expression he'd worn yesterday when she'd first said his name.

"This garage could use a coffee maker," he said.

She did an about-face, walked back into the house, and got the one off the kitchen counter for him.

"Never let it be said I force the hired help to work without caffeine," she said when she set it on the workbench on the back wall. She'd slung a bag of supplies over her arm and set those on the counter too. "I meant it when I said you should ask for anything you need."

His dark brown eyes had never been so hard. "I'll take care of my own needs."

"Really? As long as your needs don't hold things up, this arrangement will work out fine."

The Jag he turned back to was a gunmetal-gray beauty. A convertible, it was meant to cruise and hold equally beautiful people. "Harris had the upholstery redone just before we married four years ago," she said.

He nodded but said nothing.

She set up the coffee maker and brewed a pot while he ignored her. He used his cell phone a couple of times to order parts and tools and hunt down still more. His nephew, who reminded her of Tyce as a kid, was busy with the Cadillac, buffing and polishing the chrome. There was lots of chrome.

She walked over to him and introduced herself. She asked about his mother, Jenny. Tyce's sister had Jason too young and Lisa remembered him as an rambunctious, beautiful seven-year-old.

"You were the cutest little boy," she said, realizing immediately that it was the last thing a young man wanted to hear.

But he smiled and allowed her the odd familiarity. His jaw- and brow line were so much like Tyce's it took her aback but warmed her at the same time. When Tyce had been this young, there had never been a bitter word between them.

She went back into the house to get a cooler with ice and soda for Jason. By the time she returned the coffee had finished brewing. She poured Tyce a mug, determined to be of whatever help she could.

When he waved off her offer of sugar and cream, she held the mug out so he could take it. He wiped his hands clean before reaching for the mug. When their fingers brushed, the heat of him sent a thrill to her lower belly that stayed and glowed hot.

Oh my. She dug through the ice-filled cooler, came up with a soda, and rolled it across her forehead, down her neck, and across her collarbones to cool off. She caught Tyce watching her. A muscle in his jaw flexed and it dawned on her that he watched her just as much as she watched him.

That had not changed. She'd known all those years ago that he'd stop what he was doing every time she walked past his place. His hands would still, his head would come up, and whatever tool he was working with would dangle in his hand.

She'd stop at the Colorado spruce at the entrance to the park and use its thick branches to hide behind as she snugged down her T-shirt and hiked up her skirt. She would round the tree and put on a sway that would make a hooker proud, although she was too young to even know it. She thrilled down to her toes every time she made Tyce Branton stop what he was doing to stare at her.

There was nothing quite like walking past the Brantons' trailer, knowing she'd stopped his very breath. It all rushed back at once and she realized, now, what power she'd wielded then. Still wielded. Still wanted.

She looked back at Tyce, and slid the icy can of soda down inside her blouse and across her nipples, making his eyes go narrow and intensely focused. Her nipples peaked with the frigid can against them.

Slowly she bent to the cooler again and removed a fresh can. Strolling by a still and glaring Tyce, she took the soda outside to his nephew.

"Thanks!" Jason said with an awkward smile. He popped the top of the can and drained it in a couple of youthful swallows. When he tried to hold back a burp, she grinned. "Sorry, my Mom would kill me for that," he said, flushing crimson.

Tyce came up behind her and spoke to his nephew. "You've got lunch in twenty minutes. You can take a break then." He gave the boy a look that sent the kid scurrying to the far side of the car.

"I thought you were in a hurry," Tyce said, turning to her. "Don't interfere." But his eyes dropped to her blouse, his gaze hot and interested. She crossed her arms, and squeezed, creating cleavage. Her nipples remained beaded, even though the effect of the icy can was long gone.

"Are you sure one helper's enough? Six weeks isn't very long." She opened her stance and shifted her feet wider when she saw him glance down. She wriggled her toes in her sandals, and then stepped wider again.

His gaze trailed up from her toes in a heat she remembered seeing only one time before. The coffee quivered in his mug. "I don't start anything I can't finish. If you stay out of our way, the cars will be ready."

"And I'm betting you finish everything you start," she said, with a smile designed to set his teeth on edge. Tyce Branton was hot and hard and better looking than ever. And he wanted her.

He tipped his head in acknowledgment and took his first sip from the mug. His eyes widened at the taste. "This coffee's good."

It was said so begrudgingly she laughed, and laughed again when his expression turned thunderous at the sound.

The granite hard tension between them shattered with her laughter. "A girl can't work in a truck stop without learning how to make decent coffee."

His eyebrow quirked. "I'd have thought you'd want to forget all that."

"Why? Because it doesn't suit the image of the trophy wife?"

"Something like that."

Ticked that even Tyce would make the same assumptions about her that everyone else did, she strolled toward the Jag and opened the driver's door. She struck a movie starlet pose, one leg up on the running board, toes pointed, vacuous smile pasted on her lips.

His gaze ran from her pointed toes to the V at the top of her thighs.

"Is this where you expect me to be?" She goaded him and climbed behind the wheel. "Or maybe," she chirped, "I'm not capable of driving a car, maybe I need to be chauffeured." She fluttered her fingers helplessly, then climbed into the passenger's seat.

"Or maybe all I can manage is to sit here," she said, splaying her legs, one knee crooked on the seat, the other on the floor, deliberately imitating a posture against the passenger's door Tyce would remember.

She'd pushed him, she could see it in his heated gaze as it moved up from her knees to her shadowed center, then on to her chest and face. Heat flared into want and she felt her own rise in response. Moisture pooled inside her and waited for him.

She was angry, turned on and frustrated with him. "You don't know anything about me. Don't make stupid assumptions. You were never a stupid man."

Quick as a cat, he was inside the car. He leaned over her, crowding her, filling the small space with arousal and hot anger. She pressed her back into the door to get some distance but it did no good. She felt the heat from his chest, read desire in his darkened eyes, up close. She fully expected to be kissed, expected and wanted, but it didn't happen.

Instead, Tyce glided his nose along the line of her hair, along her forehead, then down to her neck, never quite touching her, scenting her the way an animal would food. She had to bite hard on the inside of her cheek to stop a moan.

Heat flared down low and burned all the way through to make her panties wet. Her nipples engorged so quickly the silk of her bra felt like burlap. His nostrils flared and his pupils gleamed black and made her think hot, hot things. She was awash in desire and, heaven help her, she knew the exact moment he picked up the scent.

She wanted to reach for his head to bring his lips into range for a kiss, but the wary look in his eyes forestalled her.

"No, Lisa, I've never been a stupid man," he said next to her ear before he climbed back out of the car. She rubbed her arms to ward off the chill his words left, then squeezed her thighs together to stem the heat between them.

She was the stupid one. She'd underestimated his effect on her and been blinded by her need to make good on her promise to Harris.

She'd always wanted Tyce to notice her, to like her, to kiss her, and to hold her. She'd always just wanted him. One way or the other, this time, she was going to have him. It was just a matter of time.

In order to join this game with any hope of winning, she had to get supplies.

First thing on her list was a large package of batteries. A very large package.

3

High Octane

Tyce was sick of being watched. It had been two days and Lisa had come to the garage every morning, afternoon, and evening, ostensibly to check on his progress. But she was just out to torture him.

He was going to have her, no doubt about it. But it would be on his terms, not hers. And it would happen in his own sweet time.

She had to be ready, had to be prepared to accept everything he planned to do to her. And he planned on a lot of different things. Wild things, dirty things she might have a problem with. But she needed dirty things. Needed to be brought to a point where anything he demanded was his. When he wanted, where he wanted, and how he wanted.

He'd start on those perky nipples of hers. The only secret part of her he got to see before. He'd suckle them until she screamed at him to move on down her body. He'd stop at her navel and play there awhile, letting his chest hair tickle and tease her inner thighs. Eventually, he'd slide his tongue along each high crease of those thighs. By then, he'd know her woman's scent, aroused, musky with the salt of her juices.

Oh yeah, she'd be screaming at him then. Screaming and so wild for it, all he'd have to do is touch the tip of his tongue to her. Once, very lightly. Maybe once more if he hadn't done his job right and she'd come, gushing and streaming into his mouth.

He was jackhammer hard just thinking about it. He adjusted his jeans to allow for the needed room. The adjustment itself was hell on his control. If he didn't keep a tighter rein on his thoughts, he'd be using the shower in the pool house just to keep the edge off. No, he didn't want his own hand, he wanted Lisa's. Lisa's hand, Lisa's mouth, Lisa's pussy.

But before he got what he wanted, he'd make her want him more. Her behavior in the Jag had startled him, and had definitely set the ground rules for the game.

But what she'd said had surprised him more. She was right. He had made assumptions about her, but with good reason. She'd been high-handed, haughty, and demanding about the cars being ready on time.

Not to mention what he'd been told by Harris Delaney's sons over the years. They'd complained like whiny kids when their old man remarried. They'd called his new wife trailer trash, made it clear she would never be good enough. That was usually when he retreated from the conversation.

The Delaney boys weren't collectors, didn't even like cars much, but they knew his name and reputation and liked to think they deserved the best.

Occasionally he squeezed in their German imports for detailing. The allure of exclusivity made them crazy and he wasn't above exploiting it. Franklin and his dim-bulb brother would pay anything if they thought they were part of an elite group of clients.

When they'd whined about the new wife, he'd hardly paid attention.

As infrequently as he'd had to deal with the Delaney boys, he knew their type and Lisa had his begrudging sympathy.

But still, she'd come a long way from the La La Land Trailer Park and she was used to getting her own way now. That much was clear when she'd enticed him into reacting to her.

He chose to ignore the fact she'd brought out her own coffee maker for him and had even gone so far as to provide an ice chest full of soda for his nephew.

At day's end, he was in the back of the garage, putting away his tools when he heard the unmistakable tap tap of Lisa's high heels. Again.

Bracing himself for another onslaught, he turned to watch her and found himself thunderstruck by the strapless dress that shimmered and slinked its way down to her pink painted toenails. She wore the same stiletto sandals she'd had on before.

She moved with a sinuous grace that held him, tightened and needy as she approached.

He dropped the wrench he'd been about to put into his toolbox and gripped the wooden workbench behind him. Jesus H. Christ, she was hot.

The sizzle in her walk said she was tired of waiting.

Her eyes gleamed with a heated sexuality he'd only seen in women in heavy heat, and the high flush on her neck dipped into the bodice of the gown she wore. Her nipples led the assault as she moved toward him.

Torn briefly between the idea that he didn't much like being used and the pounding thrum of desire, he dispatched his ideals as quickly as they'd appeared.

She was hot, she was ready, she was his.

He waited for her to close in, but she stopped three feet away.

"You've hired the delivery service?" Her voice was as cool as her gaze was hot. The game was on.

"They'll start to move some of the cars tomorrow. I've got a warehouse in Scottsdale."

"I'll be sorry to see them go." She shifted on her sharp-tipped heels, her toes splaying wide for balance in the rhinestone-studded shoes. Even her toes made him ache.

He grunted, because he was barely able to think let alone speak coherently.

"I don't know why I'll miss them," she said. "I never drove them much beyond a test drive. Harris just loved owning fine pieces of machinery." She hesitated. "In a way, I suppose it was the same with me."

"A fine piece never driven?" He taunted her because he could, because she deserved it, but mostly because he wanted to stop himself from reaching for her. If she got angry enough she'd leave and he wanted her to leave. He needed to control when and where this would happen. Because if he didn't, he'd be lost.

But she didn't get angry. Instead she looked wistful.

"Something like that." She leaned against the Jag's rear fender, her hands behind her hips, elbows bent, a posture both submissive and insolent. "After the first few months, his diabetes and blood pressure got worse."

She raised her eyes to his and he saw a glimmer of grief she couldn't fake. "We had more in common than you'd think. In a lot of ways, we were friends, Harris and I. He was proud of being a self-made man. He grew up dirt poor."

"I didn't know." He relaxed his grip on the bench. Let her talk. The comment about Delaney's poor health revealed a lot and set her up for him even more. By the time he got around to touching and tasting that sweet secret heart of her, she'd be more than willing to do whatever he wanted.

"He was the finest man I've ever known. He understood me, wanted me to be happy."

"You are happy." His cock was now even harder, straining and full. His balls pulled up and he realized he was armed with a guided missile. A heat seeker, it was aimed straight for Lisa.

She shook her head, innocently unaware of the dance in his jeans. Something about that idea made him hotter. He scrubbed his fingers through his hair.

"I'm trapped until I get these cars sold," she said. "After the auction I'm moving to Europe."

"You want me to hurry so you can leave?" Damn it, she was going to do it again!

He shifted toward her, couldn't help it, pissed that she'd talk about going away as soon as they began a real conversation. She straightened against the fender, finally aware that he was dangerously close to moving on her, against her, into her.

Taut with want, her wariness was all the challenge he needed. He faced her straight on and pressed his hips into hers, so she could feel the throb he suffered. She was soft there, soft and hot. She moved so he fit against her mound in perfect alignment. She gasped in a fragile breath but allowed the contact, as he knew she would. A subtle shift of her hips and he was centered on home.

He ground against her so she'd know his full length, his deep need, both relieved and supremely irritated at the same time. She moaned way back in her throat, tilted her head so that he wanted to bite her giving flesh. Bite and hold on while he plunged against her, inside her.

He kept his hands off her because if he touched, he'd hoist her onto the Jag and dive in. There was no way in hell he was going to do that. Not when she'd been the one to come out here dressed like this, a princess too pretty for words.

She was not going to be the one to choose the time. No way, not when she'd told him she couldn't wait to take off.

He'd been down that road before.

The timing on this would be his.

"Tyce." She raised her hands to his shoulders, ran them down his arms and tried to twine his fingers with hers. He resisted and still kept his hands to himself. His cock did the mambo against her mound, but he figured the poor bastard had that much right. She wriggled back, nearly sending him into oblivion.

Her breath came in pants, her lips shone moist and welcoming. Finally she laced her fingers behind his head and tried to pull his face to hers.

Suddenly, a sweep of headlights flashed over them.

He stepped back, painfully aware of how close he'd come to putting ass dents in the Jag's fender by ramming into her hard and heavy right there.

"I'll be home by eleven," she said, her voice shaking. She smoothed the gown down her thighs, obviously not wanting anyone to know she was messing with the grease monkey.

"So will I," he responded coldly.

She looked startled, but he didn't care. He wouldn't wait around all evening. His time, his way.

A stretch limo pulled up to the front door of the house. She took a stumbling step toward it, then straightened her back, set her shoulders and glided out of the garage as if it were perfectly reasonable to be there dressed in a slinky evening gown.

He watched her cross the cobblestones in her stilettos. The combination made her pick her way across the courtyard with a mince and sway that would have made him laugh if he wasn't on fire.

A window in the back rolled down and a guy old enough to be her grandfather watched her too.

The lights from the house limned her silhouette, smooth shouldered, long waisted, with a flare at her hips that promised a man a great fit. She had to know she was the meat in a lust sandwich. It made his gut contract to know he wasn't the only man who wanted her tonight.

On the way back to his hotel, Tyce stopped at a quiet neighborhood bar. He needed a cold beer just to get the want out of his mouth.

Lisa Brady had always affected him this way. She'd lived at the far end of the trailer park he'd grown up in.

At fourteen she had continually pestered him for attention, asking questions about every car he worked on. Eventually, he'd given up trying to tell her to get lost and started to teach her the little he knew.

Sometimes, he'd find her waiting in the moonlight filtered night under the scrubby pine next to his mother's trailer when he got home from a date. He'd sit with her awhile, talk about school, what she was doing out so late. Her mother had a mean temper and he suspected Lisa felt safe with him.

A couple of times he'd been frustrated by a bout of nearly there sex with a prudish girlfriend and he'd want to take it out on the kid. After the first flash of desire he'd remember how sweet and innocent she was. He'd never been able to stomach the idea of taking advantage of her.

She looked at him with such open longing he knew if he had her it would be for keeps and they were too young. He didn't want to repeat his sister's mistake.

By sixteen Lisa had come around less often, had started work at a burger joint, blossomed. Some of his buddies would comment as she walked past. She'd hunch her shoulders and turn her face away as if by doing so they'd stop noticing. But Lisa Brady wasn't the kind of girl who blended into the background.

If he was alone, he'd wave as she walked by. Mostly they'd just look at each other, but sometimes she'd stop to talk. It was then she mentioned finding a way out, saving all the money she could. He laughed, held up his hands, and said they were all he'd ever need.

His hands had been magic even then. That was about the time he'd begun to enter his cars in competitions. The wins were slow to come at first, but he was focused and picked his shows carefully. His reputation as a body man grew. He hadn't yet learned enough to do the mechanics.

When she was eighteen and he was twenty-two, he found her walking home one night, shoes in hand, skirt disheveled, beer on her breath. It was late and the guy she'd been with had gotten carried away, she said. Then she grinned and explained how she very likely damaged his chances for offspring.

Still made him smile in admiration.

He brushed her hair, gave her a tissue to blow her nose, coffee to chase the beer out of her system, and a shoulder to cry on. They parked by the river and watched the streaks of light as day dawned.

Lisa leaned into him and they kissed for the first time. She was warm and tasty and fresh and sweet, sweeter than all the other girls he'd ever kissed, and there'd been plenty.

She sighed into his mouth in a way that said she was glad he was with her and he'd very nearly come right then and there. They ignited each other.

Hungry, horny kids in a pickup, he had her blouse off in record time. At first sight of her pearly breasts and shell-pink nipples he'd nearly devoured her. After all, he'd waited four long years.

If he thought he'd been frustrated before, it was nothing compared to how he felt when Lisa pulled away. He spouted foolish, wild promises, but she didn't give in.

She covered her breasts and buttoned her blouse in spite of trembling fingers. "I can't," was all she said.

She looked vulnerable and confused and he considered pressing her but decided to back off. They had lots of time. He thought once he proved he could take care of her she'd relent.

He started the truck, put it into gear and dropped her off in front of her place. Then he went home and made plans.

God, he wanted her, for longer than one night, for a lifetime. That was too important to ruin with a quick fuck. Why else had he waited all this time to touch her? When she was ready, he'd make love to her slow and sweet and she'd see what it was all about. He'd teach her everything. As soon as she was ready.

Within hours he saw her again, lugging a battered suitcase out of the park entrance, waving down a passing bus.

Tyce crumpled his empty beer can and stood, told himself Lisa had got out the only way she could. Still, he'd never forget the cold contempt he'd seen in her gaze when he'd caught up to her at the bus stop. He asked her to stay, to trust that he could get them both out.

"Sorry," she said. "You can't give me what I want." Her lip curled when she saw the grease mark he'd left on her upper arm. She was still scrubbing at it when the bus pulled away.

4

Priming the Pump

Lisa climbed into Lawrence's limo, legs shaking, heart thrumming to the tune Tyce started. She didn't think she could make it through the evening. Didn't think she could wait to get back to Tyce. She'd pushed *him* to the brink and herself over it.

"Where's Felice?" she asked as soon as she saw Lawrence Griffin alone.

Lawrence pursed his lips. "A headache, she says."

"Oh. I'm sorry."

He patted her knee and the contrast between the heat of Tyce's hand and the dry cool of Lawrence's made her jump. It wasn't like Felice to allow Lawrence out on his own. Predatory and possessive, Felice was permanently on guard against what she called poaching. "And what do you say? About the headache?" she asked.

"I say she'll show up as soon as she gets my message that I'm escorting you in her absence." His hand crossed the fine leather that separated them, landed on her knee again, and squeezed. She removed it.

The limo pulled out of the courtyard and she squelched a desire to yell, "Stop the car!" and climb out.

"How are things going with the estate?" he asked, although he knew very well it had been settled weeks ago. "All sorted out?"

"Almost."

"I hear the company's suffering under Franklin's leadership. That boy never was able to think for himself. Too volatile as well. Business needs a cool head."

"I wouldn't know." Lawrence would love to move in and take over Harris's company. Ruthless to the core, he'd think nothing of beggaring Franklin and his brother in order to expand his interests.

"Anything I can do to ease your way through this widowhood, my dear?"

She gave him a cool smile, aware of the emphasis on *this*, as if her marriage to Harris was only the first of a string. "Thank you, no. I'm finding my own diversions quite fulfilling."

At least she would if Tyce would allow her to break his control. She lapsed into silence and considered how much she enjoyed the game with Tyce. The thrust and parry, the advance and retreat, and especially the touch and go they'd enjoyed in the garage. As much as she wanted Tyce to break, she loved every moment of the game.

She got wet just thinking of it.

When Lawrence's hand skimmed across the top of her thigh, she shifted away and gave him a steady look. "There's no way in hell, Lawrence."

"Can't blame a man for trying."

The evening went downhill from there.

Her body hummed all night for want of Tyce, making her more aware than ever of the men who looked her way. Her anticipation of sex with Tyce exploded into the air around her. She felt charged, hungry, alert to every sexual nuance in the crowd. Suddenly she could see things she hadn't noticed before.

In a setting that normally bored her, flirtations and lust skipped and danced around the room, connecting strangers, distancing couples. If Tyce was here they'd dance around each other, maybe let their fingers touch over a waiter's tray of drinks, perhaps he'd brush against her arm as he went past, maybe she'd slide her hand across his ass when no one was looking.

Her arousal built, her thoughts focused on everything she'd be doing with Tyce when she got home. Her mouth watered, not at the succulent desserts and wonderful wine being offered, but at the idea of sliding her tongue along Tyce's rigid chest. His cock would rise toward her seeking mouth, he'd moan and grab her head, push into—

"You look as if you've got a secret, Lisa." It was, just as Lawrence predicted, Felice peering at her with a blend of curiosity and wariness. "You came in our car with Lawrence."

"Hardly. Coming with Lawrence is your specialty, Felice, not mine, nor will it ever be."

Felice's eyes went wide with shock.

"Oh, please." Lisa waved away the phony expression.

Felice's gaze turned cool, her smile cooler. "If not him, then who are you thinking of? You've got hot sex written all over you." She scanned the crowd to look for a likely prospect. "He's not here, is he?"

"No."

"At home, then. Waiting for you." Her grin turned sultry. "Delicious, isn't it? Anticipation."

Lisa bit her lip.

Felice leaned in close, linked their arms. "Not that I care, really, but you've got me wondering now. Who could it be?" She put one long finger to her lips in thought. Tapped it, careful not to smudge her vermilion lipstick.

Lisa disengaged her arm.

"I know." Felice's gaze sharpened. "I know who it is." She grabbed Lisa's arm again, began to steer her toward the balcony doors. Lisa went, intrigued by Felice's agitation.

Safely outside alone, Felice dropped all pretense of friendliness. "It's Tyce Branton, isn't it?"

Lisa shook her head lightly.

"Of course it is. He's working on Harris's cars and you at the same time."

"What do you mean, working on me?"

"Tyce has a rep. Well deserved too. Great hands, that man."

Lisa felt the floor of her belly drop away. "I hadn't noticed."

"Right. Of course you haven't. I didn't notice either until he used them on me."

The world tilted.

"Oh pooh," Felice said gently. "Don't worry, I won't say anything to anyone. None of his conquests would. We've all just . . . enjoyed him when the opportunity arose. Never serious, our Tyce. But a lot of fun."

Lisa had nothing to say, nowhere to take the conversation. She was so much adrift in the wind she couldn't form a coherent thought.

Felice moved to the door, turned the handle and looked back at her. "But, Lisa, when you're finished with Tyce, keep your distance from Lawrence. I mean it."

"No worries there, Felice. I'm moving to Europe as soon as I can."

Felice raised one finely sculpted eyebrow. "Good idea. I'll keep it in mind for later." With that, she slid through the narrow opening in the door and closed it, leaving Lisa out on the balcony alone.

She caught her breath, controlled it, smoothed her shaking hands down her thighs, and tried to focus. Tyce had been through this circle of women like the alpha wolf he was. She shouldn't be surprised. She shouldn't even care!

She kept her body still while inside she raged. Damn that man! And every one of the women here he'd slept with. She couldn't go back into the fund-raiser and wonder how many women knew more about Tyce than she did. How many knew his unique smell, the feel of his hands, his mouth!

The irony was that Tyce's love of cars had driven her away from him twelve years ago and now that same love had brought them back together.

She'd had no way to know he'd been right all those years ago. His backyard tinkering had turned him into the "go to" mechanic for wealthy car collectors. At eighteen, all she'd known for certain was that no one would get her out of the La La Land Trailer Park but her. To depend on Tyce Branton would have been foolhardy. Lisa had never been a fool.

In deep lust, yes. Foolish, no.

She'd wanted Tyce desperately, with all the passion of a girl in love, but girls in love ended up with babies and McJobs and no way out.

She'd had to leave. She'd had no choice.

And now, all she could think of was leaving again. She stepped across the length of the balcony to peer out into the darkened gardens and think.

The other wives had been despicable in their rudeness all evening, but she expected nothing better so let it slide. When Harris was alive, the animosity had been better hidden, but now all bets were off. Harris had explained she would be seen as a threat to the other marriages and he'd been right.

More stupid assumptions, she thought bitterly. Women assumed she'd be looking for husband number two. Nothing could be further from the truth. The Lawrences of the world were safe. Felice and the others had nothing to fear from her.

"Well, well, if it isn't my own sweet stepmother."

Franklin. She turned, leaned against the balustrade, and waited while he closed the door behind him. When he got nearer she smelled alcohol wafting about his face and stepped sideways away from him, keeping her eyes firmly on the French doors.

"I thought you were still in New York," she said evenly, pleased at how easy and careless her voice sounded.

He leaned on the balustrade, in no apparent hurry to leave. "I got in this afternoon."

"I hope your trip went well." She moved to cross to the door. "Please excuse me."

"Wait. We have to discuss my father's cars."

"What about them?" She reached for the door handle and waited, ready to turn it to escape into the crowded ballroom. She didn't know if Harris had told his sons about his plan for the cars, so she waited.

"I heard you hired a service to work on them. Which one?"

"Bodywork by Branton."

"I know Tyce. He does fine work. Bit expensive, don't you think?"

"He's worth every dollar he charges."

"Ah, but what does everyone get for their dollar, eh? There's the question. If you talk to the ladies, you'll get a different answer than you'll get from the men."

She couldn't resist. She had to turn around to see his face. Franklin was too arrogant to control his expressions and allowed all his worst emotions to show. He was as easy to read as a billboard and right now ugly lust and jealousy got top billing. "What do you mean?"

He leaned closer, looked down the front of her gown. His eyes darkened. "I hear the ladies get their money's worth. You know exactly what I mean."

"I'm sorry. I don't." She opened the door a crack, preparing to sweep into the ballroom away from him. At this point, she didn't care what the brothers thought or knew about their father's plan for the collection. It was clear she'd get no support from either of them and decided it was more important than ever to keep the plan secret. "Branton's working on my cars, not yours. So you don't have a thing to say about it."

It was supposed to be a parting shot, but his hand slammed the door shut before she could do anything to stop him. She was wedged between him and the door.

The smell of sour alcohol nearly overwhelmed her, but it did nothing to hide the leer in his voice. "They're not your cars, Lisa. They're mine and my brother's and we're going to put a stop to whatever you're planning to do with them."

She wanted to cringe away from him but she dared not. To a bully like Franklin, fear was an aphrodisiac. She knew from experience that to run meant to be chased and she would not give him the rush he'd get from chasing her. "They're going to auction," she said clearly.

"No, they're not."

"Your father left them to me." He knew it well enough. He'd raged like a trapped wolverine in the law firm offices. Shuster, Townshend and Martin had never seen the like.

"We'll see about that. If I'm happy with the way they look when Branton's finished with them, I'll talk to my brother about allowing this auction. If I can convince him to part with the cars, life will be easier for all of us."

"Part with the cars? They mean nothing to you." She weighed her options. Giving Harris's sons final approval on the collection's condition was asking for trouble. Before she had a chance to form her reply, Franklin ran his fingertip down her arm from her shoulder to her elbow. Her skin crawled.

"If you were to ask me nicely, I'd speak to my brother without bothering to check on Branton. I don't care what service he gives you, Lisa, as long as I get mine. Your pouty little lips need to be put to use. Why not use them on—"

Her elbow found its mark in his ribs and when he bent over, winded, she opened the door and strode into the center of the dance floor.

When she moved to Europe no one would know her background or where her money came from and she'd be treated with respect.

She called a cab and left well before the end of the evening. Well before eleven when she'd asked Tyce to meet her.

The sweep of the cab's headlights showed empty space in front of the garage. Tyce had left.

So he was playing dirty.

She paid the cab driver and considered calling her lawyer to find out where Tyce was staying but pride stopped her. Obviously, he was far more in control of himself than she was and was engaged in some kind of waiting game. Tyce had his pride. But so did she and she would not beg.

She spent a restless night dreaming of his touch, reliving those moments when he'd leaned over her, imprisoning her in the Jag. Her nipples got so hard her silk sheets abraded them. In her dreams she felt him roam across her flesh, from her neck to her chest, past her waist. He moved lower and slower, making the most of every quivering inch of her.

He let his nose drift over her belly, allowing it to linger at her navel, then lower. He scented her thighs, sought the heated skin behind her knees. Sliding lower still, he encircled her ankles with his steely fingers and opened her legs. Keeping his gaze centered on her juicy slit he drew her big toe into his mouth and suckled and licked. The sensation was incredible and brought on another gush of cream. He continued the swirling action of his tongue until her back arched and her slit opened wider to receive . . . nothing. No finger pressed into her, no tongue eased along her outer lips. She thrashed on the bed and nearly wakened, but he moved his palm along her calf and pulled her back into the deliciously sensual dream.

One hand slid along behind her knee while his other smoothed his organ. She watched his hand slide along its length, squeezing the bulbous head. A slick tear appeared at the eye and her mouth watered with wonder at how he'd taste. His hand slid ever closer to her weeping center, her hips widened, she raised her mons in a seeking motion only a machine could ignore. Still he didn't touch, didn't bring relief.

She felt his chest hair tickle the soft skin of her calves, his chin rasp against her pubis as he dipped close, without touching. Never touching . . .

She sought relief in her tangled sheets, pulling the silk between her legs, rubbing it against her clit. Her own hand was a poor substitute for his.

When she woke, heated and unsated, she pulled out the box of batteries and loaded them into her new best friend.

Afterward, still empty and unclaimed, she climbed out of bed determined to make Tyce put out the fire he started.

A spurt of hot anger might be just the thing to push him over the edge. She was burning up and so was he. There were many delectable things she'd like to do with the energy that sizzled its way to her center.

They could enjoy the next few weeks, work to get the cars ready, and play together in bed. Their differences could be put aside, old hurts eased, and their itch for each other scratched. Maybe they could even be friends when it was over.

That afternoon, Lisa gathered her nerve and slipped into her new string bikini, another of the supplies she'd bought. The ruby-colored triangles of material did little to hide her breasts and mound. The thong backside was the worst though. She'd never worn anything so blatant in her life.

Tying the last string on her hip, she reached for her robe and covered herself. The terry warmed her instantly, and gave her a false sense of security.

Frustrated with her own cowardice, she dropped the robe

and wrapped a sheer sarong around her hips. The gathers of material across her belly and thighs provided more mystery than coverage, but she felt less exposed.

Anyone who saw her would be able to read her thoughts, she realized when she looked in the mirror. Eyes alight, rosy swatches of color across her cheeks, lips moist, and nipples beaded, she was a woman on a mission.

She would not be denied.

She straightened her shoulders, slicked lip gloss across her mouth, and picked up her novel, a poor camouflage.

Halfway out the door, she felt self-conscious enough to dash back inside and pick up her robe. She carried it, refusing to give in to the desire to cover up.

The cook looked goggle-eyed at her, but didn't speak as she strode out of the kitchen. Jason's reaction gave her a little more confidence. As she approached, he bobbed his head and blushed crimson, trying not to be obvious in his interest.

She cruised by him with a nod.

Tyce was on the phone but stopped talking when he caught sight of her. The telltale sidestep behind the car cheered her enormously. He reacted so quickly, so completely, she knew he wouldn't make her wait much longer.

She stopped on her way past and tapped him on the forearm. "When you're finished here, you should come out to the pool. It's a great way to let off steam after a hard day's work."

His jaw flexed but he said nothing.

She swam her lengths, working herself to near exhaustion until finally she climbed out of the pool to stretch out on a chaise lounge. It was cool for swimming, cooler for sunbathing, but she liked it this way. Besides, thinking of Tyce generated enough heat to keep her warm in spite of the breeze that kicked up.

She hadn't been able to stop thinking of him. Her body craved him, her heart remembered him, and her mind couldn't sort out why the hell she thought things would be any different. Tyce Branton had captured her at fourteen and never really let go.

She stretched one leg and pulled her other foot close to her body. The cool air eased the heat between her thighs. She slipped on her sunglasses and picked up her novel, idly tugging at the thong bikini bottom. Relief would take more than this.

She replayed all the mental snapshots she'd taken of him this morning. His palm, smoothing a paint blister he'd found on the Jag's front right fender. He'd smoothed and stroked the spot until she'd wanted to scream from frustration.

She moved the front piece of the thong against herself once, twice, and gave up the pretense of reading. All she wanted was Tyce's hand on her engorged nub. She tugged. *Yes, yes, just like that.*

She moaned and twisted the thong, spreading herself wide to tease and tantalize.

The whispering slide of the glass door behind her made her turn. Tyce. She set the tip of one finger to herself and pressed. *Oh God.*

"Decided to join me?" she asked. She slowly rocked her upraised knee from side to side. Tick tock.

"I used the shower." Tyce moved toward her, hair still glistening, eyes on her knee as it opened and closed. "I wanted to see the pool and when I opened the door I heard a moan. Are you all right?"

"I will be soon." She readjusted her bikini to cover herself, but the flare in his gaze told her he'd seen. A muscle jumped in his jaw as he walked around her to check out the pool and private backyard. "The hedge is tall."

His jeans bulged and he turned toward her, for once not hiding his erection from her hungry gaze.

"Yes. And thick. I like thick." Her voice held a husky tone and she wondered if she sounded as breathy as she felt.

He had his hands shoved into his jacket pockets, his jeans tented even more. His gaze traveled up from her toes, past her now still knees, and slowed at her shadowed center. Eventually, after he'd looked his fill he slid on up to her breasts. He focused intently for a long, measuring moment and she very nearly reached for her robe to cover herself.

"Cold out here."

She palmed her nipples. "Yes, it is. Are you finished for the day?"

He nodded, watching her with an intent stare that had her moist and ready. Full of ache. "The kid's gone back to the hotel. He met a girl."

"I'm not surprised. He looks like you did at that age."

He scrubbed his scalp, ruffling his hair into soft spikes that took her back to the trailer park and being fourteen. She caught her breath at the instant recognition of all the feelings she'd had. Still had?

"I was so infatuated with you," she said. Hard to believe a crush could last so long. To escape it and her foolish thoughts, she stood and gathered her robe and novel.

"This was a mistake," she said clearly and turned away.

She supposed it looked like an invitation rather than an escape because he caught up to her before she entered the pool house.

Her insides kicked into overdrive.

5

The Oil Change

Inside the small den in the pool house, Lisa felt Tyce's touch at her elbow, felt him run his fingers down to her hand and tug the robe and novel out of her grasp. He set them on the leather recliner in front of the television.

His hands tightened on the strings at her back. She confessed her heavy need and anticipation with a gasp.

"Let me," he said on a guttural whisper as he pulled her against him. She felt his lean hardness at her back. His heavy erection pulsed against her bottom and his hands cupped her breasts under her ruby-red bikini top.

He opened fingers on both hands to frame her nipples. He squeezed his fingers together and pinched, tugged, then released again and again, making erotic tingles dance south to her deepest center, flaring into moist heat between her legs.

She moved in a primal flex of hips that showed him plainly what she wanted, needed. He moved his palms to her belly and pressed in, holding her still in a claiming that promised she'd get exactly what she wanted.

"Let me," he said again, more forcefully.

"Yes," she said as he undid her top.

The triangles of material slid to the floor and she sighed, expecting him to turn her. Instead he pressed his erection between her cheeks and cupped her mound. Twining the triangle of material around his finger he tugged in much the same way she had earlier, but his hand, his heat, his strength made it seem like so much more.

The feeling was exquisite torture, and she flexed against his erection again and again, urging him silently to take what she offered and give what she needed.

Finally, slowly Tyce turned her into his arms. "Let me."

He said her name and she said his. After all these years, a claiming, finally.

His fingers trailed the line from her right nipple down to her loins. She sighed with the rightness of it.

His gaze clashed with hers as he ducked her attempt to kiss him.

"You want to get laid. I'll oblige. It's not as if I haven't fucked my share of rich spoiled women." The tone he used was aggressive and confused her.

"What? I thought . . ." Surprised, she pulled back to study his face. Fire burned in his eyes, but his lips were set in a grim line. "So you're doing me a favor?"

"I see a problem, and I fix it. You're hot as sin, and need something I can give you. Let me give it to you." His finger slid beneath the soaked triangle at her center and rubbed at her clit. He tapped it with his fingertip, causing a riot of sensation that made her legs ease open of their own accord. She was lost.

The hot edge in his voice cut through her like a butter curler. She felt churned up, couldn't make sense of his signals. His body said he wanted her, his fingers danced against her neediness, his voice and words said he didn't want to.

Her pride came to her rescue at last. "You're not talking to some cheap piece of ass," she managed on a breathy huff.

"I'm talking to the woman who's been dancing around me for three days, coming on to me like I'm her last meal." He unzipped his jeans. "Go ahead, see what you've done to me, I dare you."

His erection was huge, his rising shaft longer, wider than she'd imagined in her dream. His finger against her promised hot ecstasy and it had been a long, long time.

Lisa fought her battle of lust, anger, and pride while Tyce slid his strong, thick-fingered hands down her sides to grasp her hips. He molded her and waited without a word. He let his actions speak of his need instead.

The hard skin of his fingers tickled and scratched, setting off sparklers that ran straight to her center. A thick slide of juices at the thought of his heavy member made her reach for him.

She sobbed, dismayed at her weakness but drawn to him just the same. She spread the teeth of his zipper apart, then freed the turgid head of his penis. Daintily, she traced the rigid cap, delighted by the velvet smoothness and hot power in her hand. His jaw clenched as she worked the button of his jeans to free him completely.

He might be angry at old wounds, but Tyce Branton wanted her in a way she responded to beyond her wildest imaginings. And heaven help her because she was powerless to help herself.

She worked his shaft, watching as he closed his eyes and jutted forcefully into her hand. "That's right, like that."

He touched her shoulders and gently urged her to kneel before him. "Wet me."

Greedy for her first taste of him, she enclosed his entire head and most of his shaft in a sudden swirl of mouth and tongue.

Smooth and warm and hard and spicy, he tasted like ambrosia. She grasped his buttocks and steadied him so she could slide her mouth up and down his shaft without needing to hold it. This was what she wanted, what she craved. She moaned in anticipation of what was to come when he flexed in her mouth, once, twice, three times.

Not wanting him to come just yet, she settled back to a more sedate suction and nibbled the length of him delicately.

His large hands cupped the back of her head, firmly guiding her until the flexing started again. Her juices flowed so freely, she had to stand or risk coming by the sheer power of thought.

"I've got to get these jeans off. Then I'm going to get you off," he said with a guttural moan. "Would you like that? To come on my face? On my fingers?"

She couldn't answer, couldn't even form one, the images he evoked were too much of everything she wanted, needed. She stood on wobbly legs as he got rid of his boots, pants, and socks. He sat her on the sofa, then splayed her knees, and draped them over his shoulders.

She saw his gaze flare when he looked at her, open and ready. He slid the material aside and adjusted her legs wider so he could see more.

"Inside, you're as pink as your bathing suit. Dark pink and wet. I'm going to taste you there, Lisa."

She moaned, incapable of coherent thought. His hand was surer, larger, hotter, and demanded more of her than her own ever could. She ripened to near bursting as her clitoris swelled, plump with desire.

"You're glistening," he said as he leaned in close and finally undid the strings at her hips.

She nodded. "I'm dripping."

He dipped his forefinger into the slight indentation deep between her legs. She felt the effect immediately. Blooming like a rose, she opened to allow for any exploration he wanted. She thought of the thickened head of his penis and felt a burst of moisture in her mouth. She wanted him inside her pussy and her mouth at the same time.

Frustrated by his slow inspection she raised her hips toward him, hoping he'd get the hint and speed things up. No luck.

Tyce rimmed her outer lips with one finger, while spreading the hood over her clit with two fingers of his other hand. His eyes glittered when he saw the ripe bud straining toward him.

"Beautiful," he said on a hushed breath. "You're so ready, so full, so . . . mine." She felt the heat of his gaze, the extent of his want, and caught her breath. Too long he looked, making her wonder if he'd ever take her where she needed to go.

Finally, finally she saw his head drop toward her and she braced herself for the onslaught of tongue she felt sure was coming.

Instead, he did no more than moisten her aching, protruding clit. A cool draft of air played across the nub as he blew gently.

Ready to cry out or pull his face to her she was taken by surprise when the rimming of her lips turned into something more.

She arched with the invasion, arched and spasmed around his marauding fingers, so close to orgasm she whimpered.

"Not yet, babe. Stretch for me." He slipped another finger inside and massaged her clit with his thumb until she moaned and writhed with the onslaught. Just as she flooded his fingers, he finally bent his lips to her and sucked in the juices that flowed with her coming.

Lisa writhed and bucked and rode it out to the end. Finally, legs slack, she felt his hands leave her as he stood. "Good?"

Spent, hardly able to catch her breath she nodded. "Good," she managed.

His erection was now at eye level and she tipped her tongue across the telltale bead of moisture at the eye of his cock. He pulled back, out of range.

"I want to come inside you. I've never seen a woman so wet and ready. How long's it been?"

"Three and half years." She hadn't figured the time until her body had gone into overdrive at first sight of Tyce again. Then it all caught up to her at once.

There it was, out there, never to be taken back. She was desperate, sex-starved, and at his mercy. She held her breath, waiting for his reaction.

He looked disbelieving. "You were married four."

"Harris was ill far longer than he let on. He needed me."

Tyce nodded. He'd always understood family obligation and wouldn't doubt hers.

He absently rubbed his cock as he bent to root around in his jeans pocket. Her mouth watered again.

She nodded, trying to contain her arousal at the sight of him treating his erection as if he was the only one allowed to play with it.

He tore open the condom package. "Then I assume you're not on birth control."

It wasn't a question and for that she was grateful. He didn't doubt her fidelity and accepted her integrity, speaking volumes about the kind of man he'd become.

He placed the condom on the tip of his cock, but she couldn't resist another taste. "Wait."

The salty, heated tang of his flesh called to her and she indulged herself for long moments while he groaned and jutted into her mouth, torturing them both. Rocking his hips forward and back he mimicked the act until she moaned with want.

He settled her back down on the sofa, rolled the condom on, then draped one of her legs over the sofa back.

She felt the tip of this penis at her entrance and blossomed again as she strained toward him.

"I want you inside. Now," she said with a thrust that gave her little more than his tip. He plunged the rest of the way and she rejoiced in the sudden heat and pressure. The slide out made her inner muscles cling in a mad grab to keep him in.

Too long, she chanted to herself, toolongtoolongtoolong. The push pull of his heavy penis dragged at her insides, creating havoc along her nerve endings. The rub of his pubis against hers, the delicious tug of stickiness on her clit, the heat of him covering her, the scent of his sex and need, the feel of his taut muscles under her palms all combined into the most glorious orgasm she'd ever experienced. Exquisite pulses of sensation overwhelmed as they soothed, drove her to heights even as they eased her ache.

His pulses matched her own and he bit gently into her shoulder as he pushed into her with his own release. A cry exploded in her ear as he spurted against her inner walls and she took all he gave.

Tyce climbed off quickly, without a word, leaving her stunned and disquieted. She heard the shower while she slipped into her robe. The water ran and ran until she got the hint. He didn't want to talk, didn't want to face her.

Setting her fingers against her lips, she suddenly realized that not once during their encounter had he kissed her. There had not been one iota of affection given, not a smile, not even a buss on the cheek.

It was exactly what he'd said it would be. A fuck. Two adults: one with a problem, the other with the fix.

She couldn't remember anything shaming her as much as the idea that Tyce Branton couldn't bring himself to kiss her.

Obviously the man was still angry with her and he didn't want to talk about what happened between them today or back in the trailer park.

Fine. They wouldn't talk.

For now.

But if he thought this was over, he was sadly mistaken.

6

The Wax Job

Tyce arrived for work the next morning tired and spent. He'd had a hard night. In more ways than one.

He never should have messed with Lisa in the pool house. He'd thought to have her after all this time would put a lot of demons to rest, but the idea backfired.

Instead of clearing her out of his system, sex with Lisa had created more of a mess. Now that he knew her body, he wanted to know more than the texture of her skin, the feel of her heart pounding against his, the scent of her sex.

He'd had some great times with other bored women, had even turned some of them into allies. This was a word of mouth business and he had great word of mouth.

The fact that some of his reputation hinged on his recreational activity didn't make him proud, but he wasn't above taking the work.

But with Lisa, it was different, more, and that scared him.

His cell phone rang and he answered, half-relieved, half-disappointed to have the interruption. "Branton."

"Hey, I, uh, had something come up."

"And I've got a good idea what it was," Tyce snapped, remembering about the girl Jason had met. "Just make sure she's not jailbait and you're protected."

"I know, I know."

"Jason, make sure."

"I will."

"You be back at work tomorrow or you go home. God help you if your mother finds your sorry ass on her doorstep."

"Unh, maybe I should come in today."

Tyce laughed. His sister could kick Jason's butt from here to Sunday without stubbing her toe.

He looked at the light gleaming out from the kitchen windows. "No, you take the day off. You'll be itchy as hell all day watching the clock anyway. I know a good detailer who lives close by. You just mind yourself and the girl."

Jason was a Branton male through and through: his head got scrambled when his dick woke up.

Tyce set his toolbox down beside the pickup and headed toward the kitchen door. Lisa had always been an early riser and he'd known all along that she watched him. A telltale twitch at the frilly white curtain in the window told him this morning was no different.

He rapped once on the door, then opened it.

He found her perched on a stool sipping coffee from a huge mug that covered half her face when she held it up. She was alone. A glossy magazine lay flat on the countertop in front of her. Wrapped in a silk robe, her hair tousled like a cloud, she hadn't been up long.

Her color was high. She looked pretty sitting there, back straight, bare toes hooked over the bottom rung on the stool. She had high arches in her feet and he knew now that the skin on her soles was as smooth as the rest of her. "You need me?" she asked.

"I wouldn't say that." He stepped to the rack of mugs by the brand-new coffee maker and helped himself. He appreciated good coffee and Lisa's was exceptional.

She grinned into her mug and took a dainty sip. Surprised by her smile, he watched the fine slope of her nape as she tilted her head down. He wanted to lift her hair off her neck, then run his tongue down her spine. *Hm.* Not a bad idea. When he got to the base, he could bend her over and take her that way. He wondered if she'd like that too.

"You plan to come out to the garage today?" he asked.

She raised her long lashes and studied him intently, blue eyes warm and filled with humor. "And if I am?"

"I'll put you to work."

"Excuse me?"

He could have laughed out loud at her expression. Apparently being put to that kind of work wasn't what she wanted.

"Detailing. No more loitering unless you mean business," he said. "I'm not running a daycare."

She sputtered into her mug but managed to swallow anyway.

"These cars need to be washed, waxed and buffed," he continued, ignoring her theatrics. "My nephew's deserted me today. You can still use a buffer, can't you?"

The challenge he put in his voice was over the top, but he knew she'd take the bait. Eventually.

The red flush on her neck gave her interest away. "Have someone from that place in town come out to do it," she said in a bluff he could read a mile off.

"I don't allow just anyone to wax and buff the cars I work on. I have a reputation."

She flipped a page on the magazine, then set her mug down and looked at him. The movement caused the shoulder of the robe to slide to her elbow. He saw a thin strap and nothing but smooth, round shoulder, but it was enough to send his libido into overdrive.

"I know your reputation," she said slowly, every word husky and inviting. "Harris and . . . others . . . told me, but I already knew."

The husband again. The way she kept talking about him made Tyce think maybe she had cared for more than Delaney's money.

"How'd you meet him?" He kept his tone soft.

"You've already judged me on my marriage, Tyce, so why would you ask?"

"Believe it or not, I've been known to make errors in judgment. Correct me on this." One of the errors was thinking that once would be enough with Lisa. He wasn't sure he'd ever have enough.

She shrugged one smooth shoulder and the robe slipped down another inch. Hiding behind her mug again, she said, "I don't think so. I realized the other night that I don't have to defend myself anymore, not to Harris's friends nor his sons, and certainly not to you."

"Humor me, Lisa. All I want to know is how a girl from La La ended up here." He raised his right arm to encompass the massive kitchen. "I've heard Franklin Delaney's side of the story. Now I want yours."

Her gaze sharpened. "How well do you know Harris's sons?"

"We're acquainted. I've done work for both of them."

She cooled, looked stiff. "That explains a lot." She fiddled with a corner of the magazine. Bent it over, then smoothed it flat again. "I can't imagine why you'd want my version of my life when you've already decided to believe theirs."

He took another sip of coffee to give her time to realize he wasn't going to leave things as they were. "You're assuming I do believe them. Maybe for a short time I did. But not now."

Her lower lip firmed and her chin came up. "Why? Because of what happened yesterday?"

He didn't want to discuss yesterday. The whole episode was just this side of heaven and he'd hardly had time to process it yet. "Just tell me, Lisa. How did you get here?"

The wan smile she gave him softened into memories.

"I left the trailer park that day," she said, referring to the time she'd left him at the bus stop. "I found another job, a room to rent, and got through some business classes. After awhile, I landed a job as a file clerk at Delaney Enterprises."

She propped her chin in her hand. "This is silly. You don't really want to know—"

"All of it."

She cleared her throat. "One day shortly after I started my job, I was on the executive office floor. I shouldn't have been up there, but I'd forgotten an important file and didn't want to get into trouble. I thought I could sneak into the right office and leave it on a desk. Harris caught me and I confessed, sure I was going to lose my job."

"Obviously you didn't."

"Harris was kind and I stumbled over myself trying to say how sorry I was to hear about his wife's death. But I was young, couldn't find the words. To relieve my embarrassment, he changed the subject and talked about his car collection. When he showed me the picture he had in his hand I recognized the car as an Austin Healy. He was amazed."

"Back in the day, it was just American muscle you loved."

He caught a glimmer of a smile in her eyes. "Back in the day, I didn't know anything else. There's too much roll in a muscle car. I prefer my vehicles to corner well."

He liked tight handling too. He grinned. "And then?"

"He invited me out to his warehouse to see his collection. Three months later we married."

"Causing a ruckus in the family."

"Harris protected me from most of it, but the last six weeks have been tough." She looked up. "Harris and I respected each other and, in my way, I loved him. He was kind and I was faithful and Franklin never got over it."

"What do you mean?"

She briskly flipped a couple more pages of the magazine. "Franklin wanted to sleep with me, especially when he drank. I avoided him as much as I could. He's furious that Harris left me the cars."

Tyce knew how furious. "But he got control of Delaney Enterprises. He and that dim bulb brother of his."

"Of course. I never wanted Harris to be unfair to his family and I never wanted to create a rift. But Harris insisted I have the cars."

"And the proceeds will pay for this move to Europe?"

She glanced away from him, flipped another page. "The sale is the last thing I need to do before I leave."

"Why do I get the feeling you're not telling me everything?"

She looked directly at him, gaze steady and so sharply honest he knew his answer was going to snap like a rubber band. "Because I don't know where your loyalties lie. All I do know is what you said yesterday."

"Said?"

"About being with bored, spoiled women. It's obvious you don't like me, but I need you to get these cars ready." Her chin lifted farther. "Get this straight, Tyce. I don't want to need you, but I'm smart enough not to shoot myself in the foot. I need big dollars for that collection and I'm going to do whatever it takes to get them."

"Including inviting me into the pool house?" As soon as the words were out, he knew he was wrong. She had been too responsive, too earthy and honest in her need.

Her eyes blazed in hot anger. She slapped her palm on the counter. Then she stood so suddenly the stool tilted back and toppled over. "I'm sick to death of you and everyone else making assumptions about my . . . my . . . character. Franklin thinks

I married his father for money, you think I made—had sex with you to keep you working on the cars. Everyone thinks Harris somehow raised me out of a gutter."

She rolled over his objection and kept talking. "I did not need Harris's nor anyone else's help!" She strode over to him and poked his chest with a well-filed fingernail.

"I was way, way out of that trailer park by the time I met Harris. I had a savings account, a good credit rating. I shopped in nice department stores. No one, and I mean no one got me out of that trailer park but me!"

"Did Harris know you were going to auction them off?"

"Yes, he wanted me to, so I agreed." She sighed as if she was tired of explaining herself. "Like my wedding vows, I take my promises seriously."

Nodding, he accepted what he should have known all along. Lisa Brady had taken care of herself, just as she'd always had to.

7

The Buff and Shine

Hours later, Lisa applied a thick coat of wax polish to a five-inch square of gunmetal-gray fender. The wax took a couple minutes to dry into a white paste, so she sidled over to the other car where Tyce lay on his creeper under the chassis. The front end was jacked up and there were tires, parts and tools strewn on the floor all around him.

When she nudged his thigh, he rolled out from under the car just enough to see her. "Yes?" He sounded impatient.

"I'm almost finished. It's been awhile since I buffed a car. I hope you're happy with the results."

"I'll go over it and look for any spots you missed. If I find any, you'll do it again tomorrow."

"Okay." She grinned. Her arms were killing her, her back, thighs, and calves were sore from crouching and bending, but she wouldn't have traded her afternoon for anything. She arched backward to give her back a good stretch.

"I can see up your shorts from here," he said. "Open your legs."

She did and felt a cool rush of air against her private heat.

"Very pretty," he said.

"Thank you." A slide of rough fingers from her ankle to her knee made her melt. His fingers danced a tattoo behind her knee, making her want to ease down so he could do more.

"My hands are dirty," he said. "That doesn't bother you?"

"Not really."

He rolled out from under the car with a strange expression on his face. His brows knit as he frowned. "There's a grease mark up your leg."

She shrugged. "It'll wash off."

His gaze cooled. "You're not finished with the Jag. I want to keep to schedule."

"Okay." She backed off, disconcerted with his response. True to form, Tyce advanced and retreated. She just hoped she wouldn't have to wait another two days before he advanced again. "That reminds me, when will your nephew be back?"

"Tomorrow. Bored already?"

"No, but my timetable has changed. We'll have to speed things up. The collection has to be ready sooner than I thought."

"Why?"

"It just does. I'll continue to help, even with Jason here. I'll go finish up." She stepped off and picked up the buffer again, her forearms protesting. When she'd started, the handheld machine hadn't seemed very heavy, now it weighed a ton.

Suddenly, Tyce's heated body braced her from behind, his arms supported hers as he grasped the buffer to help. His hands closed over her smaller ones and she felt his breath in her ear. Tingly sensations trailed down her back, already hot from the press of him against her. She felt his cock rise against her ass and knew his newest advance had begun. She shifted forward so her belly pressed against the fender. She tilted her ass up and out, letting him know he could take her against the car any time he wanted to. She thought of his hard dick sliding between her lips and deep into her. He'd have to angle her upward to get the best ride, his plunges deep and hard would send her flat against the trunk. She'd come with her mons pressed against the smooth fender, his plunges taking her over the edge with a sharp scream.

"This won't take long," he said against her ear as he touched the spinning buffer head to the paste wax. Smoothing the head across the spot, the whitened wax came up to a beautiful crystal shine.

Disappointment and reality struck with twin force. She sagged with the truth of how pitifully needy she was.

When they finished with the buffer, Tyce inspected the car from headlamps to taillights, checking around all the chrome, inside the doors, and even inside the grill.

"Not bad, Delaney," he said with a wink when he was done. "Looks like you haven't forgotten much."

She grinned, feeling positively goofy with delight at how little it took to please him. "I had a great teacher," she said with a chuckle.

He swept her into his arms and blessed the tip of her nose with a kiss. It was close to what she needed but not nearly enough. He set her aside as quickly as he'd grabbed her.

"I just need to replace a set of brake pads and I'll be right with you," he said with enough heat to ignite her.

She set about putting her supplies away while he rolled back under the car. Her mind kept drifting off into fantasies about Tyce and everything they'd done in the pool house.

"I'm going for a shower," she said, needing to cool off.

He rolled out from under the car. "I'll be inside in an hour."

"Inside?" Her voice hollowed out into a breathy sigh.

He cocked an eyebrow at her, gave her a steadying look. "The house. Give me an hour and I'll be in the kitchen." He rolled back under the car.

But it was too late, she was already weak in the knees at the thought of him being inside. *Oh good grief, woman, get a grip.*

She wobbled her way across the cobblestones, telling herself the kiss on the nose meant nothing. The way he'd helped and held her meant nothing. The heat of his gaze meant nothing.

Later, after a long bath, she dismissed the cook for the day. She watched Tyce cross the courtyard toward the kitchen door. Even from here he gleamed from the top of his still-damp hair to the toes of his boots.

He'd scrubbed himself into a shine, as fussy about his appearance as he was about the cars under his care.

Heat bloomed in the pit of her stomach and she swore she would not go another day, not another hour without being kissed, thoroughly and completely.

She scampered to her favorite stool and took up her position, trying to look cool and unaffected.

This time he didn't bother knocking, sure as he was that she'd be waiting for him. The arrogance of the gesture both piqued and thrilled her.

Just like this morning, Tyce found Lisa perched on her stool. But unlike earlier, something wild in her eyes slowed him, made him cautious.

"Thanks for your help. Are you tired?"

"Not very." She released the toes of one foot from the bottom rung and swung her leg like a pendulum. Like the first time he'd seen her he marveled at the smooth length of skin. Except now he knew exactly how soft, how smooth the skin behind her knee was. How she liked to have that skin licked.

"You mentioned you may have to speed up the schedule. Care to elaborate?"

"Franklin's unhappy I'm selling the cars. He doesn't particularly want them, but he hates that I've got control of the collection. He's threatening to stop me from selling them."

"You figure the sooner they sell the better."

"My lawyer says there's nothing he can do legally. They're mine."

"Could he say his father was incompetent when he left them to you?" He tapped his temple.

She shook her head and grinned in such a carefree way that he felt something inside crack and warm to her even more. "If he tried something like that, the control of Delaney Enterprises would be affected. After all, if Harris was incompetent leaving the cars to me, he must have been just as incompetent when he left the company to his sons, right?"

"Makes sense."

"I'm not as stupid as Franklin assumes. I've got my bases covered, but I'd just like this to be over. The sooner the better."

"So you can leave."

Her gaze hit the floor. "So I can leave."

Angry that all she could think of was escaping again he was on her in two strides.

Cupping both her shoulders, he lifted her off the stool and ground his mouth against hers. He wanted, needed, to claim her, bind her, brand her. He heard a deep moan that he assumed was hers, but couldn't be sure. She met his mouth with equal strength, equal power, and it shook him to the core.

She went limp before reaching up and slipping her arms around his neck. He hoisted her onto the counter and she wrapped her legs around his waist. He settled himself exactly where he wanted to be and pushed against her.

Her lips were soft and welcoming and oh so sweet. Her mouth was hot and soft and wet for him. His tongue met hers, ran the tip of it along her bottom teeth, tasted her, drank from her, claimed her.

He gathered her close, felt her nipples graze his chest and reached up to cup them. She shivered but didn't let go. He kissed the side of her mouth, licked her bottom lip and tugged it into his mouth.

She froze for a still moment out of time, and he was just about to pull back out of the kiss when she turned fierce.

Lisa gave as good as she got and tore into his mouth with a fury that took him aback. She was ravenous, demanded all of him, and he knew damn well she'd get all and more than she wanted.

His mind blew at the sweetness, the spice, the raw need he tasted.

Again. And again, as the kiss went on.

It was as if yesterday hadn't happened. The raw sex in the pool house receded, and his decade-old memories resurfaced.

Lisa was clover sweet. As sweet as she'd been at eighteen. Her kisses were exactly right, her mouth possessed him, drained him, and excited him beyond arousal. He strained and pushed against her and she strained and pushed back.

She swept her arm across the counter, clearing it, pulling him down. He stretched her out, kissing and nipping her neck and shoulders.

Her breasts were less perky when she was flat on her back and he was happy to see she hadn't bothered with a bra. Gathering both soft mounds in his palms, he squeezed gently, pushing them together. "These are real, aren't they?"

"All me all the time." The look she gave him made him laugh. "You thought they were fake? I'm disappointed you don't remember them better."

"They've haunted me. The scent of them," he trailed his nose across the straining tips, "the delicious raspberry-cream taste of them." He suckled and licked at her.

"I remember you too." She stretched up to meet his lips with a hunger he couldn't ignore. She kissed him again and again as if she couldn't get enough of his mouth.

"What do you remember?"

"The taste of your mouth, the feel of your hands. You made my panties wet. I tasted your kisses for months after I left."

Mind blown, he fed her the kisses she craved. He tweaked

each nipple as their lips met time and time again. Each tweak brought a flutter of noise in her throat. The flutter grew to a moan when he finally mouthed the pink buds.

"You taste the same," he said. "I can't believe you taste the same." He could hardly recognize the sound of his own voice, grating with need.

"Upstairs." She was even more tousled, flush with want. Her eyes were bright and swam with come-fuck-me. "Please, Tyce."

His erection pressed between her thighs, a zipper away from being inside her. He'd been ready to tease, to entice and seduce her, not give in to his own randy need. He'd wanted to give her a taste of her own medicine, but now he just wanted to taste.

He slid his hand under her short, tight skirt. Sighed at what he found. "No panties. Good girl."

He found her cleft, moist and ready and gathered her moan into his mouth. They were exposed here, bound to be caught, and while it wouldn't be the first time he'd been found with his hands full of woman, he didn't want it to happen with Lisa.

He'd felt protective of her when she was fourteen and it blew his mind that he still felt that way.

He rubbed his thumb against her clit, felt it go rubbery and engorged, to be certain she wouldn't change her mind, then withdrew. He heard a small, strained sound of frustration so he leaned over her, clasped the back of her head so that her neck was exposed. "Open your eyes."

When she did, they were foggy with desire. He took his damp fingers into his mouth, tasted the salty flavor of her. "Delicious," he muttered and watched while her eyes widened again.

"Your room," he said. "Now."

He helped her stand and slowly resettled her T-shirt and skirt to cover her. She clasped his erection, rubbing his straining cock, one finger tapping insistently on the head.

One more kiss, he thought, before he let her go, but one kiss turned into ten as they pressed and bucked and strained toward each other. Whatever game they'd played was played out.

They won.

He picked her up and walked through the silent mansion, releasing her lips only long enough to find and walk up the staircase.

He carried her into the room she pointed out as hers and set her down inside the door. He got an impression of feminine elegance from the furniture and draperies while she locked the door. She turned to face him, holding the knob at her back.

Curious as he was about how she lived, he was more interested in removing her clothes. The skirt puddled at her feet with a tight shimmy. He shoved her T-shirt up over her breasts and feasted for a moment.

She clasped his shoulders to steady herself and cried out when he nipped and marked the underside of one breast. "Mine," he said.

Kneeing her thighs open he settled on the floor in front of her. She'd shaved her hair into a heart-shaped thatch and he smiled. "This is cute." *Also mine.*

"I think so."

She was already so wet he didn't think she needed much tongue to get her off, but he took his time, causing shudder after shudder as she came in his mouth. She nearly fell once so he hooked one of her knees over his shoulder to help keep her upright.

"No more," she whispered. "Your turn. My turn."

He carried her to the four poster bed that stood dead center in the room and set her on top of the down comforter. Reaching for his zipper she freed him, laving him with her tongue. She dragged her tongue around the head of his shaft, causing an ache in his balls he relished. He was ready to explode, but her lips were so delicate she managed to drive him crazy and help him stay sane at the same time.

"Lick my balls too."

"My pleasure."

He barked out a laugh and let her play all she wanted. She undid the tab button of his jeans and he shucked them. When her pink tongue went lower and her mouth took in one of his testicles he nearly hit the roof. Her pleasure turned into his.

"Enough." His cock flexed, once, twice. He had to come soon. Had to come with her. Setting himself at her entrance, he nibbled at her mouth again, just to tease. "I've waited a lot of years for this, Lisa. Are you sure?"

"What about the pool house?"

"Doesn't count." He kissed her slow and deep until her eyes glazed. "We start from here."

She blinked back tears and took a sharp breath.

"Tell me what you want, Lisa."

"Love me, fast and hard." Her response sent heat from his ears down his spine and he did as she bid.

Only slower.

He grasped his cock and slid the head along her slit, rubbing against her clit. He felt fresh juices slide out of her to smear along his length.

Using two fingers he eased opened the hood that hid her throbbing nub and tapped the head against her most sensitive nerve ending. Her eyes went wide as she grabbed his ass to bring him closer. She shuddered when he slipped his tip along the slippery entrance.

8

Fill 'Er Up

Something had changed, Lisa thought. Tyce was different, in his touch, in his gentleness, in his whole approach.

He kissed her again and again, deep, lingering kisses that teased and fulfilled all at once, each brush of his lips a promise of more to come. She felt the rasp of his beard on her chin, her cheek, her neck, but still she sought more.

The tip of his cock slicked against her slit, never quite entering. He was a tease! A man so perfectly controlled she was mad with want long before he was.

Perfect pressure, perfect alignment, perfect tongue, each kiss blessed her, rocked her, made her yearn. She tried to keep up with him, to match him kiss for kiss, touch for touch, caress for caress, but he was fast devouring her. She drowned time and again, drowned and felt lifted, curled in on herself, and splayed wide to take and receive each of his blessings.

She'd never felt anything like what Tyce was doing to her. His body shook with need, trembled beyond desire, shaped hers into a honeyed, formless blob he could do whatever he wanted with.

When he slid down to sip at her cleft Lisa thought she'd go crazy. She thought he was going to enter her, slide into her to the hilt, but instead he circled her clit with his tongue, delved his fingers in deep, time and time again. Strokes from his tongue kept her on the fine knife edge of orgasm, rocketing her close to implosion only to fade back to gentle swirls and ripples.

She melted into honey, slick with desire, she cried out in frustration. "Tyce, now!"

"I'm not done with you yet. Open for me." He straddled her head and tapped her mouth with his engorged penis. She clamped her mouth shut, turned away her face. Her need was too great, too burning.

"Now, Tyce."

He tapped again, smeared the bead of moisture across her lips until she tipped her tongue across for a taste. When she opened for more he slid inside her mouth. She felt his palm cup her mound again. Firmly, he pressed up and into her, shaking her labia gently while dipping one, then two fingers, into her honeyed warmth.

She sucked and lapped at his burgeoning cock, felt him flex at the same time her hips arched off the bed.

With a speed and strength she didn't know he possessed, he turned her so they were face-to-face.

"I have to come inside. Let me in."

He rolled a condom on. But before she could form permission, he was pressing into her, filling her, spreading her hips so she could take him in one strong slide.

"I have to . . ." his voice trailed away into a groan.

Everything fit, everything swelled, and the moment she reached to tunnel her fingers through his hair to bring him down for a kiss, he obliged. She felt low, deep shudders building, the roar in her head deafening as he gathered her storm into himself.

They came that way, hips locked, mouths melded, moans covering moans.

He raised his head and she watched warily as his eyes came back into focus.

"You finally kissed me," she said, on a note of wonder.

He rolled and gathered her close to his chest. She felt his lips brush her hair.

"Aren't you getting up?"

"Give me a minute, I've got a fast recovery but that's asking a lot."

Too weak and languid to laugh, she said, "No, I mean yesterday . . ."

He tilted her face up with a single finger to her chin. "Yesterday was before."

"Before?"

"Yesterday was sex, Lisa. Just sex. And I'm sorry for yesterday. You deserve better."

He looked at her steadily, his brown eyes gentle for the first time and she knew she'd been right. Things between them were different now. She wasn't sure how or why, but she accepted the difference and decided not to question him further for fear of ruining the tenuous peace they'd found.

They showered together then wandered downstairs to the darkened kitchen. Tyce wore his jeans and Lisa snuggled into her terry robe.

He pulled out a leftover roast beef from the fridge and sliced it thinly, while Lisa peeled fresh potatoes. Finding a container of gravy, she laughed when she saw his expression of relief.

"Let me guess. A meat and potatoes guy?"

"Through and through."

"You eat in my kitchen," she wagged a carrot at him, "you eat your vegetables."

He cocked his eyebrow at her. "That's not all I'll eat in here." With that, he advanced on her and ignored her delighted squeals as he nibbled his way across her bared shoulder to her neck and up to her ear. She giggled at the tickling sensations of tongue and nipping teeth.

"Tyce! I'm—" but she couldn't finish because he was relentless in his desire to make her laugh.

"I love the sound of you laughing. We didn't do much of that when we were kids."

"There wasn't much to laugh about." She put the potatoes on to boil and poured the congealed gravy into a pan to warm it. She turned to him. "How's your mom?"

"She's good. Still working at the hair salon except she owns it now. Calls herself queen of the blue-rinse set. Some of those ladies have been going to the shop since beehives were in style."

Lisa grinned at that. "I always liked your mom. She had a great sense of humor." Unlike her own, but Tyce never knew Lisa's mother was a hard-drinking, bitter woman.

"Yeah, she needed it with me in the house. The neighbors hated living next to us." He swung open the fridge door and bent in for a look. He started digging around. "Mom had to keep promising them I'd stop working on my car. Then I'd sell it and buy another one and start work all over again."

"At least you didn't keep spare cars around for parts."

He laughed. "I wanted to, but didn't want to be disowned."

"And Jenny? What's she doing now?"

"Working too hard. She's the bookkeeper for me and for my mom's shop. She has a large client list of small businesses."

"Jason's her only child?"

"Yeah. After he was born, she put her nose to the grindstone. Jenn's too busy to have a life. I keep telling her to live a little, but she pushes herself so hard I doubt she ever will."

"Maybe someday."

"She's in New York right now for our cousin's wedding. I told her I'd take Jason to the auction with me to give her a couple weeks off. I doubt she'll take them though."

Enjoying the comfortable memories, they prepared the rest of the meal together. Eventually, they sat across from each other at the island, and served each other. She offered him ice tea and he took it gratefully. "I was looking for a beer in the fridge earlier."

"It's in the bar fridge in the den. I'll get you one."

When she returned, he was putting the finishing touches on a bouquet of roses he'd obviously filched from the vine beside the kitchen door. "It looks funny," he said around a rueful grin. "I wanted it to be perfect."

"They are perfect, just like your thoughtfulness."

"Then what's wrong with them? They don't look right."

She smiled at his desire to give her perfection in the blooms. "They're not long-stemmed roses. They're climbers. More leaves around the blossoms and short stems. It may be better to put them in a shorter vase."

He pulled one out and smiled. "Do roses float?" He went through the cupboards until he found a cereal bowl. He filled it with water and roses and set it on the island.

When the roses looked presentable, he wrapped his arms around her, looking pleased with himself. He plucked a stem out of the bowl, removed the thorns and twined the bloom behind her ear. His warm brown eyes studied her, taking in everything from the crown of her head to the tops of her breasts, now plastered against his chest. He snugged her hips close to his and held her there. His hands massaged her behind, sending signals to every part of her body.

If she wasn't careful, she could get addicted to this kind of attention. It had been too long since she'd shared a simple meal in the kitchen with a man.

"Beautiful," he said, sliding his hands under her robe so he could palm her backside without the terry in the way. "You haven't told me how your mom's doing."

Talk about a mood wrecker. She shifted away from him.

"I think I'm sorry I asked," he said.

She might as well tell him. "The drinking caught up to her a couple years ago. She's gone."

"Sorry. I didn't know. She moved out of the park a few years back."

"Harris paid for her care but she was past help." She shrugged. "She loved the bottle more than anything. She used to say it was her best friend."

He nodded and went still. He blew out a breath. "I knew about her screaming at you."

She turned, looked into his face, saw nothing but the kindness she'd seen back in the trailer park. "So that's why you let me hang out at your place?"

"At first. Then you became useful."

"Now you're teasing me," she said, suddenly glad and wanting to share the burden of her memories. "It was safe at your place. Like I said, I always liked your mom. As tough as it was for Jenny, I used to watch her with Jason and tell myself if I ever had children, I would be like her."

"Not like your mom?"

"Never. I rarely drink. I see exasperated mothers in the mall and hate it when I hear them scream at their kids."

"Jason wasn't always the polite kid you see today. Jenn had her moments, but she always pulled back, reined in when she got too hot."

"Drinking can take that away from some parents." She rubbed her arms, determined again to be evenhanded and consistent if she was ever lucky enough to find a man who wanted to give her children.

"I don't drink much," he offered. "I like to keep my hands steady." He grinned. "You know that saying, 'one day at a time'?"

"Sure."

"For me, it's one beer at a time, always will be. My old man was a drinker. Left us flat."

"I don't remember him."

"Neither do I, but my mother was steady as a rock. Jenn started too young, but she did a great job with Jason, so things worked out fine. My mom invested well, which is how she bought the shop, I've got a good business with an unending supply of work, and Jenn's getting her education now that Jason's older. It's all good."

"Stay tonight," she offered and held her breath, hoping.

He resumed his position. Hips squared with hers, chest to chest, his hands on her bare bottom. "Just tonight?"

Her response was in her kiss. Tonight and every night from now on, she thought, but couldn't say. It would be dangerous to think about every night. Dangerous and foolish.

"Ever thought of making your clients come to you?" she asked as they walked upstairs to bed, arms entwined.

"You mean open a shop and put up a shingle? Something permanent?"

"Yes."

He stopped, looked down into her face, and one side of his lips turned up. "It would be good to have my own hoist and paint shop. There would be a lot less travel."

When he didn't back away from the idea, she couldn't help but ask, "Would you like less travel?"

He kissed the tip of her nose. "Mrs. Delaney, is that a proposition?"

Suddenly afraid she'd gone too far, had put too much hope into her question, she backed off. "No, just curiosity."

"Oh, right, Europe's calling." He ran a finger down her nose and pressed it between her lips. She rolled her tongue around it and just like that, lost the thread of the conversation. His eyes darkened into burnt umber and he swung her into his arms again.

He kicked open her bedroom door and dropped her onto her bed, then followed her down. He rolled her over, hoisted her hips up to receive him. Shoving pillows under her belly for support, he said, "You wanted it this way out by the car, but Jason was due back."

"Yes," she said, raising her pretty ass even higher. She held her knees steady with her small, elegant hands while he looked his fill.

From this angle he could see all of her, from her rosy little ass button to the hood over her clit. He opened her outer lips to expose the inner ones. They fluttered with the cool air he blew across her. Cream filled her slit and he lapped at it with one quick swipe of his tongue. Her belly jerked with his action. "You like that? What else, Lisa? What do you want?"

"More kisses like that one. But higher, inside. Fuck me with your tongue."

He thumbed her clitoris to prime her and set to work with his mouth. She writhed and moaned and pressed her open lips to his, begging for release. He thought of holding her off, of making her wait, but the time for games was over. He slid two fingers into her slick channel to allow her to prepare for his burgeoning cock.

He slid home with a deep grunt and filled her. She arched and cried out, slipped her hand between her legs to cup his tight balls and sent him to heaven.

In spite of having Jason back at work, Lisa insisted she help every day. If Tyce didn't have her on the Internet hunting down parts, she was on the phone ordering them or passing him tools.

They worked well together and Lisa laughed more all the time. Tyce got comfortable with the idea of sleeping in her bed, using her shower, and sliding into her body every night.

One night they argued about chick flicks versus action movies and agreed to see a moody suspense.

"I'll drive," Lisa said. "I want to show you my baby anyway."

"You've got a whole vintage car collection to choose from and you drive this?" he said when she pulled up in front of the house in a little red bomb he didn't even recognize. "What is it?"

She climbed out and opened the hatch and unlocked the T roof panels. "Climb in," she said when the panels were stowed. "And buckle up."

He settled into the low-slung passenger's seat, stretched his legs full length and buckled his seatbelt. "Okay, I give. It's a Nissan, but what model?"

"1992 NX 2000. Goes like stink and handles like a Porsche." She laughed at this expression and took off, running through the gears like silk, the car responding in a rush of power he felt clear down to his toes.

"It's a gut sucker, all right," he said, reaching for the handhold. "But it's awful small in here. Tight."

She slanted him a glance and grinned. "I thought you liked tight." The wind above their heads caught her hair and it sailed up and out of the roof. She laughed and he laughed with her.

When they got to the movie, he discovered even more about Lisa he didn't know.

Her focus on the screen was total. Completely enthralled with the story, she followed the action closely. When the music turned threatening, he felt her tension almost before she did. Stealthily he took the box of popcorn out of her lap before she jumped in her seat and sprayed everyone around them with flying kernels.

The murderer leaped out, Lisa screamed and clung to Tyce, heart pounding, breath coming in gasps. He wrapped his arm around her shoulders and held her close while she ducked her face into his shoulder.

Her intense concentration aroused him. He wanted her to look like that when he kissed her. She often did. He wanted to see if he could distract her, so he slid one finger up her thigh. Her eyes closed. Interesting.

He slid her skirt higher, felt the soft curls at her mons. Dipping his finger lower, he felt her shift in her seat and he suddenly had more room to maneuver. He pressed his thumb to her clit, slid a finger inside her dripping pussy, and let her move, slowly and subtly in her seat.

By the time the next crescendo of music rose all around them, she had her face buried in his neck while she came on his hand. Her shudders faded as the music slowed.

Every week after that, he took her to the movies and let her drive her girly car. The car she'd bought straight cash a year before she married.

It was a marvel he was getting any work done at all. He was a walking hard-on these days. Lisa could give him a look at ten in the morning that simmered through him all day until he couldn't take it anymore.

He would grab her hand, drag her into the pool house, shove down her shorts and his zipper, and have her against the wall. She was always ready, always slick, always hot.

Once, they stepped back into the garage to find Jason blushing crimson. "You rattled the clock off the back wall," he said as he backed away. "I just came in to check out the noise."

After that, Lisa brought a CD player out from the house and set it up on the workbench.

But still, they moved farther into the small den and took more time with each other on the sofa. They practiced some of the best mouth work he'd ever experienced, learned each other thoroughly, taught each other how to wring the most exquisite pleasure out of each stolen moment. He'd be so hot by the time he actually got her naked that his cock would be weeping before she'd so much as touched it.

Lisa was wild for him. Wet and juicy and heavily primed for

him with just a glance, she would come with the merest flick of his fingers or tongue. Then he would drive into her with one powerful slide, hold his position for her while she built into another orgasm. They would rock together, cling to each other as if they planned to never let go.

The days turned into weeks, the nights turned into heaven, and Tyce fell further under Lisa's spell. In spite of remembering that she was on the move again, in spite of the obvious difference in their financial stability, in spite of his drive to avoid deep commitments, he fell.

One afternoon when the sun heated the courtyard beyond bearable, Lisa sprayed Jason with the water hose and started a water fight that had all three of them soaked to the skin. Tyce grabbed her around the waist while Jason wrestled the hose from her hand. Squealing in his arms and dancing with the icy water streaming over her, Tyce held on. She was like a wet seal, sliding and slipping against his chest.

He tightened his arms around her and nuzzled his nose against her hair, drank in the scent of her heated, damp skin, and used her wriggling as an excuse to cop a feel.

She squealed with laughter when she felt his hand, not caring that Jason saw her tilt her face to his for a kiss. She was so open with him, so giving, so ready to show the world she was his.

Tyce turned her into his arms, away from the stream of water, warming her with his heat.

He wasn't sure if love felt like this, but if it did he wanted more.

With a hot, sensual glance, she whispered against his ear. "Take me for a ride in your truck."

He decided to oblige and lifted her to drape her over his shoulder. She squealed, still dripping, but the show she made of kicking and fighting didn't fool anyone. She loved the he-man bit and played right along.

He walked to his truck, opened the driver's door, and slid her into place. She scooched over to the middle, giving him just enough room to drive.

Jason waved, laughing as Tyce drove off. "Where to?"

"There's a pond next to the warehouse at the far end of the property. It's quiet there."

"And no one will see us?"

"Right." She slid her hand up his thigh to his crotch, let her fingers dance.

"Tit for tat," he said, and let his fingers rove in tight hot circles from her knee to her apex. She opened her legs, giving him room to comb through her curls. Lisa was slick and hot beneath his hand. "I love your skirts. Have I told you that yet?"

"Not in so many words." She pointed to a bushy lane way up ahead. "Turn there," she said on a sigh. "And hurry."

The truck slewed left when he tried to negotiate the turn one-handed. She had his cock sprung free of his jeans. "Head down now," he said between gritted teeth.

She obliged and her hot mouth encased him. She kept her lips tight like her pussy and plunged downward in one long action that had him jamming his foot to the floor on the brake. The truck slammed to a halt.

She eased back up and swirled her tongue around his thickened head. He pulsed and flexed and jutted up toward her. "Do me."

"Not yet. Not 'til we get there."

"I'm there, believe me."

She ran one finger from the base of his cock to the tip. "You have to wait." She cocked her head toward the right. "Behind those bushes, there's a pond. No one will see."

He bumped and rumbled his pickup over the rough ground, grinding his teeth against the jarring he felt from his balls to his heart.

He pulled up in front of the prettiest little slice of heaven he'd ever seen. One hundred yards across and twice that wide, the pond was just big enough to float a dinghy in. "If you had a rubber dinghy I'd take you out in it. Naked."

"I'd like that, but I'd like this better." She set her shoulders against the passenger door, the way she had in the Jag.

He lifted her left leg and set her foot on the back of the seat.

While he shucked his jeans he studied her. Spread open this way, she looked wild, wanton, and wet. He saw her curls, dewy and secretive, waiting for him. He combed through them again, and shook her labia gently before putting his mouth to hers.

She sighed and lifted her damp shirt up to expose her breasts. She tugged at one nipple while reaching between his legs with her other hand. Her grip was exquisitely pleasurable, firm where he needed it, harder when she stroked. She guided him to her entrance, paused with the tip of his cock at her outer lips.

"Love me, Tyce. Love me hard. The way you wanted to back then."

Needing no more encouragement, he lifted her ass and entered her in one plunge that took him in to the top. He slid in smoothly and stilled, holding onto his thin tether of control.

"Now," she said on a sexy purr, "do me. Hard. Make me come." The last was said on a moan because her rolling shudders had already started.

He spurted and spewed into her, mouth to her shoulder, too crazed to see one lone tear track down her cheek.

9

The Brake Job

Five weeks into the project found Lisa feeling stronger than ever in her commitment to sell the cars and weaker than ever in her resolve to move away.

Franklin cajoled, whined, and finally demanded that she stop work on the collection. She refused, infuriating him even more. Eventually she called her lawyer to let him know of the harassment and had him handle it. When the phone calls stopped she breathed a sigh of relief and continued to work with Tyce and Jason.

Cars were leaving for Arizona daily, each one a reminder that soon she'd be leaving too. The fact that she didn't want to move away anymore weighed heavily sometimes. Other times, she set her feelings of doubt aside and resolved to enjoy the time with Tyce.

She couldn't deny she was in love with Tyce all over again. Probably had been for all those years apart, she realized as she waited for him to come to bed one night.

He was doing his window and door lock check. He'd noticed her nerves were shot and he put it down to living here alone. She hadn't told him about Franklin because she wasn't used to sharing her problems. With Tyce or anyone.

She stretched under the sheets, her muscles comfortable with the labor she'd been doing. She'd grown stronger, more toned with the work. Holding her hand out she inspected the remnants of her last manicure. Sorry state, she thought, seeing the shortened version of her nails.

Her left hand wasn't quite so bad.

Except her simple wedding band still gleamed on her finger.

She touched it, surprised to find how loose it was. She turned it. Once. Twice. Then slid it off.

Tyce came back from his rounds just as she was putting the ring into her jewelry box on the dresser. He stood behind her and cupped her shoulders as he watched her close the lid on the box.

Their eyes met in the mirror and he pulled her left hand up so he could kiss her fingers. She turned and took his heat and strength and comfort.

She loved him. She couldn't question it anymore. It simply was.

He led her to the bed and climbed in first. He held the covers up so she could slide in next to him. She settled her head on his chest and slid her fingers through his chest hair. He didn't speak and she couldn't have spoken if she'd tried.

She loved him. Tyce Branton. There wasn't a thing she could do about it. Nor wanted to.

At fourteen her love for him had been a first crush, delicate and young and exuberant. By sixteen she'd been confused because when his friends were around he paid her no attention, almost drove her away whenever they were with him. But alone, he'd been his usual interested self, kind and always willing to talk.

But that night at eighteen, all her passion had risen when he'd kissed her. Powerful, raging passion had consumed her when his lips had found hers, then moved on to her breasts. It frightened her, especially because she'd felt nothing when her date had tried so hard to arouse her. She'd even had a beer, thinking to relax, but nothing had helped and eventually she'd had to convince him sex wasn't going to happen.

Now she knew why that other boy had left her cold. Quite simply, he wasn't Tyce and Tyce was the only boy she wanted.

Wanted so badly that when she felt overcome with desire, she'd had to stop it. She couldn't, wouldn't, be stupid enough to end up like so many other girls in the trailer park. Like Jenny.

Babies, responsibilities, low-paying jobs. None of that was what she wanted. And all of that was what Tyce was offering back then.

At least that was what she'd thought. So, she'd stopped Tyce from loving her and run the next day as if he was a demon bent on possession.

He continued to hold her while she thought, while she remembered, not realizing that inside her resting body rose a whirlwind of memories and emotions. Her childhood had been a pit of screaming rages, drunken accusations, and bleary demands for forgiveness.

Nothing, but nothing, could stop her from getting out.

Not even the feelings that stormed inside her for Tyce. Like a terrified child, she'd hidden those feelings, even from herself, and run like hell.

At eighteen she hadn't been ready for the kind of love she felt for him.

But she was ready now.

The problem was that she wasn't sure how he felt. Yes, he kissed her, yes, the sex was hotter than she could imagine, yes, he made her laugh, but did he know her? Did he see beyond his assumptions?

By the time she screwed up her courage to ask, she heard his breath deepen into sleep and for the first time, slept with him without making love.

Early the next afternoon Lisa was supposed to be washing the Thunderbird so Jason could finish the detailing, but she'd been staring into space most of the morning.

"I'm taking off to pick up those parts we ordered," Jason said as he lifted his motorcycle off its kickstand. "You okay?"

"What? Oh, sure," she scooped her hair off her neck. "I'm fine," she lied. She waved as he pulled out of the courtyard.

She heard a curse from behind her and turned to see Tyce climbing out of the Austin Healy. He got onto the creeper and slid under the chassis.

By unspoken agreement, the subject of Europe hadn't come up again since the night he'd first stayed with her.

They'd talked about everything else: the cars, their families, their interests, all the mundane details of their lives.

All but the important things, like love and commitment, marriage and children.

Tyce was a magnificent lover, rough and gentle, demanding and submissive when she wanted to be in charge, and she enjoyed every aspect of their lovemaking. And he wanted a lot.

At one point he mentioned making up for lost time, but she wasn't sure if he meant the years they'd been apart or her three years of abstinence. At the time, she hadn't much cared. She'd been delirious with sexual satisfaction and had barely been able to move let alone decipher the deeper meaning to everything he said.

But the time was fast approaching that they would need to discuss the future. If they were going to part ways, she wanted to know soon so she could prepare herself.

She also needed to know so she could make her plans to move. In spite of now wanting to stay here, she would never be able to live in the same country with him if he didn't want her.

It would be horrible to know he was close at hand but unapproachable. That he didn't want to see her.

A cloud crossed the sun and the sudden chill raised goose bumps on her bare arms. The house loomed over her, quiet and dark in its Tudor splendor. How lonely it would be. How silent without the activity she'd lived with for weeks now.

Suddenly determined to chase the chill and her dreary thoughts away, she strolled over to where Tyce lay and straddled him. "Hi."

He stilled as she crouched down onto his lap.

"Hey!"

"Hey, yourself," she said, rocking against his crotch. "Whatcha doing?"

"Getting hard."

She heard a fine-toned clang as he dropped the tool he was using. She felt the truth of his words rising to meet her.

"This is interesting," she said, "having you trapped beneath me and the car. There's not a lot you can do to stop me having my way with you, is there?"

"Not a whole helluva lot, no." But she heard curiosity in his voice. Curiosity and heat.

"Stay here," she ordered, then stood and went to the wall. She hit the garage-door button. As the door descended, she caught him trying to wheel out from under the car and shoved him back. She laughed. "You didn't put your overalls on."

"I didn't think I'd be under here today."

She dropped her shorts and panties to the garage floor. She heard a long, low whistling sigh from him.

"You're naughty and need to be punished," she said, using a prim voice she knew turned him on. She got busy unzipping his jeans.

"I need to be ridden awhile . . ."

The next sound she heard was his deep moan as she sank onto his swollen shaft. The wheels of the creeper made for a wild, back-and-forth motion as she pressed down on him. Stomach clenching, she took him inside, rocking with him, impaled and loving it.

"Lisa!" The urgency in his voice was half-sexual, half-demand.

"Don't bother me, I'm working here," she bent over him, letting her nipples brush against his T-shirt. It wasn't nearly enough so she lifted the cotton away from his chest so she could feel more of his heat.

He rolled out from under the car, dislodging their connection. Groaning in frustration she scrabbled back and reached for him again, but he covered himself.

"You didn't use protection."

"I forgot."

"Or didn't care?"

She barely registered that he sounded half-amused instead of angry. "I'm safe. I counted." She grasped him and slid her hand up and down his slickened cock. The idea of having his child increased her arousal. God, she wanted him, wanted his babies, wanted to share his life. If these few days were all she had left of him, she'd take every moment of pleasure she could get. Her memories would have to last a very long time.

"Wait." He groaned but did nothing to stop her hand. "Let me clean up. I want to touch you too." He held up his hands with a rueful twist to his mouth, but his eyes were feverish with need and Lisa reveled in it. "But I won't touch you with grease on my hands. Not ever."

"Whoa, that sounds . . . ominous." She cupped his testicles and squeezed, loving the resulting catch in his breath.

"It's important to me," he ground out on a groan.

She replaced her hand with her lips, in a slow, smooth slide, opening deeply to take him all in.

"Sweet Jesus!"

She loved having him at her mercy. Under her control, powerfully focused on her every move, every flick of her tongue, every stroke of her hand, Tyce hung suspended, waiting for whatever she chose to do next. Waiting, anticipating, needing.

If he was going to walk away from what they had, he was going to walk away a marked man. She would make certain he'd never forget her, would always think of her whenever he thought about mouths and tongues and deep, deep kisses.

"What the hell—"

Befogged by her own desire, Lisa couldn't understand at first why Tyce pulled back and covered himself.

"You slut!" a man's voice screamed.

She looked up to see Franklin Delaney outlined in the doorway to the pool house. Just as quickly Tyce stood between her and the door, giving her time to wipe her mouth and scramble for her panties and shorts.

"Get out," he snarled at Franklin.

As Lisa got to her feet, she saw the veins in Franklin's neck stand out. He ignored Tyce and strode toward Lisa with his hands raised to grab her. "You bitch!"

10

Burning Rubber

All Lisa wanted to do was cover her ears, close her eyes, and wait for the blow, but she didn't. She faced Franklin straight on, without blinking.

When he continued his advance on her, she wanted to run, but she'd never hidden from her mother's raised fist and she wouldn't hide now, even as frightened as she was.

Heat rose into her face, and fire burned in her belly as she prepared herself for Franklin's attack. She braced for the feel of his hands on her, ready to fight back with all she had.

Before Franklin could reach her, Tyce stepped in front of him and grabbed him by the shirt collar. He brought the older man to a dead stop.

"Be very careful what you say, Delaney," Tyce said with an intensity Lisa hoped never to have directed at her.

Franklin finally seemed to realize that Tyce had hold of him, and quieted. He tried to smooth his shirt front, but found Tyce still had a firm grip.

"All right now?" Tyce asked in a tone frigid enough to form crystals.

Franklin looked at him, cleared his throat and nodded. He was a fussy man, always manicured and pressed. Lisa doubted he'd ever owned a pair of jeans, let alone faded ones, and here he was with his shirt front wrinkled and pulled out of his waistband.

My, my.

She finished righting her clothing and pressed the button to open the garage door. The garage filled with light and fresh air, bringing a trace of normalcy to the charged atmosphere. In spite of her desire to run and hide, she turned to Harris's son to have this out once and for all.

"Why are you here?" she asked Franklin, wary because her lawyer had told her Franklin had accepted the idea of the auction.

"I came to talk sense into you, but I can see that's a useless endeavor." The sneer on his face and disdain in his voice was used to make her cringe, but she refused.

She would have shriveled under his degrading stare a couple years ago, but not now. There was nothing wrong in her feelings for Tyce, nothing wrong with her having a relationship. Harris had taught her that in the first weeks of their marriage.

Whispers and gossip couldn't hurt if you knew the truth he'd told her. The truth was she was in love and women in love took crazy chances.

"Talk to me about what?" she asked in the cool tone she'd taken four years to perfect.

Tyce took a step back, leaned against the workbench, and watched Franklin closely. She was grateful Tyce had controlled his temper. The rigid control he exerted made it clear that if she wasn't here, he might have let loose.

Unused to displays of control under such circumstances, she fell in love with him all over again, aware that he would always, always keep a rein on his temper around her.

Every word she'd told him about her mother's rages had been heard.

Other people's anger still tended to bring out the worst in her, something Franklin would soon learn.

"I know you've been shipping Dad's cars out of the state. I want them back."

"No." She stood her ground, eyes firmly on her adversary.

Something dangerous shifted in his eyes and he turned them to Tyce. "Branton, I can see why your business is doing so well. Lucky man, you. Blowjobs in the middle of the afternoon, and a fine piece of ass all night. No wonder most of your references come from women."

As steady as Lisa felt, his sick comments rocked her. Even so, Lisa stepped forward to snag Franklin's attention. "Get out," she said.

"I don't take orders from trailer trash who can't keep her hands off the hired help." The sneer he gave her again said it all. The feverish look in his gaze was sick, as if it turned him on to catch her in the act. He'd watched her like a hawk for four years and had come up with nothing filthy he could take to his father. He must feel vindicated at finding her like this.

Suddenly Tyce lashed out and grabbed Franklin by the throat again. The other man made a gurgling sound. Tyce's knuckles were bloodless against the navy collar of Franklin's shirt. Still, he showed iron control.

"It must burn you to find me with a man now, after all this time," she said. "After you finally realized I wouldn't sleep with you, you tried so hard to set me up, to catch me with someone else. Your father knew everything you were up to. You're a sorry excuse for a man, Franklin." She shook her head, feeling empty pity for a man so small minded, so consumed by jealousy of his own father that he would want to deny his father his happiness.

Franklin's eyes bugged out in shock and fear. Lisa touched Tyce's bulging forearm.

"Stop, Tyce. He can't hurt me. He's never been able to hurt me. That's what irritates him most."

Tyce let him go and wiped his hand as if he'd dirtied it on something.

Relieved, she set her sights on Franklin again, noted the sharp scent of fear that radiated out from him. "All those times you propositioned me, all those times you tried to buy me, got you nothing, Franklin."

"My father bought you even when I—"

"When you what?" She was no more than curious now and relieved that Tyce's temper was again under control. She wouldn't want him to suffer for something he'd done to protect her.

"I found out exactly where you came from. I told him about the trailer park, Lisa, told him you were the daughter of a drunken slut."

She laughed and shook her head. "So did I, you pompous freak. That first afternoon when I saw how much he liked me. I never tried to hide where I came from and that was one of the things your father liked about me. My honesty."

Franklin glared at her. "That's not true."

Tyce moved toward him again but Franklin quickly stepped back out of reach. Lisa moved in and took Franklin's hand in both of hers. She patted it gently as she leaned in close. "It is true. Do you know what else is true?"

"What?" he asked softly, clearly taken by surprise at her touch and nearness.

She raised her hand then cupped it next to her mouth and his ear and whispered to him.

He jerked his hand away from hers. "No! That's such a fucking waste," Franklin snarled. "I'm telling my lawyer."

"The paperwork's already done," she said, stifling an urge to laugh. "Your father approved and set everything up before he died. He knew if he left the cars to you it would never happen."

She stepped back and crossed her arms, gave him a dismissive glance from head to toe. "You know, Franklin, I don't see the tiniest resemblance between Harris and you. He had integrity and honor, worked hard all his life and faced his battles head on, while you, you're—"

"I will not be spoken to this way!" he cried, trying to sound imperious but only succeeding in a whine.

"It seems to me you've made a lot of wrong assumptions about your stepmother here, Franklin." Tyce's voice cut like glass. "One of them being that she's above physical violence. I'm going to do you a favor and give you a chance to run before she kicks your ass."

Lisa lost it at Tyce's boldface lie and burst out laughing at the look that came over Franklin's face.

"Whatever it was she whispered to you, you'd better believe it, because Lisa Brady Delaney does what she says she's going to do. She got out of that trailer park on her own long before meeting your father. And you wonder why he married her? Look beyond the beauty, Delaney. She's got integrity, strength, and endurance, and I don't know how the hell she put up with you all this time."

He snarled at the cowering man, while Lisa did her best to control her laughter. But when Tyce stamped his foot and made Franklin jump in fear, she broke out into peals again.

"Now get!" Tyce said.

Franklin pushed past them both and scurried across the courtyard and climbed into his car. The engine roared and the rear tires squealed as he made good his escape.

"What the hell did you whisper to him?" Tyce demanded with a chuckle.

"My secret," she said, trembling from the adrenaline rush. Now that it was over, shock set in and she had to lean against the workbench to stay on her feet. She hated screaming scenes.

He noticed her reaction and swept her into a hug. Rubbing

her arms he soothed and crooned to her. "It's okay, Lisa. Take it easy. He's gone. You're right. He can't hurt you."

She nodded, but didn't speak. The tension had been so high and she'd been trapped by it. If Tyce had lost control, she might have too. Nothing frightened her more.

11

Pride and Joy

Tyce wiped his hands on his rag and patted the fender on the old Ford. She was a spectacular ride, a highway cruiser with elegant lines, strong fins, and a full backseat that made a man think about hot women and hotter sex.

He'd bet she'd seen a lot of action on that cool two-toned upholstery.

Lisa opened the kitchen door and turned to him with a smile and wave.

As she approached, he took stock. Weak smile, lifted chin, suspiciously moist eyes. She'd tied her hair back today and covered herself in blue jeans and a fleece vest the color of daffodils.

Jason carefully drove the Ford up onto the trailer and secured her for transport. The driver gave Tyce a thumbs up.

"That's it?" Lisa asked as she drew near. Up close she looked more fragile than she had since Franklin's untimely visit the week before.

"The last one."

She nodded, folded her arms under her breasts. "It's going to be strange around here. Too quiet."

Jason climbed down off the trailer and ambled over. He looked at Lisa, then swung his gaze to Tyce's. "You're following, right?"

"I'll be along soon. Stay with the truck and trailer."

Beside him, Lisa shifted then wandered over to the flowerbed that rimmed the courtyard. She knelt and touched some of the blooms.

"Your mother phoned," Tyce said to Jason. "The cousin she went to see get married got jilted at the altar."

"Too bad. What'd Teri do?"

"Took off this morning on her honeymoon. Alone."

Jason snorted. "Makes sense."

"I guess so. Take it easy on the interstate. Your mother doesn't know I'm letting you ride your bike. She thinks it's going in the back of the pickup." He gave Jason a couple of other instructions and clapped him on the back. "Safe ride."

Lisa stood and waved goodbye as Jason donned his helmet and started his bike. The transport driver cautiously turned the truck and trailer, carrying the Ford around in the courtyard. With a heavy sigh of brakes, rubber, and metal on metal, the truck and trailer pulled out.

Tyce walked over to her but she turned her face away, pretended interest in the hedge. Her shoulders looked stiff and straight. He put a hand out to touch her, let it fall to his side.

He'd loved her last night with all that he had, all that he was, and still she'd said nothing about today's leave-taking.

"Will you be at the auction?" he asked.

She shook her head once, quickly, but didn't look at him. He wanted to ask her to come with him, but it didn't feel right. He kept getting waylaid by the memory of her scrubbing his grease mark off her arm on that damn bus. Stupid, but there it was. She'd walked out once and he couldn't go through it again.

Hell, he'd been a kid then, with his whole life fresh and

stretched out ahead of him. She'd been broke and he'd been golden and she still hadn't wanted him.

Now, she was rich. Independent. She didn't need him. Not for security, stability, nothing. He'd seen that clearly when she'd stood up to Franklin Delaney's poison last week.

There was no reason Lisa Delaney needed Tyce Branton. She had what she wanted. Her car collection was ready to sell. She'd get top dollar, take the money and run to Europe like she planned.

"Franklin called off his dogs," she said. "I made a preemptive strike and had my lawyer mention some jewelry the boys took while Harris was ill. I never would have kept it, but they didn't know that. They assumed that I'd want their mother's rubies." She made a bitter sound in her throat.

"Was that what you whispered to him in the garage last week?"

"No." She turned and looked up at him, her eyes wide and still. Calm. "I told him I was auctioning off the cars and giving the money to a charitable foundation Harris set up."

"What?" He was floored by the confession. "None of this work was for you?"

She shrugged. "No. Harris left me comfortable without the money from the cars and he knew if Franklin got them he'd sell them all and keep the money. Harris and I agreed the proceeds should go toward something meaningful."

"Which is?"

"A high school in the inner city will get a course on mechanics and body work added to the curriculum. The auction dollars should build a whole garage and paint shop."

"Sounds like a school I'd have loved when I was a kid."

"I know." She looked at him and smiled so sweetly that his heart jumped into his throat. What he saw in her gaze caught at his vitals.

"Lisa, you blow me away. These weeks have been a lesson for me."

He marveled at the valiant effort she put into her smile. "For me, too."

"You're so strong now. Sure of yourself."

The shake of her head was so slight he doubted he saw it.

"I don't feel very strong. I'm weak and afraid."

"You? The woman who stood up and took it when Franklin caught us? The woman who looked so fierce I thought he was going to crap his pants?"

"You did?"

"You were awesome. Most women would have run like hell if they were caught that way."

She raised her hand to his cheek. Her fingers felt cool and delicate, small. He turned his head and kissed her palm. Her eyes flared heat and he responded as if he'd never had her before.

She moved into his arms, pressed her hips to his.

"I've been thinking about Europe," he said, trying to stay focused on the words, but Lisa was moving against him, sliding her hips across his, rubbing. Her eyelids drooped in the way that signaled her eagerness.

"You have?" She sniffed and nuzzled his neck.

"Yeah, it's so damn old over there. The whole place is crumbling."

She nodded. "Some parts, I guess."

He placed his hands on her ass and held her still. Which did nothing to clear his mind. Pressure built behind his fly.

"And I know the French don't bathe," he quipped.

She giggled, swiped at her eyes, which had filled. "I'm not sure I'll even go to France."

"Yeah? Well, Italians grab ass."

"And you're worried about this. Why?" She tilted her face

up and her lips quivered as he slowed his breathing, held her chin, and brushed his nose to hers. A tiny squeak escaped and he lapped at her lips once before tracing them with his tongue.

"Let me in, Lisa."

She opened and took him inside. He ran his tongue across her teeth, felt the one that was turned slightly, caressed her lower lip, sipped at her mouth. She whimpered.

"Ask me, Lisa."

She whimpered again.

"Ask me." He pushed into her mouth and pressed against her crotch at the same time. She groaned and clasped at him, pulling him into her, taking, receiving, needing more, demanding all he gave. She was powerful in her need and he responded full blast.

"Jesus, ask me!"

"Love me, Tyce. One more time."

He stepped away, and shook with the need to move back into her. But he couldn't. He wouldn't. She had to ask!

"I need to show you something." He walked over to his pickup and pulled out a large manila envelope from the glove box, certain this was the stupidest thing he'd ever done in his life. He was leaving himself wide open again.

He undid the flap, pulled out legal documents and passed them to her. She was pasty except for the high spots of color in her cheeks. Her hands shook when she took the sheaf of papers.

She read the top page. "A deed?"

He nodded. "Free and clear title to a garage and body shop."

"This is wonderful," she said, sounding shaky. "I wish you luck with it."

"I figured you'd be interested. In case you ever want to drop by." Now his own voice was sounding wobbly.

"I'd like that." She sniffed and lifted an arm, showed off the muscle definition wielding the buffer had created. "If I ever need work I know where I can get a job."

Her smile crumbled and she walked straight into his arms. "Oh, Tyce, I don't know if I can let you leave. I'm sorry, I know you don't get attached to the women you . . . sleep with, but . . ."

He tilted his head back so he could see her face. "What gave you that idea?"

She smeared her nose against his denim jacket. "I, um, asked a couple questions and found out more than I wanted to know about the women you—"

"Fucked?"

She nodded.

"Some of them became friends. Some of them weren't looking for anything more. None of them were enough."

"Enough?"

"Enough for me. Shallow, bored, lonely, you name it, not one of them would have shown the confidence, the guts you showed Franklin. What you've always shown me." He tucked a wave in her hair behind her ear. "Ask me, Lisa."

She stared up at him, confusion etched into her features. He kissed her nose, her chin, her mouth for a long moment, setting them both on fire.

"I assumed you felt the same way about me as you did those other women."

"What have you taught me about assumptions?" he demanded. "I saw you and jumped to conclusions without even thinking about them. I assumed you were like all the other women who'd wandered out to the garage. Franklin assumed you were a gold digger, assumed you'd want everything, assumed you'd sleep with him, even when you were married to his own father."

When she still didn't get it, didn't speak, he felt kicked in the gut. "Lisa, ask me, damn it!"

He tugged her to him, drowned in her mouth over and over, demanding she understand.

She pulled back, stepped away from him, dragged her sleeve across her mouth. "Back in La La, you asked me to stay, but I couldn't, Tyce. We were kids, and everything I felt was too much, too big, too strong. We'd have been swept along and life would have overtaken us. I had to run. I had no choice."

He nodded. "I know that now. I think. I knew about your mother. I knew how afraid you were of turning out like her. But, Christ, that night in the pickup, you blew my mind. All I wanted was to be inside you, loving you. You made me shake."

She crossed her arms. Looked cold. Lonely. "You asked me to stay. I couldn't."

"And now?" It was as close as he could come to saying it. He wouldn't beg.

He watched her. Saw the light dawn slowly, in tiny rays that crossed her features. A small cry came from her throat as she launched herself into his arms.

"Oh, Tyce! Love me, please, the way I love you."

"I do."

"Marry me and I'll never ever leave you again. I'm ready now. We're both ready now."

"I'll hold you to that," he said, pulling her into a deep kiss that ended upstairs beside her bed, dead center in the room.

She pulled him down, took him inside her slick heat, and they found heaven.

An hour later, Tyce raged into her, biting her shoulder, pumping his seed, gasping and grasping as he felt her tilt and go over the edge with him. A few minutes later he said, "Come with me, Lisa."

"I just did."

He laughed against her neck. "No, I mean, come with me to Arizona. I can't go without you."

"I wasn't planning on letting you." She picked at the sheet, kept her eyes down. "What you said last week in the garage meant a lot to me."

"You mean when I told Franklin about your integrity and strength?"

At her nod, he rolled onto his side of the bed and tugged her close. "I meant every word. You're an incredible woman, Lisa. I'm just sorry I didn't see it twelve years ago. If I hadn't pressed you, if I'd given you more time to grow up, things would have been different."

"So you forgive me for leaving that way?"

"Of course. You did what was right for you."

"I never forgot you. I never stopped loving you, but I thought you'd find someone else."

Thinking of all the women he'd wasted time with, he said, "Believe me, I tried. Thought I might have a time or two, but in truth, no one ever came close to you. Actually, no one ever stood up to me the way you did. You really turned my crank."

She laughed, and slid her hand down his belly. Blood rushed, desire rose.

"I'd love to do this all over again, but . . ." he said.

"We've got to catch up to Jason before he drag races all the way to Arizona," she said, finishing his thought.

She propped herself on her elbows and gave him a saucy look. "Which car do we take? Yours or mine?"

"My truck's ready."

"Yeah, but—"

"But yours is more fun to drive. Is that it?"

"I told you I like good handling."

"That's exactly what you'll get." He growled and pulled her into another kiss.

"If we take my car we can put the seats back . . ."

"Don't even think about it. There's absolutely no room for two in one seat, no matter how deep inside you I am."

"Well, okay, I guess we'll have to use the pick up. But I get to drive."

"Like hell you do. My truck, I drive."

"Have I ever told you you're no fun?"

She rose from the bed and headed toward the bathroom, giving him a come-hither look over her shoulder.

He grinned, already hot and imagining the soapy foam and water sliding and slithering down her breasts and across her smooth belly into her curls.

The shower was better than he'd thought, the water warmer, Lisa hotter, slicker, holding him deeper. They toweled off slowly.

"I can already see you stretched out with your back against the passenger side door."

"Really?"

"Yes, and I've got your legs draped over my shoulders."

She shuddered against his chest. Her breathing changed and her voice went soft and husky. "I can hardly wait."

Chinatown

Sunny

To my editor, Hilary Sares. For your gracious warmth, generous praise. And for opening the door.

1

It was as if Lily Huang had stepped out of a black-and-white movie into a world of color. The black eyes and black hair of China was behind her. America's vibrant colors and people welcomed her now. The airport's runway came into view as the plane descended.

Twenty-four days after meeting with a government agency specializing in exporting labor, Lily had left China and flown to Singapore with a genuine Chinese passport and a Singapore visa. The group of them—six men and another Chinese woman, a twenty-year-old computer clerk from Fuzhou City, young and pretty like Lily—had stayed in Singapore for two weeks. It was here that legal crossed the fine line over into illegal. The agency had provided them with photo-substituted Singapore passports, their photos replacing the original passport owners' pictures.

Excitement coursed within Lily like an electric jolt as she stepped foot into JFK International Airport, the gateway into the golden land of America. How easy it was to enter this land when you were willing to pay for it. Everything could be had for a price.

Lily was met at the gate by the *ma zhai*, enforcers hired by the smugglers to collect the rest of the fee each person owed—$26,000. The enforcers were a well-dressed bunch, four Chinamen altogether, sticking out like black crows among white pigeons. The leader introduced himself as Billy and hurried the flock of eight new arrivals like sheep into two white vans waiting outside the airport.

They drove to an old two-story brick building in Flushing, Queens—their safe house. There was nothing alarming about it, Lily thought, nothing to warn her that she was about to step over the threshold from heaven into hell.

The foul stench of unwashed bodies hit Lily on the way down to the basement. A man's sharp wailing cry of agony pierced her ear. Lily tensed and hesitated for a second. So did the rest of the flock. The *ma zhais* gave them a shove, pushing them down the stairs.

A man was shackled between two posts. He had been severely beaten. A young *ma zhai* was doing a good job whipping him with a bamboo stick. The last vicious thud struck the man's body, making him jerk horribly. "That," the enforcer said in Fukinese to his new captives, "is what happens if our payment is late in coming."

He released the restraints and the half-conscious, beaten man fell to the ground and began crawling back to his room.

"Did you all see what happened? You men go in there," Billy said, pointing to a room where several other male immigrants were, "and pray to Buddha that your family is good with the money."

Lily and the other girl turned to go to the other room where a half dozen women were huddled, some of them showing signs of being beaten as well. "Stop," Billy commanded. "You two girls go upstairs now."

Don't panic, stay calm, Lily told herself. It was just telephone time.

On the first floor, the white walls were scuffed and dirty and the cheap linoleum floor was peeling in places. A fat cockroach scuttled its long body unhurriedly across the worn flooring. Rusty bars barricaded the finger-smudged windows.

"You first," Billy said, shoving the telephone to Lily. She dialed with a trembling finger the number that she had committed to memory. Someone answered on the first ring. "Mama," Lily whispered in Fukinese. "I have arrived, safe. Pay the rest of the money. Right away."

The phone was snatched out of Lily's hands. "I would listen to your daughter and do as she says," Billy said. "We are going to charge you $100 a day for every day we keep her. If you don't pay in a couple of days, we will sell her to a house of prostitution." He hung up on her, midbabble.

The other girl, Mei-Ling, made her phone call, interrupted by the same warning delivered by Billy. An enforcer started herding them back to the basement when Billy said, "Wait. You two can stay upstairs."

Don't panic, don't panic, Lily told herself. She and Mei-Ling were better clothed, their accents less coarse, obviously from better families than the others. It wasn't unusual for the wealthier immigrants to be treated better. But it was only after the enforcer showed them to their room and left that Lily breathed a sigh of relief. Now all she had to do was wait. Wait and be ready.

There were beds and a bathroom, even a small TV on the floor. Luxury indeed. Lily fumbled around in the bathroom, looking for the light switch. A blind and lengthy search finally yielded up a string, which when pulled, illuminated a bare 15-watt bulb. Presto—dim light. No matter, it was enough wattage to sit on the cracked toilet seat—yuck!—peel off her clothes and step into the grungy tub. Rusted water from pipes a half-century-old came groaning out. After two minutes, the orange finally cleared from the spewing gush and she turned on the shower and hurriedly undressed. Cool, refreshing water washed off the grime and fatigue of her long journey, slicking away the sweat and stench of fear and helplessness.

It was only after the shower, as Lily was drying herself off with an old towel, that she noticed her clothes were gone. Her heart revved into overdrive and adrenaline washed away her fatigue in a surge of panic.

Clutching the threadbare tiny towel, Lily peered through the partially open door into the bedroom. Fuck! The black crows were there, waiting for her. Two of them held Uzi pistols in their hands, held them in a manner that was way too comfortable. Billy lounged on her bed, the arrogant asshole, his eyes cold. Lily's shirt dangled from his hand. Mei-Ling was huddled in a corner, frightened.

"Give me back my clothes!" Lily cried from behind the bathroom door. She could feel the men's eyes creeping over her flesh.

"Come get it," Billy said, "if you want it so badly."

Asshole, Lily thought. She had to get that shirt back at all costs. But which part did she cover with this little patch of a towel? She stretched the rag to cover the slopes of her breasts and, barely, the tops of her thighs. Using her left palm to shield as much of her bare bottom as she could, Lily gingerly stepped into the room.

Inches away from her shirt, Billy asked, "Is this what you are looking for?" He flipped the shirt over to reveal a small, round device no bigger than a dime under the back collar. Oh shit! They'd found her tracking device.

Lily saw her death in Billy's cold eyes.

"What is this?" Billy snapped in English.

He was trying to trick her. She couldn't let him know she spoke English.

Lily shook her head and said in Fukinese, "I don't understand you."

Billy switched to his native dialect and snapped out the question.

"I don't know," Lily said. "I've never seen it before. A neighbor gave me the new clothes as a farewell gift."

"Who is this neighbor that you speak of, little girl?" Billy asked.

"Mr. Ho, a good friend of my mother's. He's an officer in the Fujian Public Security Bureau." Lily's eyes widened. "*He* must have put it there. I didn't know, I swear. I didn't know. Please, I don't even know what the thing is."

"You don't know?" Billy mocked. "I will tell you. It's a tracker."

Standing abruptly, he viciously smacked Lily, sending her stumbling against the wall, pain stinging her face.

"You work for somebody. Who is it? The police?" Billy demanded.

"No one. I am only here to make money for my family."

"Police or FBI. This is one of their toys," Billy sneered. "You don't fool anybody. Tie her up!"

"No, I am innocent!" she protested as the two enforcers roughly roped her hands behind her.

"We'll see how innocent you are," Billy said. "Strip the other bitch, Johnny, and search her too."

Johnny, the younger and better looking of the two enforcers, turned his Uzi to Mei-Ling and barked out instructions. Sobbing quietly, Mei-Ling took off her blue-flowered shirt and pants.

"Everything!" Johnny barked. With trembling hands, Mei-Ling removed her underwear.

Johnny patted Mei-Ling down, fondling her breasts, causing her to weakly protest. "Open your legs," Johnny snapped.

"What are you going to do?" Mei-Ling cried, shielding her crotch with her hands.

"I'm going to put this in you," Johnny said, holding up two fingers, "to see if you're hiding anything bad like that girl."

Johnny pried Mei-Ling's legs open, stuck his fingers up into her and circled his fingers around. "She's clean but her cherry's already been popped."

Billy tsked tsked. "How loose girls are nowadays. What is China coming to?" He pointed at Lily. "Ed," he said to the other enforcer, "tell me if this one is a virgin."

"Spread your legs," Ed commanded, pushing Lily onto the bed. Fatty boy seemed to like his food. He yanked her legs roughly open, so damn far apart Lily had to bite down on her lip to hold back a frightened cry. She closed her eyes, bracing herself. He thrust his fingers inside her. God, it hurt and burned like hell. A goddamn whimper escaped.

He withdrew his pork-knuckled digits and brought it up to his face. A repellent pink tongue slithered out and licked his offending fingers. His eyes disappeared when he smiled. Lily shuddered.

"She's a virgin, at least," he said in English.

"Then we won't kill her just yet," was Billy's cool response.

Lily trembled uncontrollably.

A smile came to Billy's mouth. "Let's switch the girls' clothes. Mei-Ling, you put on Lily's clothes. Lily, you wear her clothes. Your friends," he said to Lily in English, "will be tracking the wrong girl."

Ed untied Lily's hands and shoved her toward the clothes on the floor. "Put on her clothes!" he ordered in Fukinese.

Lily hurriedly donned Mei-Ling's shirt and pants, a bit too big for her, but clothing nonetheless.

Billy smiled. "Now say good-bye to Mei-Ling."

They took the crying girl downstairs. Lily heard the door open and shut, and then she was gone.

2

The following evening they took Lily out of the basement through a tunnel dug to the adjoining house, trussed her up, gagged her, and tossed her into the trunk of a waiting car. She heard the engine start, the garage door crank up, and they drove her away.

She was truly alone now, lost without her tracker. The task force would be following the wrong girl. She lived and breathed only because of one stupid membrane: her hymen. What would they get for it? One hundred dollars, five hundred? They'd pop her cherry, and then pop her. A mixed blessing.

As the car bumped along, Lily pondered her fate and how she had come to this moment.

A couple of dead bodies, unidentified Chinese men who had been beaten and tortured, had been fished out of the Hudson River several months ago. Billy Lim, the leader of the Red Lion Gang, had made quite a name as a ferocious enforcer of an international smuggling ring. On the street, people whispered that he used deadly force if smuggling fees weren't paid promptly.

Billy Lim had become a priority and Lily had been pulled onto the joint Homeland Security, FBI, and NYPD Asian Criminal Enterprise Task Force. Why? Because not only was Lily Chinese but, even more importantly, she spoke fluent Fukinese, the dialect of the Fujian Province where 95 percent of the smuggled immigrants came from. Oh, what a fateful day that was and how happy she had been. She shook her head at her own naivete.

Her thoughts drifted to her roommate at the police academy—how long ago it seemed now. Linda Chavez had been her name. Late at night, lying in bed, they would play the worst-case-scenario game during their twenty weeks of intense training.

If you were at the mercy of a monster like Billy Lim, an undercover female cop and a virgin to boot, whose cover had been blown, which would you choose? To be shot dead? Or to be raped, carved up, and then shot dead? The wild, untamable part of Lily—a legacy from her father—chose to live, any way, any how—raped, filleted open, whatever.

She thought of her mother, her own mother—not the fake mother planted as her contact in China whom she had phoned—her beautiful, caring face came to Lily's mind. She did not know whether to pray that her mother would never know how she had died, saving her the pain. Or that she did, so that she would not wonder up to the last moments of her life what had happened to her child.

When Lily had joined the force, her mother had kissed her, her soft lips so cool and tender against Lily's guilty cheek. *Anything you want, Lily,* she had said. *So long as you are happy. But be safe. Be safe for me. You are my only child."*

Mama, she thought. I'm sorry. So sorry.

Lily lay in the cramped darkness of the trunk, trussed up like a chicken about to be slaughtered. She didn't know how long they had traveled or where they had taken her. Once, over the noise of the engine and the grinding of the road, she had heard a helicopter roar past overhead. At another point, she heard a ship horn blow in the far distance.

After what seemed an interminable amount of time, the blind journey finally came to an end. The trunk door opened, shocking Lily with a blast of cold wind. Two new *ma zhais* met her, one with a scarred face. The other guy's face was pitted. The narrow streets were quiet, without a soul. She glimpsed a few blinking Chinese signs at the end of the alley. Chinatown, she realized.

The two thugs picked her up and carried her into the back door of a rundown building. The stench of rotting garbage attacked her nostrils and the smell of frying food permeated the air. A Chinese restaurant, Lily thought, and a busy one. Two cooks were busily minding their own business, chopping fish heads and lobster tails, without even glancing once at her. Scar Face snatched a knife from the fish chopper and cut the rope tying Lily's wrists. The gag was removed. Before circulation could reenter her limbs, Lily was pushed forward. "Walk upstairs," Scar Face grunted.

Lily dragged her numbed legs up step by step, leaning on the sticky railing. Pit Face kicked open the door and Lily stumbled in.

Oh great, Lily thought, a shabby remake of *The Godfather* plus *Chinatown*.

Behind the desk sat her old friend Billy with his fellow *ma zhais*, Ed and Johnny, looking smugly amused. On the black leather couch sat three white guys, ponytails and all, with cheesy black leather jackets bulging with weapons. Mafiosos, to be sure.

Don't bother to stand up, assholes, Lily thought.

"Is this your merchandise?" one of the mafia guys said. He stood and Lily almost wished he hadn't. He was a brute of a guy, well over six feet with a bullish build, heavy cheekbones, a cruel mouth, a bent Roman nose, and sharp, piercing blue eyes that took in the red marks around Lily's wrists. She felt his gaze touch upon the tender skin around her mouth where the rough gag had chafed her skin. He looked like a bad guy. An aura of thugly menace radiated from him.

"You like her, Tony?" Billy asked.

"A little worse for wear, isn't she?" Tony said, circling Lily. He stopped in front of her and ran a finger down her bare arm.

"All that matters is what is between her legs, does it not, my friend?"

"I don't know." Tony studied Lily once more. "Do you have any more virgins?" Deliberately, he pushed first one sleeve up his massive forearm, then the other.

Their prearranged signal, Lily thought with stunned surprise. Could this dangerous-looking brute be her contact? God help her, only one way to find out.

Lily signaled him back, coughing, one hand flying to her throat.

Tony gave no sign of recognition. Instead, he reached out and toyed with a lock of her hair where it had fallen over her breast.

Yes, I'm your undercover agent, Lily screamed in her mind. Like, duh, can't you tell from my photo? Or do all Asian girls look the same to you? Stop fondling my breast, asshole! Pay attention to Billy, he's getting suspicious.

She had to do something to distract the *ma zhai*. Lily fell to her knees before Billy. "Please, don't sell me," she babbled in Fukinese. "Don't sell me to these white devils. I'll do anything for you. I am innocent. Please do not punish me."

And herein lay the crux. Did Billy think she was or wasn't a cop? She looked young. Hell, that's why she'd been in the Juvenile Division, undercover as a high school kid for two years before being pulled onto this task force. But many Asians looked younger than their age.

If I were him, Lily thought, I'd kill me, just to be safe. Kill me in such a way that my death wouldn't be linked to him. I'd sell me to the Italian Stallion here, earn some money while doing so, and then pop me on their turf, shifting the blame onto the mafia.

Do it, Lily screamed silently. Sell me to them!

But Billy, damn his yellow soul, didn't want to follow the script, even if it was one he himself had written. He straightened his tie—everyone had a prearranged signal, it seemed—and suddenly Scar Face and Pit Face had their guns trained on the Italians. They shoved Lily back toward the frozen three mafiosos so that now all targets were grouped and centered.

"Keep cool, guys," Tony said, hands carefully splayed in front of him. His two henchmen weren't moving, not a twitch, not a tickling sneeze, not even when Johnny and Ed whipped out their Uzi pistols, illegally converted to fully automatic, the law-breaking scum.

"What's the meaning of this?" Tony demanded with just the right amount of outrage in his bass-sub-woofer voice.

"I don't know, my friend. I was hoping you could tell me why you suddenly, tonight, show up at my door asking for some tender virgin flesh."

"Come on, Billy, I told you. I've got a buyer. We've done business before."

"So we have. So we have. In other things but never virgins, which you ask for, oh so coincidentally, tonight. Buddhist I may be, but I am not a believer in such coincidence. Unfortunately our mutually beneficial business relationship will have to come to an end." He kicked back in his leather chair and laced his fingers together. "Are you a cop?"

Tony's eyes widened, then narrowed. "Are you out of your freaking mind?"

"No, I am not, my friend," Billy replied. "She is a cop."

Languid fingers gestured to Lily. "We found the tracking device she wore. You came for her, didn't you? Strip the three of them," he told his men.

"Hold it!" Tony said, seething, then more quietly, "We'll undress ourselves."

"After we frisk you first," Johnny said coolly.

"Agreed."

They submitted to the rough, thorough patdown. Big guns, small guns, hidden guns—an unbelievable amount—were removed from them, piling up like a gun swap on the marble desk. Then they began to strip. If Tony had seemed big wearing clothes, naked he was a monster. Uncovered, every thick, heavy, delineated muscle was revealed.

Lily trembled uncontrollably. *Don't be wearing a wire! Don't be wearing a wire!*

For once, her prayers were answered. She caught a glimpse of an impressively sculpted naked behind as Tony dropped his last item of clothing, his boxers. No tape. No wire. No incriminating tracker.

She'd barely breathed a mental sigh of relief when Billy said in Fukinese, "Take out the two guards."

Two muffled gunshots rang out and the backs of the two mafia henchmen exploded with gushes of blood. Their bodies fell to the floor with heavy thuds, twitching.

God! God! What just happened? Lily screamed frantically in her head.

"What the fuck! What did you just do?" Tony thundered. "We're not cops! We're clean. No wire. We came in good faith. You're going to pay for that, you motherfuckers!"

"You may speak true," was Billy's surprising response. "Those two indeed may not be cops. But you? I do not think that is the case. But no matter. You shall serve quite well either way."

Tony breathed heavily as they tied him up, his muscles

straining. "You don't want to do this, Billy. You don't want to start a war with Coretti."

Billy nodded in agreement. "Do not worry yourself. This will not start a war. You see, you are new to Coretti, less than a year, I remember. You are a plant. Coretti will thank me for this."

Billy opened a drawer and took out a leather case. Flipping it open, he removed a vial and began filling a syringe with the clear yellow liquid. "This shall ensure that you do not worry unnecessarily about my welfare, my friend. It is a new drug that my chemists have concocted—an aphrodisiac like Viagra but much cheaper, without all that expensive FDA-required testing. So much unnecessary money wasted on safety issues, do you not think? We have been giving it to uncooperative girls in my massage parlor—makes them wild with lust. The customers have been most appreciative and business has been booming. But we haven't tested it on men yet. You have the honor of being the very first one." He stopped and appraised Tony. "Such a big man," he said in English. "I think, double . . ." another generous gush, "no, triple." He drew the plunger all the way back so that the entire 5-cc syringe filled with the eerie yellow fluid.

"What if I say no?" Tony said.

"I'll make sure you don't," Billy replied. At his nod, Scar Face and Pit Face pistol-whipped Tony in the head from behind and pinned him down on the floor.

Billy the doc plunged the needle into Tony's naked butt. Tony didn't flinch or curse. Instead he turned and spat in Billy's face. Billy wiped the spittle off with a white handkerchief.

"A little pain at first, but a lot of pleasure to come, my friend. And you will have me to thank for it." Billy turned to Lily. "It will not be long before this stallion roars to life. He is going to rip you apart, my little one."

3

Scar Face and Pit Face dragged Lily and the naked Tony, if that was really his name, down to a cement-walled basement. A bare bulb illuminated a single cot and a tiny bathroom. A knife flashed. Lily's clothes were sliced open. Then Scar Face ripped off her pants and underwear, the tearing sound loud in the silence. They turned to cut Tony's ropes.

She could seize this second and jump them now, Lily thought. The least she could do was make them shoot her and she would die clean. But then they'd kill Tony. After all, there was no need for him once she was gone, and he'd risked his life coming for her. Or had he? Maybe he'd pushed back his sleeves because he had a habit of doing so . . . maybe he *was* part of the mob.

Lily jumped as the heavy door clanged shut with ringing finality and the footsteps faded away.

Tony just stood there, hot energy pumping off him in almost palpable waves. The only sound in that little room was his heavy breathing.

Lily held her ground, five feet away from him. She glanced at him in the dim light, frightened and embarrassed.

I'm butt naked, all alone with a butt naked brute who's jazzed up on some freaky yellow shit!

The man was flushed red all over, gleaming with perspiration, his penis rising up like a sword. Sweet Jesus, Mary, and Joseph, he was a freaking club, jutting straight up, ready for some serious plowing. And he was ripped. Wide shoulders and heavy arms tapered down to a slender waist, a tight behind, and thighs like tree trunks. At least 250 to her 100 pounds. Would he crush her, she wondered? Without a doubt.

He would have been any other woman's erotic fantasy come true. Rich hot chocolate with whipped cream on top. Not just beautifully built but revved up and raring to go. Maybe a little too raring to go. But, unfortunately for Lily, he was a virgin's worst nightmare.

Lily cringed with fear.

Wes felt the yellow shit hit his bloodstream. His heart was racing and his skin was scorching. Hot sweat trickled down his slick skin. Nothing had gone as anticipated. She wasn't supposed to have been at Billy's office. They hadn't even been sure if she was still alive. Her tracking signal had traveled up to the eastern tip of Long Island, near Montauk's lighthouse, and then just disappeared. The task force had moved in on both the location in Flushing and the one in Long Island and had found nothing. All the illegal immigrants had been moved. They'd pulled him in on this op because of his previous dealings with Billy Lim under his tough-guy persona that he'd spent almost a year carefully cultivating.

All he was supposed to do during the meet was to send out feelers: *Hey, I got an order for some cherries. Got any you wanna sell? I have a buyer willing to pay big.* That sort of stuff.

Instead, Billy Lim had pulled her out like a rabbit from his magic hat.

And she'd looked nothing like her police photo. There, her hair had been neatly pulled back in a bun. Cool, intelligent almond eyes had stared out of that picture with a cop's knowing cynicism. Jesus. For one second he would have sworn on the Holy Bible that the girl who had stumbled into that room, tousled, tangled hair flying wildly, had been a genuine illegal immigrant straight from China. Everything had been reflected in her eyes: her terror, her ignorance, her incomprehension of the English language. And the way she'd spoken Fukinese . . . even to his uneducated ears, it had sounded like the real deal. No way could she be the steely-eyed cop he was looking for. No way could she be that good of an actor, could she?

Only the features, the eyes, the delicate nose, the small pointy chin—they were the same. So he'd checked, pushing back his sleeves, signaling her. And she'd signaled back, to his complete and utter amazement. His fatal mistake, he knew that now, under Billy's suspicious gaze. Hell, Billy had already been suspicious to begin with at the timing of it all. That little gesture of his—and hers in return—that had sealed their fate and had gotten poor Nick and Vinnie shot point-blank like some useless shitty animals. He laughed, an ugly laugh completely without humor, and the girl jumped. Fuck, Nick and Vinnie may have been the lucky ones.

His body was on fire. He burned with heat as if caught in the merciless grip of a fever, only the part of him that burned the hottest was a part that usually shriveled up when he got sick. Not so now. His dick was long and thick and so engorged that he was afraid he actually might burst. God, he ached.

And the girl, Lily was her name, she was practically quivering with fear, eyeing that rigid part of him that had stiffened and lengthened against his will so that it stood straight up against him, past his belly button. He didn't want to move. It would just scare her more, but Jesus Christ, he couldn't stand still. Everything was on overdrive—his pounding heart, his heaving lungs. His blood pressure felt as if it was going to shoot through the top of his head and his balls were so tight they felt as if they were turning blue. Blue balls to go with his purple dick. He felt like one giant bruise down there, so exquisitely sensitive that he knew it was going to be painful to touch. Fuck. He began to pace and sure enough, the girl edged back from him. Yup, he definitely frightened her. And he couldn't look her in the eyes and reassure her. He couldn't look at her without remembering all that creamy skin that he'd glimpsed, those small but beautifully shaped breasts, those gently flaring hips, and that teasing black tuft of hair between her legs that he'd seen as they'd cut her clothes open.

Yeah, that's right. Don't look at her. Just keep walking. Look everywhere else but at her. Look at the walls, the ceiling, the floor. It was all freaking cement, like a bomb shelter, only the bomb that was about to go off was locked inside the room.

He bent down, picked up the remains of Lily's ruined pants, and gave a few violent rips, sparking that Chinaman's nightmarish prediction again: *He's going to rip you apart.* No, he promised himself, promised her silently, that's not going to happen. He tied her modified shredded pants around his waist, covering up his too-fucking-sensitive self. He sucked in a breath as the cloth touched him. It was as if a bolt of fire flashed through him. Coarse curses and pants escaped his mouth, and he bent over in agony, his hands braced on his knees.

"Are you okay?" She spoke in English, sounding so American that it was a shock.

He looked up at her briefly. She clutched her torn shirt together in front of her. It covered her, just barely. She was a little thing, a whole foot shorter than him. Why, then, did her legs, the entire ivory length of them, seem so long? He tore his eyes away.

"Yeah," he grunted, then threw himself against the door, slamming against it like a human battering ram, once, twice, three times. *Bam! Bam! Bam!* The door didn't even shudder. And no lock to pick, just a goddamn iron bar that locked them in from the other side.

She didn't say anything. She just did her own exam of their little prison. Carefully, she went over the floor, walls, bathroom, gazed up at the ceiling. She even moved the cot over in a fruitless but thorough search.

"Nothing," she said. "No wires, no cameras."

"No way out either."

"Does anyone know where we are?" she asked softly.

He looked at her, met her eyes. "No. Sorry."

She smiled, a bittersweet smile. "I'm sorry too."

He looked away and went back to business again. The door, the one obstacle that held them trapped here in this room, bore his weight, his silent fury as he battered himself against it again and again. The tenth time he struck it, she cried, "Stop, please . . . you'll just hurt yourself."

The soreness in his shoulders was the least of his hurts. Not a good thing to say. He leaned against the icy bitch of a door. "I won't hurt you."

Her eyes were so expressive, a swirling sea of emotion. It was easy to read what she mistakenly thought he meant: *I won't hurt you when I take you.*

"I mean, I won't touch you." Then more quietly, he said, "You don't have to be afraid of me."

She didn't bother replying. Her silence screamed her skepticism.

Agony flared up like a burning conflagration, throbbing mercilessly between his legs, gripping him so fiercely that he had to bite back a moan and bend over once again and let it roll over him like a monstrous wave. Once it passed, he staggered over and swiped up the splash of white lying on the drab gray concrete floor—the tattered remains of her underwear. Clutching it, he made his way to the cot as he felt another wave coming. The flimsy cot groaned as he sank his weight down onto it.

"Turn around," he said harshly.

She just stayed there, frozen.

"I won't jump you. Promise." Harsh panting. "Trust me. I couldn't walk over to where you are . . . even if I wanted to. I just need to . . . relieve myself." He groaned, sweat running down his face as the ache began to swell like a tidal wave.

She swung around, granting him the visual privacy he'd requested, but she could still hear him. She had to have heard him fumble his loincloth open. Had to have heard the cot squeak, again and again and again as he pumped himself with his fist, and yeah, he was so primed it hurt like the devil to touch himself. She had to have heard his harsh panting and soft groan as he spurted into the white fabric of her panties.

Then silence, stillness. His breath soughed out in a deep sigh and every single muscle he had relaxed.

He must have slept. But not long enough. Not damn near long enough.

He woke up with a gasp, with his body on fire, his dick swelled with that awful pain again. Lily was sitting down on the ground, huddled in the far corner. She looked away without him having to ask. Closing his eyes, hating it, he worked at bringing himself to release again. It wasn't as easy this time, a bad portend of what lay ahead for him. The pain from pumping himself, so much that he had to stop several times, made it harder to achieve climax. It was many long interminable minutes before he finally finished, tears mingling with the sweat dripping down his face. Tears of pain, tears of fury, tears of humiliation, tears of this cursed, unwanted lust. He rolled over onto his side, his back to the room.

Ten fucking minutes and then he felt it building once more. He uttered a string of the foulest curses he knew and swung his legs over the cot. Staggering over to the bathroom that had no door, no privacy, he rinsed out the white cotton cloth and wiped himself all over—his face, neck, arms, shoulders, stomach, legs, his balls, and lastly, that part of him standing tautly upright, so tight that it slapped his belly when he released it, sending a ripping, jolting pain though his groin. He breathed through the agony, then drank from the faucet. Cool water soothed his parched throat.

"Drink more," came Lily's quiet voice. "Not just to rehydrate yourself but to help flush out the drug from your body. My mom's a doctor."

It made sense. Cupping the water in his hands, he gulped down more, and then more, drinking until he could drink not another drop. Only then did he return to the cot and cover himself once more with the loincloth.

"Those other two men . . . were they undercover too?"

She meant Nick and Vinnie. "Nah, the poor bastards." The poor unlucky stupid bastards. "They were real mob. The enemy, but . . ."

"I know." And she sounded as if she really honest-to-God did know. "They're humans too," she said softly.

"I was undercover for six months. You can't help getting to know someone in that amount of time." He expelled a rough breath, remembering. "Nick used to make those really dumb Pollock jokes, the same ones over and over again. Got old real fast. But he used to laugh and chuckle each time he told them. As if they were the funniest things he'd ever heard."

He got up and began to pace, unable to sit still anymore as the urgency began to grip him mercilessly again.

"And Vinnie, he used to slurp his spaghetti. Refused to cut it. Tried to suck the long strands into his mouth all in one piece, the dumb fuck." His breathing sped up, not from the pacing but from the chemicals racing through his system, revving him back up again. "He could bust a guy's kneecap without blink-

ing. But once he had us stop the car in this really shitty neighborhood . . ." He stopped speaking a moment to suck in a deep
breath, which didn't seem near enough what he needed to oxy-
genate himself. "This big guy was"—pant, pant—"pounding
on this kid. Maybe eleven, twelve years old. Right there in the
street. Out in the open. And no one was doing squat. Vinnie
got out. Told the guy to stop. When he didn't, Vinnie kicked
the shit out of him . . . warned him not to touch the kid again . . ."

And then he was sinking down onto the cot and loosening
the cloth from around his waist, groaning and then crying
when he wrapped his big, rough hand around his too-sensitive
dick, forcing himself to squeeze down tight and start pumping
and pumping and still goddamn pumping until he couldn't take
the pain anymore and he had to stop or burst into sobs.

"You didn't . . . What's the matter?" she asked.

He shut his eyes, squeezed them tight. "I need to come but I . . .
can't. I'm finding it a total turnoff having to jerk off in front of
you. And my body's so fucking sensitive, it hurts to touch myself. Pain's jamming the system and I can't get the relief I need,
it seems, without hurting myself to get it. Real neat drug Lim's
made himself. The bastard." He cursed the smuggler weakly,
unable to generate any heat even though a fire was engulfing
him.

Something cool touched him and his eyes flew open to see
Lily's hand, so white, so contrasting against his flushed purple,
vein-rippled penis. She ran her small white fingers lightly down
his shaft.

"Does this hurt?" she asked, not looking at him, her other
hand keeping her shirt modestly closed, her actions a ridiculous
dichotomy.

His jaw tightened, his teeth clenched. He could only dumbly
shake his head no. She moved her fingers lightly back up, the
barest pressure, and a groan escaped his lips. Her hand jerked
away.

"Did I hurt you?"

He gave a shaky laugh. "No, it felt . . . good." Massive understatement. It had felt fucking great. There had been that edge of pain, but—oh, the pleasure. Not just from the feel of her but also from the picture of her—her ebony-black hair half-veiling her face, her moist red lips, her small, silky hand touching him. "But you don't have to . . ."

"I want to."

And his dick wanted her to too, so badly that a thick pearl of lubricant gathered and wept from the single-eyed opening, pleading its want more eloquently than he could.

Her hand moved slowly, so slowly, and touched him once again like a shy bird alighting on a strange branch of a strange tree. With gentle care, she wrapped her entire delicate hand around him near his tip. Her fingers didn't meet all the way around. He swallowed down another groan, not wanting to startle her, and watched in agony as she reached up with her thumb and smeared the pearly essence around his fat tip. That was it, that one little gesture, and he started to pulse and spurt. He barely got the panties there in time before he spent himself in a powerful release.

She was looking at him, her wide eyes fixed curiously on that part of him that had leaped and jerked, and was now relaxing, softening.

"I'm sorry," she said when she looked up and saw him watching her. Pink tinged her cheeks. "I just . . . I hope you don't mind that I watched. I'd never seen that before."

"Thank you."

Her brown eyes were as solemn as a nun's. "No, thank you for coming for me."

4

Thank you for coming for me.

The pun hit Lily a moment later. She'd meant his trying to rescue her, not the orgasm. She clamped a hand over her mouth, but not before a giggle escaped. "I'm sorry," she gasped amidst more giggles that just wouldn't stop, "my brain's still not engaged."

"Thought that was just a guy's problem," Wes said, "thinking with that other head."

That did it. She chortled and so did he, both of them laughing so hard over something that wasn't really all that funny. But it was as if something else controlled them. She laughed and gasped so hard that she was crying. And then she was just crying.

"Hey." The cot squeaked and arms, so hot, came around Lily and pulled her into his chest. Her hand, still holding her shirt closed, was caught between them. "Hey, it's okay." He stroked and soothed her, rubbing her back, murmuring sweet little nothings that she couldn't hear, could only feel as comforting vibrations against her. He held her until she quieted.

Lily pulled back and he released her instantly.

"I'm sorry," she muttered, wiping her eyes with the heel of her hand.

"I'm not. It's a good way to release tension. You needed that. We both did." She heard him sigh.

"Are they going to be looking for us?" she asked.

He took the time to tie the ridiculous blue-flowered cloth around him before glancing at his watch. "Not yet but soon. They'll know something's wrong when I miss my normal check-in." He lay back down on the cot and closed his eyes, looking exhausted.

"There's room here if you want to lie down," he offered, scooting over.

Lily shook her head. "No, I'm okay. Go ahead and rest." She scooted down to sit against the wall, leaning back and closing her eyes.

The cot shifted again as he resettled, old metal rattling, and then there was just the sound of his even breathing.

Even with her eyes closed, Lily could see him clearly, as he had been in that moment of release. She could see that almost blind look that had hazed his electric blue eyes, feel the soft jetting pulsations as he'd thickened, and then spewed out a white, creamy stream. Felt again that surprising sense of intimacy with him. Felt again her unexpected pleasure at his pleasure.

The size of him was still frightening, yes, but she no longer feared him. He was a kind man, maintaining control of himself in a situation where many others would not even have bothered, indeed, would have used the drug as an excuse not to. His size no longer struck terror in her heart, even though he was far bigger than Ed's dirty little fingers.

He'd been as soft as velvet, softer even than a baby's skin, with an oddly supple hardness underneath. She'd enjoyed touching him, she found to her great surprise. It hadn't been at all as repulsive as she had thought it would be. And he'd been almost helpless beneath her touch, had wept that perfect pearl of his desire. An incredible feeling of power had rushed through her—how odd, that—in this miserable hole in the ground where she should have felt no power at all.

How odd that such a moment shared would make her feel bonded with him somehow, make her care more for him, make her want to ease his sufferings. Make her wonder what it would be like to have that long, hot male organ slide within her, joining them. Would they feel even closer?

The change in his breathing brought Lily out of her thoughts. His muscles were tenser, tighter, his reprieve brief, his turmoil beginning yet again. He swung himself so that he sat with his back against the wall, his long, hairy legs swung over the cot, his feet on the cold floor. He had big feet. Wide, solid, largely proportioned like the rest of him. At least a size twelve.

"How old are you?" he asked.

Lily blinked. "Twenty-two. Didn't you know?"

"Yeah." He laughed. "Yeah, I did. Just wanted to be sure. You, uh, look much younger."

"Don't worry. I won't be bringing any statutory rape charges against you." Her attempt at humor tripped and fell flat, serving only to remind them of their dismal future. It was unlikely she would be bringing any charges against anyone. They would come back, Billy Lim and his men, and kill them, make sure they were dead. Or they could just leave them down here to starve and rot to death. Neither was an attractive option.

"How old are you?" Lily asked in return.

"Twenty-seven."

He looked older, like in his early thirties. Maybe it was the size thing. Like the smaller one was, as in her case, the younger one looked, while the taller, bigger, broader a person was, the older he seemed.

But it wasn't just his exterior. He had presence. The force of it had struck Lily when she'd first seen him, an air of cool confidence, almost cockiness. And his eyes . . . they'd been cold and calculating. But not cruel. Not like Billy Lim's dead snake eyes.

Shit, shit, shit, shit, shit, Wes thought. That was the litany going through his head as he shuffled into the dingy bathroom, emptied his bladder, and gulped down more metallic-tasting water, drinking as much as he could until nausea stopped him.

It had only been ten frigging minutes before he'd gotten a raging hard-on again instead of the normal physiological hour. Man had that natural circuit breaker built in for a reason. He'd come three times in an hour. He hadn't even done that as a randy teenager.

Pleasure was no longer pleasure. It had become a hellish, demanding bitch that wouldn't let him get the rest his body was screaming for. He burned too much energy cranking up and was completely wiped out afterward, so weak that he shook. How long could he keep this up before he collapsed? And once he did—collapse, that is—there was no guarantee even then of a respite.

He leaned over the sink, made himself gulp down two more mouthfuls of water. Breathe evenly, don't throw up, he told himself. That's right. Flush it out. Get it the hell out of his body before it killed him.

He cleaned and rinsed out the white cloth—her underwear. She'd been . . . amazing. His cock surged and twitched and he slammed the door shut on the memory. He set the cloth down by the cot—he was really coming to loathe that dirty, stained mattress—and began to pace again, back and forth, back and forth, until he was almost jogging. Until he could actually see the steam wafting off him in vapors. Until he couldn't stand upright anymore and stumbled to that stupid cot, fumbled with that stupid cloth, her pants. Impossibly his dick swelled even more and he groaned with agony. And then her cool hands were against his chest, gently pushing him to lie down. He resisted.

"Let me," she said, kneeling at his side.

"You don't need to," he muttered between clenched teeth, hating it. Hating that she touched him only because he needed it, not because she wanted to.

She held his eyes and smiled—a slow, unhurried curving of her mouth at both ends, a tantalizing flash of beautiful small, even, white teeth. A siren's smile. Knowing and luring. Totally bewitching. He allowed himself to fall back onto the cot, unable to look away from her face, from the promise in her eyes.

"I want to," she said huskily. Her hand fell away from her shirt. It parted and his eyes fell down to feast on the soft fullness of her breasts, the brown velvet of her nipples. They were erect. He looked back up, searching her eyes with sudden, searing intensity that made her take a deep, involuntary breath. Her nipples hardened even more, plumping into dark raspberries.

"What are you doing?" he rasped in a thick voice.

She reached out that lily-white hand of hers—so small, really, to have become the most important thing in his world—and laid it over his swollen staff.

His jaw locked, his hands fisted, and every muscle in his body clenched at the light contact.

She stroked her hand down his entire length. Lightly back up. Circled his sensitive head, making a pleased sound that had his muscles tightening even more at the pearly essence she found there. "I'm pleasing you," she murmured.

She lifted his hand, uncurled his fist, and brought it up to her chest. He resisted, holding back that last inch before he would have touched her. So she leaned forward instead and his hot hand covered her breast, rubbed against her sensitive nipple.

It felt good. So good. Lily cried out, opened her eyes. Found that the blackness of his pupils had swallowed up his eyes and his irises now were a thin, narrow rim. Found that his incredible blue eyes had deepened and darkened so that they were almost violet. So beautiful.

"And I'm pleasing myself," she whispered, cupping his big hand over her breast. Oh, the sensations . . . she'd never known.

"Lily." It was the first time he'd said her name. "You don't have to do this for me." His face was so hard, so harsh and unsmiling, even as his rod twitched beneath her hand. "I don't *want* you to do this for me."

She stood up then, forced herself to pull away from his hand, to pull her own hand away from that living, stirring part of him that was beginning to fascinate her. She stood up and let her shirt fall to her feet, let him look at her, knowing and liking that he was unable to do otherwise. His eyes so hot, so hungry, stirring a similar hunger within her.

"You're wrong," Lily said and climbed onto the cot, straddling him, knees braced on either side of his narrow hips. He made a strangled noise and his hands bit into her waist, holding her there, unmoving. Not pushing her away, not pulling her to him. Just holding her and trembling.

"I'm doing this for me," she said fiercely. "Make love to me. Please."

"Lily, you don't know what you're . . ."

"If Billy Lim comes back, you're dead. And so am I. But they won't kill me right away, do you understand? Only after . . . I'm not doing you a favor. I'm asking you to do one for me. The first time . . . I want it to be with you."

Gently, Lily laid her hand on his powerful forearm, slid it up to his wrist, brought his hand from her waist and placed it over her stomach, long fingers spread. His hand almost spanned the width of her waist. Eyes locked on his, she guided his hand lower. "Please . . ."

"Are you on birth control?" he rasped.

What did it matter? But in this she could ease his mind some. "Yes. Depo-Provera shot. Good for three months."

He didn't look any happier. How grim he was. Her fingers ached to smooth away his frown but she didn't dare. Touching his face was somehow more intimate than touching his cock.

"I'm clean," he said, his voice a deep rumble. "I've always used a condom."

He was trying to reassure her, and he did, but in a way other than what he meant. He was a good man. The right man.

And then he was touching her, down there, and it was Lily's turn to tremble as he lightly brushed over her curls, as he ran a gentle finger over her wet portal, and then away. "Oh!"

It was his turn to smile, a pirate's smile, transforming the lean, rugged planes of his face, making him younger and devastatingly handsome. Lighting up his entire face. It was shocking how different he looked when he smiled and to realize that women would be drawn to his bad-boy looks—buxom, built blondes ten feet tall. They would be drawn to his darkness, his danger, his confidence. It came as a shock to realize that he could have any woman he wanted and to realize that had they met in any other way, he would never have looked at her, and she would never have looked at him, so different they were.

He touched Lily again and her thoughts scattered. He ran his fingers with smooth confidence through her black tuft and just curled his fingers over her, cupping her so that he felt her heat, her wetness. A sound escaped Lily and she pressed down against his hand, asking for more.

He smiled that devilish smile again, speeding up her heart, speeding up her breathing so that it matched his. He ran his hands up her belly, so terribly slowly so that when he finally cupped her breasts, Lily almost cried out in relief. And then she did cry out as he rasped her nipples with his thumbs, shooting pleasure through her entire body so that it spread and spread, and then arrowed down to her groin.

He heaved up, rocking her world, sitting up. Then he lowered his head, took a nipple into the hot, wet cavern of his mouth and sucked. And rocked her world again.

"Oh my God," she gasped. Her hands gripped his head, found the elastic tie that held back his hair and ripped it out, diving into the long, silky cloud. So soft. So unbelievably soft when she'd always thought of men as rough and hard. But there was nothing rough about this man. He licked and sucked and laved her breasts so tenderly, first one, and then the other, until she pressed against him, rubbing her lower body against his hard length. He groaned and she pulled back. "I'm sorry. Did I hurt you?"

His face was clenched in agony. She *had* hurt him, rubbing against him like that.

"In the best way," he managed to say with a tight, reassuring smile. "In the best possible way, sweetheart."

"We can wait, until the next time," Lily said hesitantly.

"No." He lay back and centered her over him. "Let me see if you're ready."

He seemed to be awaiting her permission. She nodded and he gently opened her. He rubbed a light finger over an exquisitely sensitive part of her in front that had Lily crying out and clutching his hips. A thick, long finger slipped into her and her breathing stopped. It was . . . indescribable, the feeling of fullness, of sweet, slick, slippery pleasure. Full, so full from just that one finger. A bit of pain. A lot of amazing pleasure. She wanted more.

"Ride me. Sink down on me," he urged.

She moved over him, slowly taking him in, lifting back up. "Oh, Tony."

"Wes. My name's Wes. Say my name."

His eyes . . . she couldn't look away from his burning eyes.

"Wes." She sank back down, taking his finger as deep as it could go in her, not stopping even when it hurt.

"Yes." His nostrils flared as he watched her. "That's it. You're incredible," he breathed. "Another finger. Take another finger."

It didn't seem that she could take that as well. But she did. She did, frowning, biting her lips.

"I know it hurts, baby. I'm sorry but I need to stretch you. Help me. That's it," he murmured as she took him in. His other hand smoothed in a possessive sweep over her belly, his fingers burning hot. His thumb came to rest just on top of her swollen nub, just resting there, touching so lightly she couldn't believe how it could generate such lovely, deliciously sharp sensations within her, making her breasts swell even more, making her nipples so unbearably sensitive, making her move, riding him, up and down. And each time she did, he touched her more firmly, harder, so that it was all she concentrated on, so that she plunged harder, sinking his two thick fingers into her, rocking on him, having him touch her more, just there, until she was panting and on the edge of something so terribly huge it scared her and enthralled her and beckoned her with maddening desire.

"Wait," he panted, sweat rolling down his face, sheening his beautiful, sculptured body.

He removed his fingers. Using her own juice to lubricate his head and upper shaft, he positioned himself. "Take me in," he rumbled, his lavender eyes mesmerizing Lily, holding her willingly captive.

And she did, with her hand over his. She brought him to her wet opening and sank down.

He was big. Bigger than two fingers. And he wasn't going in. Lily cried out in frustration. "Help me!"

His hands came up to grip her waist, anchoring her. With one controlled surge he was in, just barely, just the tip, and, oh my God, did he feel big.

"Is this going to work?" she couldn't help but ask.

He laughed, and then groaned. "Yes. Yes, it will. You've got to trust me."

Trust him—how easy Lily found it to do that. "All right," was her soft, gasping reply. She smiled tremulously at him.

He smiled back and she relaxed, her muscles loosening up, no longer desperate, no longer afraid.

"Take me in," he urged again.

She had to work hard to do so. Shifting and lifting, pushing down, rocking up and down, even around, nudging him in inch by incredible inch. And always there was his thumb, right there over that most swollen part of her, rocking her with terrible, incredible sensations, so that she forgot the burning and stretching and just concentrated on reaching for that looming, building, peaking promise.

Her hand reached down and measured him. "Only halfway in," she panted, wanting to cry, knowing he must be hurting, prolonging it like this. The need within him must be tremendous. "Take me," she said urgently. "Make me yours. Now."

"Lily . . ." His eyes were almost blind.

His hands gripped her hips and brought Lily down as he surged up into her, breaking that thin virginal membrane, filling her beyond what she had ever imagined she could take, so far deep inside of her that she felt him touch her womb. His thumb touched her once again, rubbed, pressed, squeezed. His other hand squeezed and plucked a hard nipple and she exploded, convulsing, shattering. "Wes . . ."

Then it was his turn. One wild thrust, another, and he arched his back, lifting Lily up, jetting and pulsing within her, hot gushing streams that she felt within her, finding his release even as she experienced hers. And his satisfaction, his release, his relaxation was as fulfilling and satisfying as her own. She sank bonelessly down onto his chest, wrapped in his arms, rocked by his soft breathing. Sweet heaven.

5

Hell returned quickly enough for Wes as he stirred, lengthening and hardening within Lily. Hell was lifting her up and slipping out of her. He got up, sat her down, and grabbed the damp cloth. "Let me."

And like that she acquiesced, lying back, relaxing, parting her legs. It killed him when she did that. Trust him like that, so completely. Gently, he wiped up the blood staining Lily's thighs—her blood. Gently he cleaned her up. In the bathroom, he cleaned himself up, cleaned the innocence of her blood off the part of him that had impaled her, hurting her and bringing her pleasure.

He closed his eyes, hands braced on the sink, glad that there wasn't a mirror, glad that he couldn't look up and see the man who had taken a young girl's innocence. Glad that he couldn't see the triumphant satisfaction he knew would be there, mixed with the guilt and shame at having done so.

Make me yours, she had cried. And God help him, he felt that way about her. She was his. She had offered herself to him and he had taken her. As she had taken him. For the time they had left, they belonged to each other.

A long, unbroken stream of water hit the toilet for an entire minute as he emptied his bladder, his urine an unusual frothy yellow like that damn drug they'd poisoned him with. Good. He was pissing it out of his system.

Thirty minutes they had slept, still joined. Thirty minutes of bliss that would have to last him for the rest of the night, perhaps the rest of his life, which was looking to be quite short. He drank and drank, handful after handful of water, and rinsed out Lily's panties and wrung them dry.

She was his now. He had to take care of her. No more penetration. She'd be sore enough as it was from that one time. She needed time to heal a little. A day. Lord, please grant them at least that much time before that bastard Billy returned.

If he was Billy, he'd definitely come back to tie things up. Kill both of them with his semen in Lily's vagina, and make it look as if he had raped Lily, murdered her, and then killed himself.

She was still lying there, naked, her skin gleaming like a luminous pearl, so white against the inky blackness of her hair, her dark eyes slumberous, watching him as he began to pace, one foot in front of the other. Walk. Don't look at her. But her image, the picture of her lying there with that sweet, satisfied smile was imprinted in his mind. He didn't need to look at her, didn't need to lay his eyes on her to remember how she'd felt, so incredibly soft inside, hot and wet for him.

He clenched back a groan, tried to shut the image, the memories, out. Tried to close his ears to her remembered cries, to that remembered moment when she had called out his name as she'd broken apart in his arms and let him put her back together again, a different woman. Tried and failed.

"Come here." Her husky voice beckoned, filled with promise.

Had he thought her a little girl? He couldn't imagine it. She was a goddamn siren.

He resisted her call for a minute longer, trying to rid himself of as much as he could of that excess artificial energy, then gave in.

The cot squeaked as she sat up. Squeaked again as he sat down beside her and leaned back against the wall, playing with the dark fall of her hair. "You have beautiful hair. So thick, so black, like the dark, mysterious night."

She scooted back, bringing her knees back. "I love your hair too. So long and silky. I want to feel it over my face. I want to feel it brush over my breasts."

She ran a finger, one finger, up his thigh. And he shuddered. He grabbed her wrist before she could reach her final destination and brought it to his lips, laid a gentle kiss on her soft hand that surprised her. Then he watched as surprise darkened into desire and he just barely found enough strength to say, "I'm better now. Drinking all that water like you suggested, it's working. I can take care of myself. Why don't you lie down, get some more rest."

She stopped him with one hand to his chest as he moved to rise. One tiny hand that physically couldn't stop him. But her power over him went far beyond physical strength.

"Oh, no," she drawled. "This." She wrapped that tiny hand around him and gently pumped him, making him groan, making him almost whimper. "This is mine." She smiled, part angel, part devil. Wholly witch. And he was totally under her spell.

"I'm not going to make love to you again," he gritted, sweating as she stroked him in that agonizingly gentle way. "Your body needs time to repair what I tore."

"How long?" she whispered. Lowering her head, she kissed his chest, his neck, his jaw. Licked a drop of his sweat. His cock bobbed fiercely.

"A whole day."

"A night," she countered and opening her mouth, lightly bit his neck.

He whimpered as she kissed her way back down his chest, down his belly. "Twenty-four hours," he gasped, almost mindless with the feel of her soft lips pressing against him.

"Twelve hours," she whispered, and then the sweet hot wetness of her mouth covered him.

"Oh, Jesus! Lily . . . Oh God! . . . baby . . ."

Her little tongue flicked and laved him, totally destroyed him. He prayed, he cursed. He called her name. She took him soaring so high he thought he could touch heaven but he stopped just short of it. She tongued him, sucked him, almost swallowed him, and it wasn't enough. It wasn't enough! He couldn't come. He plummeted back down to earth, suffering the torment of the damned, his balls, his cock, his entire self on fire.

Just when he was going to pull away from her and pump himself to completion by hand despite the hellish pain, she reached down with one hand and cupped his tight balls and squeezed them. He groaned. He died. But still he did not come.

Her hand slipped down farther, touching him where he had never been touched before, pressing down on the taut, sensitive tissue of his perineum. And he came spurting like a high-pressured geyser into her mouth.

He collapsed against the wall, amazed, awed, embarrassed that she had been able do that, make his body react like that against his will, against his volition. He pulled her into his arms, rested her head against his chest, the top of her head tucked under his chin. She fit him well. Felt so perfect against him, so perfect for him.

Limp. Utterly limp. Jello possessed more gelatinous firmness than he did now. Every muscle in his body was lax, relaxed. Only the wall held him up, otherwise he would have been sprawled on the cold, hard ground.

"How did you . . ." He cleared his throat. "How did you know how to do that?" She had been a virgin, untouched and never having touched a man before. He would have sworn it on his grandmother's grave. She had been a virgin. And she'd just used a whore's trick on him.

She pulled back, hearing more in his voice than perhaps he had wanted her to hear. A little smile teased the corners of her mouth. "I was in Juvenile Division. You'd be surprised at what high school girls know and talk about."

"High school girls." He closed his eyes. "Jesus Christ."

But when his eyes opened again they twinkled with humor. "Makes me want to go back to the twelfth grade."

She snickered, giggling and snorting, her vibrations shaking his chest as he settled them down on the cot so that they were lying side by side, so that he spooned her from behind. "Close your eyes," he whispered, kissing her lightly on the cheek. "Rest."

6

The door crashed open and the cot almost tipped over as Wes sprang to his feet, shielding Lily with his body, facing their attackers.

Machine guns faced them, a multitude of them. It was a bowel-loosening tense moment until one of them said, "Wes?"

Another called out, "Lily?"

It was her friend and fellow NYPD. "Sara," Lily said with a crashing wave of relief, her voice husky from the heart-wrenching fear.

"Hey, Gus. What took you so long?" Wes said dryly. "We're unarmed, as you can see."

Gus, the FBI agent, yelled, "Guns down," snapping everyone out of that frozen moment. "Everybody outside but Lieutenant Wang and me. Get me some blankets."

Wes handed Lily her shirt, then a medical team rushed in and wrapped them in blankets.

"Are you injured, hurt anywhere, detective?" a young paramedic asked Lily as he pumped the blood pressure cuff.

"No." She turned and looked at Wes. *Don't leave me.*

Wes's eyes locked with hers. *I don't want to.*

The cuff deflated. "I'm going to examine you," the paramedic said gently.

Lily nodded and competent hands ran lightly over her.

Stretchers were brought in.

"I don't need a stretcher," Wes said.

"I can walk out," Lily protested.

The young paramedic cleared his throat. "It's, um, cold outside."

"And you've got no shoes," the other paramedic, a crusty older man, said to Wes. "Not to mention clothes."

Lily lay down on the stretcher without another word. Wes sighed, then gave in to Lily's silent urging and sat down, compliant, on his stretcher. Lily's eyes never left Wes's as they were strapped in. *Will I see you again?*

One last look from him. *Yes.*

And then they were taken away.

Living, it seemed, was going to be more of an ordeal than dying would have been. The doctor and nurses in the hospital were kind. Too kind. Pity was in their faces, in the way they talked to her, in the careful questions they asked. That was easy to shrug off. Just as it was easy to politely refuse a pelvic exam, a test for sexually transmitted diseases, and a test for pregnancy.

She had looked around futilely, hoping to see Wes, and was told only later that he had been taken to another hospital—FBI protocol. Lily was released after three hours, a complete waste of time. She could have told them she was all right, but it was a necessary waste of time—NYPD protocol. Besides, she couldn't return to work until after she had been medically cleared.

For the next several days, Lily spent hours between debriefing and writing a lengthy and detailed report about her entire mission. Somewhere in those busy hours she found out how she and Wes had come to be rescued. Sara Wang had gotten a call from a suspicious motel manager about "all these people who look like they've just come off the boat." NYPD had gone in and swooped up a dozen illegal Chinese immigrants. One of them was Mei-Ling. Under Sara's deft and gentle coaxing, Mei-Ling told her the story, leading them to Ed, Johnny, and the other *ma zhais*. Billy Lim, though, was still at large.

Ed had spilled everything on the promise of a lighter sentence, knowing had he not made a deal, they could have gotten him for accessory to murder: the two mafia henchmen whose bodies had been found. Charges for human smuggling was a much lighter sentence to bear.

How strange, then, to feel as if she had been lost instead of found. Lily felt abandoned. First by Wes, who didn't call, then by her own commander, who ordered her off the job on a forced vacation once they had sucked all the little details out of her.

"I'm fine. I don't want to take leave," she had told Commander Gerrity.

"You've got no choice," he had replied, his bulldog face set. "And see Janet Meyers." The psychiatric specialist for their precinct. "You can't come back until after she's cleared you." Oh joy.

So she went to the shrink. Let the doc poke and prod with her cold, sterile voice into Lily's privacy, into her mind, which was even more invasive than submitting to a pelvic exam. And Lily had played along, babbling on the couch. She had learned early on not to fight them. Fighting would only result in more couch sessions, more probing, more prying. You agreed with them and said everything they wanted you to say. Yes, the closeness Lily had felt for Wes was a mere creation borne of a dangerous situation. Yes, there was no need to feel guilty for submitting to him. Yes, Doc Meyers told her, you might think that your act of submission was voluntary, my dear, but your subconscious understood that you had no other choice. You made the only choice you could make under the situation, therefore what you did was involuntary, and what you gave up was a dear sacrifice. Your intense feelings for Wes are unreal and will fade with time. He is experiencing the same artificial emotions and, on top of that, suffering guilt over having robbed you of your virginity. It is a castle built on sand. It would be better, my dear, if you two could leave this baggage behind and get on with your lives.

And if Lily heard another *dear* come out of that prissy mouth, she was going to brain her. God almighty these couch sessions could really fuck you up.

Lily swallowed down the crap and left the session with her stomach churning, in disgust for having had to submit to that mind rape, and in fear that the psychiatrist may be right. Maybe Wes's feelings for her *had* been a result of their forced captivity together. Maybe Wes's feelings for her would fade with time. Maybe it had been a castle built on sand.

The fact that seven days had passed without him calling seemed proof that it was.

7

W es waited in darkness, calling himself all kinds of fools for doing this, for coming here to Lily's elegant prewar apartment on the Upper East Side, with her generous view of Central Park, decorated with good taste and lots of money.

Idiot. Stupid dumb fuck. There had been a fifty percent chance that Lily would want to see him again, but that had been ten days ago. Ten days during which time she hadn't returned a single one of his calls. That fifty percent had slipped down a mucky, slippery slope to one percent now. But one percent had been enough to bring him here like a smitten swain. One percent refused to go away and die. One percent was keeping him roasting on a simmering spit in this purgatory of hope. One percent had to know . . . from her own lips. And so he was here after having finessed her lock, waiting patiently, impatiently, hope fighting against hopelessness. Finally, after two fucking long hours, his wait was over. The door opened and the lights flicked on.

She was wearing an expensive wool jacket and skirt, her black hair neatly pulled back in a polished bun, the mail clutched in her arms as she swung the door closed and looked up. And screamed.

And Wes realized that he had the wrong woman. "I'm sorry, I was looking for Lily Huang," he said, forcing himself to remain sitting. Standing would only frighten the woman more. "I must have the wrong apartment."

"No . . . no," the strange woman choked out, her eyes wide. She looked at him then, with an intensity that made him feel like a squirming insect under a microscope. "You must be Wes."

"Yes, ma'am."

She snorted at the polite address. "Ma'am, huh?" and grimaced. A grimace so much like Lily's that Wes's breath stopped.

"Yes," she said with amusement. "I'm Anna, her mother."

Oh crap.

Lily's mother set her purse and stack of mail down on the side table, and perched on the sofa across from him. He could see it now, the soft lines that time had touched upon her face, but it had been gentle in its stroking. She looked ten, fifteen years younger than what she must be, and Wes saw where Lily had gotten her genes.

"She's not here," she said.

"Is that a polite way of telling me to get lost, Dr. Huang?"

She smiled. "No, if I'd wanted you gone, I'd be calling the police and filing charges against you for illegally breaking and entering a private residence. I'm simply telling you the truth. My daughter left three days ago. I came to water her plants and collect her mail."

"Where did she go?"

"She went to our cottage in Key West."

Cottage in Key West. That phrase, tripping so lightly off her tongue, drilled in again how far apart Lily's world was from his, with his middle-class Bensonhurst, Brooklyn upbringing. If any other cop had lived like this, Internal Affairs would have been all over them like buzzing flies on hot dung. But Lily had come from money. Lots of it, it seemed. A fact that had stunned him after he'd finally grown desperate enough to call in a favor and have a report run on her. A fact that had stopped him from coming here two days sooner.

"She doesn't want to see me," he stated flatly.

Anna Huang tilted her head and studied him like the doctor she was. "No, I do not believe that is the case."

"Then why did she run away? Why didn't she return my messages?"

"Ah, so you did call." She arched an elegant eyebrow.

"I left fifteen messages for her at work," he gritted, and realized now that none of them had been delivered. The cops had been protecting one of their own from the outsider, the Fed.

"I want to see her," he said. "Will you give me the address?"

"Why?"

He splayed his hands in front of him. "I miss her."

Silently she got up and fetched a paper and pen from an antique desk, a Henry XVI. Scribbling down the information, she handed it to him.

"Thank you," he said and walked to the door. With one hand on the doorknob, he hesitated, turned around. "Did she tell you what happened?"

"Yes."

"Do you have any questions for me?" he asked.

"No."

"Does she blame me?" A pause. "Do you blame me?"

"For what?" she asked.

"For having . . . touched her."

Her dark eyes looked at him coolly, mysteriously, her emotions unreadable. "As I understand it, you did not touch her until after she had touched you first."

He blushed.

"You feel guilty," Anna said and sighed, those midnight eyes softening. "There is no need. I know my daughter. You did nothing to her that she did not wish you to do."

"How do you know? She couldn't have stopped me. She might have felt forced by the circumstances to submit."

Anna laughed. "I'm sorry," she said at his affronted look. "I know it's not funny. That you must have suffered thinking that." She laughed again. "It's just that Lily holds a black belt in kung fu and a brown belt in . . . what do you call it . . . that Israeli fighting art. She put a mugger in the hospital once with three broken ribs and a dislocated shoulder. A man outweighing her by over a hundred pounds. Did you know that?"

Wes shook his head.

"Put aside that worry. I know my daughter. She could have stopped you, big though you are." A wry smile curved her full lips, which she had passed down to her daughter. "Have a good trip."

8

Lily left Poppies, a quaint little dive, alone and unsatisfied. The date had been a lousy mistake, though the food was delicious.

A block from the cottage a young man suddenly came out of a dark alley, charging Lily, the smell of liquor and chemicals oozing from his pores, polluting the night. The metallic gleam of a dagger gripped in his hand glinted under the glow of the streetlamp.

Jesus, Lily thought. There was just something about petite women that seemed to proclaim *victim* to all would-be muggers. Totally annoying, as if stature had anything to do with strength, or knowledge, or skill, or determination.

The defensive moves came naturally, without thought, to Lily. A swivel to the side, a grab to the forearm, bend, twist, and he went flying in the air, knife falling from his hand as he hit the ground with a satisfying, bone-wrenching thud, groaning.

"I hope you broke your tailbone, asshole," Lily said, standing over him in her ridiculous two-inch heels. Stupid things. Shouldn't have worn them.

"Better than breaking three ribs and an arm," said a gravelly voice, a voice she had not forgotten, would never forget. A voice that she still dreamed about, damn his abandoning soul.

She turned and watched Wes cross the street. A different Wes with his hair cut short. A Wes who, even in his civilian attire of khakis and white T-shirt, still looked big and menacing, still looked like the guy who should have been mugging her instead of the kid at her feet.

There was a brief scuffling noise, and then the sound of running as her incompetent assailant fled.

"He's getting away," Lily said evenly.

Wes's right brow lifted. "I didn't fly all the way from Virginia to New York, then from New York to Florida to chase after a punk."

"Why did you come then?"

"I came to see you, Lily."

"You're FBI."

He nodded.

"I didn't know that, not until after we were rescued."

"Now you know."

"You live in Virginia, three states away," she stated.

"We are only inches apart now."

"How long are you here for?"

He hesitated. "I have ten days."

Ten days, Lily thought. So little time compared to the lifetime she wanted. What then, after ten days? Was that all he wanted? Would that be enough for her?

Wes's heart dropped like a cut anchor when she turned and walked away. She didn't want him.

At the end of the block, she stopped before a white picket fence. She swung open the gate. "Well," she said, looking at him coolly, "are you coming in?"

And like that, his world was bright once more.

The cottage was shaded by tall palm trees, cooled by the balmy breeze from the Gulf of Mexico. The ocean was only a small walk away. It was like stepping into another world, of seclusion and privacy.

Lily looked different from Wes's memory of her. She wore a red floral dress, her lips painted a matching red, her eyes accented so that they appeared even more exotic. Her hair was loose, falling in straight black contrast. She was sophisticated and beautiful, inhabiting this persona as naturally, as believably, as all her others. This cool, confident woman was nothing like the frightened girl or the awakening virgin just discovering her pleasure that he remembered, that he couldn't forget.

"You had a date," he grated and felt something that he had never felt before. Jealousy.

A short hesitation, a guilty lowering of her eyes. Defiantly, she looked back up at him. "Yes."

"Did you kiss him?"

Her coolness suddenly vanished and the hot turmoil that seethed beneath broke through the calm surface. "I was going to. I wanted him to help me forget you."

His muscles tightened into an unbearable ache. "Did you kiss him?"

She made him wait for one long, terrible moment. "No. I couldn't bear to let him touch me." She laughed softly, bitterly. "I couldn't even finish dinner with him. I just walked out on him."

"Lily . . ." He went to her then, put his arms around her and held her. She fit tinily, perfectly against him and wrapped her arms tightly around him for one moment of bliss before pushing and shoving him back, her small hands pounding his chest.

"You"—pound—"stupid"—push—"jerk!" Big shove. "Why didn't you come sooner?" she hissed, her glittery almond eyes narrowed like a cat's.

"I called," he said, holding her tight, not letting her get away. "I left fifteen messages for you at your precinct."

She stilled. "You did?"

"You have to believe me, Lily."

Her eyes welled up with tears. Her beautiful lips quivered, forming a smile. "I do."

"God," he groaned and held her tight against his chest, rocking her. "You destroy me when you do that, baby, when you trust me. Please . . . don't ever stop." He stroked her back.

"It must have been the shrink's influence, discouraging contact with you."

"I thought you didn't want to see me," he confessed raggedly, "but I wanted to hear it from your own lips. Why didn't *you* call *me*?"

She shoved away from him and began to pace, an agitated little feline. "How? I don't even know your last name." She closed her eyes as Wes pulled her back against him and held her.

"I'm sorry, Lily."

"I've been intimate with you in the closest way a man and woman can be, and I still don't know your last name."

"Penzatti. Wesley Penzatti."

"Wesley's not an Italian name."

"My mother's Irish. She named me."

"We never even kissed." Her voice was so sad, held such longing. "I don't know how your mouth tastes."

He turned her around and lowered his head. Gently, he touched his lips to her lips. Sweet. So sweet. They both shuddered.

He kissed her softly, reverently, lightly, skin gliding against skin, learning her feel, her shape. Gently, he opened her mouth and learned her taste. Like honey. Like pure nectar. He breathed for her, then took in her breath.

She was crying. He licked away her tears. "Shh. Lily, baby. Don't cry. You know me, the real me. And I know you. We know the important things about each other. The rest will come in the next ten days."

Those ten short days again. Well, if that was all she would have with him, she didn't want to waste a moment of it.

"Yes." Lily drew his head back down so that she could press her lips against his, so that she could caress his cheeks and learn the rough angles of his face with her hands. "I thought you didn't want me," she whispered. "That you weren't really attracted to me. That it was just the drug that made you need me."

He growled and cupped her breasts, brushed his thumb against the hardening bud of her nipple. She moaned and her eyes grew heavy. He slid his big hands possessively down over the curve of her buttocks and pulled her against him so that she felt his taut arousal against her soft belly. "This isn't because of any drug. This is from being with you, feeling your soft skin, breathing in your scent, hearing your voice."

His hands flew, touching her everywhere. She rubbed herself against him, making him catch his breath, making him suddenly impatient with the barrier of cloth. He lifted her dress up and off, undid her bra, and ripped her obstructing panties off in one sharp, rending tear that had her laughing softly, seductively in his ear. She nibbled teasingly at his earlobe as he hastily undid his belt and kicked off his pants and underwear. Ran her hands greedily over his chest, his sides. Scraped a nail over his nipples, making them pucker up pebble hard.

"Christ!" he breathed, shaking, looking down into her knowing smile as he lifted her up and brought her down on him. The smile faded into a look of sweet ecstasy, sweet agony as he slid, pushed, worked his way slowly into her.

He was so big. Lily had forgotten just how big. She felt fullness, the sense of being stretched and crammed and stretched more, with him thick and hard and so long within her, the fit seemed almost impossible. But no pain. Just pure, molten pleasure.

"God, you're so tight, baby. So tight, so tight," he panted, pulling out slowly and carefully sinking back in.

Her lids fluttered shut.

"Look at me, Lily. Open your eyes, baby. Let me see what I do to you. Watch what you do to me." His eyes burned into hers, intense flames, so tender, so hot, possessing her as surely as his body was possessing her, powerfully, intimately.

He watched her with his churning violet eyes, moving in long, slow, easy strokes that made her wetter, that made her whimper, that made her want more. He was being too gentle.

She lifted her legs up and wrapped them around his waist, taking control of the motion, riding him as he had once asked her to, lifting up, falling down, impaling herself down on him, faster, harder, rubbing and grinding her pelvis against him where that most sensitive part of her was. Rubbing and grinding her erect nipples against his hard muscles, against the wiry hair on his chest, everything stimulating her until she was almost mad, almost sobbing, and still it wasn't enough. "Wes, please . . . I need more," Lily urged, her nails biting into his thick arms. "More. Harder."

"I don't want to hurt you," he rasped.

"You won't," she panted, writhing against him. "Please."

He moved, stirring, jolting inside her, hot, delicious jabs as he walked a short distance, and then her back was pressing against the cold wall, and he was pressing against her, surging into her with incredible strength, making her cry out with each hard and fast thrust, lifting her up with each forceful stroke.

"Are you okay?" he asked, pausing, his hot breath striking her face.

"Yes, yes, don't stop," she cried frantically, clutching his hips to her.

He took her at her word and began pistoning into her, strong hard thrusts, with his teeth gritted and muscles straining, sweat beading on his skin.

"Oh God . . . Oh yes . . . Wes . . ."

She clutched him so tightly within, it was h[...]
sweet hell. He wasn't going to last much longer. T[...]
so that his cock surged against her sensitive, swollen nub with
each thrust, he took a peaked nipple into his mouth and pressed
it hard with his tongue up against the roof of his mouth, and
she rocketed into climax, convulsing in a powerful release that
clamped her inner muscles around him like a velvet iron fist,
squeezing him in her spasming grip. He pounded into her even
harder. With an exultant cry, he came, spurting hotly within
her, shuddering and shaking in her arms, heaving and groaning
her name.

The quiet aftermath was like after a battle. You were surprised that you had survived. But oh, what a battle. She stroked
Wes's hair, loving the cool feel of it against her hand, loving the
feel of his solid weight pressing her against the wall, loving the
pounding of his heart against hers. Loving him.

He stirred and pulled out of her, kissing away her murmur
of protest.

"I'm sorry," he said, regret in his eyes.

"Well," Lily declared. "Now I feel cheated. Makes me wonder what the sex is like when you don't feel like you have to
apologize afterward."

He laughed and grew serious once more. "I was too rough."

"No." She touched his face, relishing the right of being able
to do so. "You were perfect."

"I wanted to make love to you slowly, gently." He turned
his face into her hand and kissed her palm, making her heart
twist at the tender gesture. He swung her up into his arms with
impressive ease.

"Where's your bedroom?" he asked huskily, taking the
stairs.

"First floor. Second door on the right."

He set her down on her bed, went into the bathroom, and

returned with a damp washcloth. He eased open her legs and wiped the wet cloth over her gently, examining her down there.

"I'm all right, really," she murmured. "Will I have to bargain with you over how long I have to wait before you make love to me once again?"

He laughed. "No, not this time." His eyes darkened as he looked at her, the spill of her hair so black against the white sheets, the pretty flush of satisfaction and renewing desire on her face, her red lips swollen from kissing him, her body lushly open to him, wet with desire, wet from his seed. His cock lengthened and surged. "No, you won't have to wait," he said, his voice a low rumble. "Do you want me again?"

For answer, she crawled up and pushed him down on the bed. "Yes. Yes, I do. And you're right, this time we should take it nice and slow and easy."

She started down below, touching his long toes, stroking the arch of his sole, making him realize for the first time that feet could be an erogenous zone. Her fingers glided over the insides of his ankles, making his breath catch. Her dainty pink tongue reached out and licked his calf, making the breath he had been holding whoosh out. The soft touch of her fingers behind his knees made him squirm and reach for her.

"Oh, no." With one dainty finger she stopped him. "Keep your hands . . ." Languidly she pushed him back, stretched out his hands wide with her own, and pressed them down firmly. "Here . . ." Her wicked, knowing smile made him break out in a sweat. It promised pure torment before he glimpsed heaven.

"Uh, maybe you're right," he said nervously. "We don't have to go slow . . ."

She kissed him softly on the lips. "Let me . . ." she said quietly. "I want to explore you. I want to know you in these next ten days."

And he found himself unable to deny her anything when she looked at him like that.

Wes relaxed back, keeping his arms out, pinned voluntarily to the bed, and Lily smiled a sultry, triumphant smile full of wicked promise. His muscles tensed again when she kissed his knee, then flicked out her tongue to taste the skin of his inner thigh.

"You're soft here," she said, her voice purring with happy discovery.

He was dying. She was so close, so damn close to where he was aching most for her.

She rasped her tongue over his tender thigh, more roughly this time, and he groaned and squeezed his eyes shut, hating his voluntary bondage and yet incredibly turned on by it. So turned on, it was impossible for her to miss. She laughed, pure temptress, her hot breath wafting over his jutting staff begging for her attention. He felt the cool wash of her hair brush over him for one incendiary moment and his body left the mattress.

"Have mercy," he breathed.

Her cat eyes, filled with her power and pleasure, held his gaze as she pressed him back down. "No."

He looked at her with awe, with trembling body, with trembling soul as he watched her unfurl and blossom before him, reveling in her newfound power as a woman.

Sweat covered him, dampened his hair. His chest lifted rapidly, as if he had run ten miles. He gritted his teeth, prepared to endure.

She brushed a finger over his belly and every muscle in his stomach locked tight. Her finger ran down, brushed lightly over the coarse hair framing his genitals. Ran back up his tense, ridged abdomen, making him groan. "Lily . . ."

"Yes, say my name." She bent down and nudged aside his stiff cock with her soft cheek to kiss his belly button, her hair spilling once again over his engorged, sensitive rod, over his tight sacs like a thousand silky, flickering tongues.

He cursed, groaned, and almost cried when she moved to his

chest, when she ran her hands up his side, following his V shape. And then he did cry out as she touched his armpits, surprisingly sensitive, curiously brushing over the tufts of hair there. He swallowed loudly as she ran a finger up the underside of his arm.

"Your skin is soft here too," she murmured. She stroked again, a barely there touch, so light he couldn't imagine how it could send such rippling pleasure streaming through him, making him shudder, making goose bumps prickle his arms.

"Ah, you like that," she crooned, stroking him there again.

He laughed, groaned, shuddered again. "Yeah. Lily . . ."

"Shhh," she whispered, tracing his long fingers, running her fingers over the webbing, sliding and gliding her fingers against his, making love to his hand. His cock surged and strained and she laughed. Slowly, she took his forefinger into her mouth. His cheeks flushed as he watched his finger sink slowly in. "Jesus, Lily, where did you learn that?"

She nipped his fingertip and released him. "From you. From finding out what pleases you."

She ran her soft hands over the rough calluses of his palm and rubbed her cheek against them, purring. Her hands glided over the taut tendons and rippling sinews of his forearm. She ran a finger over a bulging vein, depressed it, and watched with fascination as it popped back up. Her eyes lifted to him. "You're like that down there . . . covered with veins."

He held his breath as her gaze lowered.

Yes, yes, please, he chanted silently as her head bent down to study him. He felt her hot breath fall like a soft blessing over him. He groaned when she lifted back up. She soothed him with soft kisses on his chest, petting him, tugging experimentally on his wiry hair. Unexpectedly, she took his nipple into her mouth. He shot straight up into the air.

"Did I hurt you?" she asked.

"No," he said hoarsely. "Christ . . . it just surprised me. No one's ever done that before."

"No?" She ran a curious fingertip lightly over his taut disc. "Your nipples peak like mine when I touch them. Do you like it?"

He swallowed, nodded.

"And when I do this?" She licked his nipple and the hot rasp of her tongue, deliberately rough, had him arching his back and swallowing a cry.

"Yes," she purred, "I think you do. And this?" She covered his tiny bud with her mouth, pressed down gently with her teeth and tugged.

"Oh God," he cried, lifting them off the bed. They bounced back down and Lily kissed her way up his corded neck, her soft breasts brushing against him, her peaked nipples a tactile caress. She pulled back, and holding his hot gaze, explored his face with her fingers, touching the rough stubble of his jaw, scraping it with her nail.

"How different men are from women," she said.

"Lower your hand a few feet more, baby. That's where we're really different," he suggested.

She laughed and he smiled up at her. She traced his mouth with a light finger, brushed it over his full lower lip, outlined the twin peaks of his upper lip, then pressed her finger gently into his mouth. He sucked her all the way in, laved her with his tongue, and watched her eyes dilate, her breath catch. He eased back, out, then pulled her finger in again, watched her eyes close, watched her breasts swell, and smelled the sweet perfume of her arousal fill the air. "Lily," he breathed, in want, in pleading agony.

She opened her eyes and with a sweet, tantalizing smile, swung up and over him, hanging there for an agonizing moment before lowering down to sit on top of his cock. He was so aroused that his dick lay flat and upright against his abdomen. She placed her wet slit over him and rode the entire length like that, wetting the entire underside of his cock with her juice, murmuring soft, appreciative sounds. "Um . . . nice." She sat back, her eyes slumberous. "Do you mind . . . if I play a little?"

"No," he lied, his voice rough, almost unrecognizable. It was sweet hell.

She wrapped her hand around his dick and pulled him straight out and vertical. He made a sound as she pulled and pulled until he was angled with his tip right there against her gate. She leaned back, closed her eyes, and rubbed his fat mushroom head against her slit, up and down, around and around, soft moans coming from her throat as she grew wetter, hotter. She leaned back even more, lifted her hips the tiniest bit and his thick head slid just barely into her. His sensitive tip burned with her wet heat, her incredible softness. Her nipples puckered even harder and she rotated her hips the tiniest bit, moving just his ridged head into her. She straightened, sliding him in another inch more and opened her heavy-lidded eyes. "Touch me."

Wes didn't wait for a second invitation. He had her flat on her back with one twist. He linked their fingers together, anchored their twined hands by her shoulders, and looking down into her beautiful, exotic eyes, he slowly sank into her. One inch only. Pulled out. Slid in, that one bare inch again. Lifted up. She moaned, her lips parted, her breath held as he stroked again, deeper. Two inches. Pulled back until he was almost out.

"Look at me, Lily." He wanted her to remember him, to never forget him, to make it so good for her that she'd continue seeing him after these ten days were up.

His eyes glittered with heat, with restrained passion. She whimpered, sighed, purred as he filled her again, pushing in, that thick, bulbous head sliding in past her vulva, pulling out again, and then filling her once more, stretching her again.

"Feel me."

She did. Every single bump and ridge. Every single bulging vein as he poled her ever so slowly, killing her with unyielding gentleness, filling her up with too little. Another inch. Her lips greedily sucked him in, her muscles involuntarily spasming around him, squeezing him. He cursed, his jaw clenched.

"Ah . . . Lily."

She tried it again, deliberately clenching around him. He grimaced, he groaned. He trembled against her. She smiled, spread her legs wider, and squeezed him again with a wet inner caress.

"Oh God . . ."

He panted and pushed all the way in, burning, stretching her in the most wonderful way.

"Slow," he muttered, pulling his hips back, then surging back in with gentle force.

She released and squeezed him, rewarding him as he filled her, relaxing as he dragged himself out. In again, squeeze. Out, release. In—a forceful clench, muttered prayers, soft curses. Out—exhale, relax.

A drop of sweat fell from Wes's face onto her chin. Lily's pink tongue flicked out and lapped it up. His eyes blazed like purple fire. A muscle jumped in his clenched jaw. He lowered his head and filled her mouth with his tongue the same time he filled her with his cock. In. Out. Squeeze. Release.

His tongue danced with hers as Lily's muscles brushed and glided sweetly, hotly, tightly, around him. He moved faster, deeper, more forcefully against her. She panted harder, clenched him tighter. He surged suddenly, a swift, sharp stab deep inside her, touching her womb, and she started shuddering sweetly, convulsively, wringing him with her soft, strong tissues, and then he felt himself coming, pulsing hotly within her, spurting, filling her with his seed. He collapsed on top of her for one brief moment, crushing her into the bed. No protest, just her hands wrapping around him, holding him, gliding down his back in a smooth caress. He grunted and rolled onto his side, pulling her into his arms, still deep inside her as he drifted off to sleep.

9

They didn't come out of the house for three days. Didn't leave the bedroom except for brief raids down into the kitchen, then he'd carry her back upstairs to satisfy another, more urgent hunger. They played and frolicked, teased and tormented each other in bed, and yes, making love did make Lily feel closer to Wes. Closer and closer with each stroke, each thrust, each kiss. When Lily stopped and caught her breath afterward, holding him cradled in her arms, his head pillowed on her breasts, the feelings she found within her for this tough-looking man were almost overwhelming, frightening in their intensity.

Lily had always been extreme. All or nothing. And for so long it had been nothing. No close friends other than her mother. First school, then her job, her commitment to it. And now him. No middle road for her. If she allowed it, her feelings for him, her need for him would overwhelm him, smother him, drive him away. And so she kept them in check, covered them with an easy smile whenever he gazed at her, intently, moodily, making her worry that he'd had enough, making her fear that he would go even before their time was up. But then he'd just murmur her name, open her legs, and sink back into her to start that delicious dance all over again. He couldn't seem to get enough of her and she didn't know if that was normal or not. It couldn't be normal—how often they made love, day and night, five times, six times a day—could it? Made love so often that Lily felt raw, tender, and abraded, the muscles in her thighs, back, and neck sore. But she needed that intensity from him to match and balance her own. She needed his concentrated, unflagging desire for her, just as she needed those quiet moments afterward when they talked.

He kissed her and tucked her against him, their bodies damp with perspiration, their muscles wrung out, limp. And the thought came to her once again. He had to feel something more than just lust for her to hold her this tenderly afterward, didn't he?

"Why did you become a cop?" Wes asked, twining a strand of her hair around his finger.

Should she tell him the truth? "My father."

"Your father was a cop?"

"Quite the contrary," she said quietly. "I knew him even though my birth certificate lists my father as unknown. My mother fell in love with him when she visited Fujian during a student exchange her senior year in college. He told her that he loved her as well but he didn't really. When she returned home and found out she was pregnant, she told her parents she was going back to China to marry him. Paranoid as my grandparents are—but this time with good reason—they hired an investigator, who took pictures showing my father with not one but several women after my mother returned to America. Some were intimate pictures she couldn't misunderstand or find an excuse for. And so she had me and he didn't know he had a child until I was six years old. She had finished medical school and her residency by then, had become the doctor that her parents wanted her to be.

"She took me back to Fuzhou and I saw my father for the first time that year. I can still remember how tall, how handsome he seemed. One smile and I fell at his feet as easily as my mother had, as many women had. I saw him for the next three summers. Mama had warned me not to tell him about our homes or about my nanny or driver. He knew we were rich Americans, you see, but not how rich. He was so good to me, giving me presents, buying me treats each time we visited, spending a lot of money on me that only afterward I found out came from the two thousand dollars my mother gave him every summer we visited. Two thousand dollars a year is a lot of money to someone in Fuzhou where the average annual income is eight hundred dollars. But I was just a child. All I knew was the toys he showered me with. I loved him and hated it each time we had to leave him."

"That was natural," Wes murmured.

"Foolishly I thought my father would want to be with Mama always and come live with us if he knew how much money we had. And so I told him that third summer when I was eight. I told him about our houses, about our car and driver, about our cook and nanny, the fancy parties that Grandma and Grandpa threw and attended. I told him we had lots and lots of money and that he should marry Mama and come and live with us. He didn't react the way I thought he would." An understatement.

"What happened?" Wes asked.

"He kidnapped me," Lily said simply. "He demanded a hundred thousand U.S. dollars, a fortune in his mind. I think he was expecting my mother to bargain and agree to something much lower, but she didn't, and I heard him curse after he hung up the telephone and say that he should have asked for more, much more."

"Did he hurt you?"

She shook her head. "No, he . . . He told my mother that

he'd cut off my fingers if she didn't have the money for him in twenty-four hours. He pinched me and made me cry so that she would hear me on the phone. He frightened me . . . his anger, his bitterness. When I cried and said I thought he loved me, he laughed and told me he had fussed over 'the brat' to please my mother. The rich American doctor, he called Mama. He had played the devoted father to keep Mama and the money she gave him coming each summer.

"When he took me to meet her the next day, he held a gun to my head," Lily said, her voice shaking. She could still remember it, the feel of the metal, the hurting roughness of his hands.

Wes muttered curses under his breath.

"They shot him, the police. One moment he had the gun pressed to my head, the next second there were loud sounds and I was free. I turned and saw him sprawled on the ground like a broken doll, the gun still in his hand, blood oozing from the wounds in his head and chest. Blood had pooled around him like a crimson halo." Lily remembered vividly the horror she had caused. "He died."

"Oh, baby, I'm sorry," Wes muttered, rocking her, his heart breaking for her. It all suddenly made sense to him, her virginity, her untouched state. "You learned not to trust men, didn't you?"

"Only their actions, not their words."

"Why did you trust me?" he asked roughly.

"You came for me. And you didn't attack me even when your body needed relief."

He hugged her tight. "Is that why you joined the force? To fight the bad guys?"

"No, to defend the defenseless, and to fight my own fear."

"What do you fear?"

"I fear being so helpless ever again. I fear misplacing my trust again. I fear losing another loved one. And I may be serving a little penance for causing my father's death."

"Your father deserved what he got," Wes said, his voice hard. "His actions caused what happened to him, not yours. You should not feel any guilt over that."

"Are you my shrink now?" She laughed wryly. "Ironically, the actor in me, what makes me a good undercover cop, comes from my father. He was a good liar. Mama's a believer."

"Are you a believer also?"

"I'm learning to be."

He smiled, threw back the bed sheet, and set her down on her feet. "Come on. We've been holed up here too long. Let me take you out for dinner, and then we can grab some groceries. The frig is almost empty."

"And who is to blame?"

"You," he growled. "You make me hungry, all the time." Laughingly, they ran into the street.

How strange it felt to reenter the real world after being immersed so many days in their own private one. With Wes beside her, his hand in hers, their fingers interwoven, the Florida sun felt soothingly warm. We're holding hands, just like boyfriend and girlfriend, Lily thought. It was such a normal thing to be doing, and something she had never thought to experience. She had never expected to trust someone enough to let him get that close.

She stopped and pulled his neck down and kissed him.

"What was that for?" he asked, smiling.

"You make me happy."

"You make me happy too, sunshine."

They dined at Effie's, a charming little bistro overlooking the ocean. The sea breeze whisked away the humidity and riffled through her hair with airy fingers. Delicately, she chewed her sausage and savored the refreshing, bitter taste of broccoli rabe, smiling with amusement as Wes tucked away his cavatelli with bacon with gusty appreciation, but left his arugula untouched. She ordered tiramisu while Wes went for plain old cheesecake.

When the bill came, Lily snatched it up. "It's on me. You're my guest."

"But you are my date."

"But *I* have the bill." She hid it behind her back.

"I may not make six figures, but I can afford to pay for our meal."

There was a long moment of discomfort before Lily yielded the bill to Wes.

She mulled over the incident, worried about it in silence as they walked along the beach. "Are you uncomfortable with my family's money?" she finally asked.

Wes rubbed the back of his neck. "It certainly doesn't make it easier."

Two little *thud thud*s hit the ground near their feet, kicking up the sand.

One moment Lily was standing, the next minute she was sprawled out on the gritty sand, behind a small boulder. Wes had tackled her and rolled them both to the ground, his weight heavy on her as he shielded her with his body. A moment later, Wes flinched, letting out a soft cry of pain. Lily felt something wet trickle down onto her cheek. Wes! He'd been hit!
Someone was shooting at them.

Wes shifted and pulled out a gun. It glinted blue-black under the silver moonlight. He looked suddenly like what he was, a warrior, his face harsh, cold, implacable. Two more shots flew their way, hitting the boulder. Wes returned fire, shooting blindly at the source. His aim must have been good. There was a muffled curse in the distance. "Stay here," Wes said, leaping over the boulder and running into the darkness.

Lily watched him, heart in her throat. Don't go, she wanted to shout, but she bit back the words. It would only distract him and put him in peril. Her hand reached automatically for her own gun but it wasn't there. She hadn't brought it. She hadn't thought she'd need it. This was the Keys, paradise. It contained the blue sky, white beaches, coconut trees, long naps, exotic drinks. No guns. No weapons. Why was someone shooting at them?

Silently Wes returned, a dark, looming shadow. She almost screamed.

"It's me," he said. "He got away."

"You're hit."

"Just grazed my arm. Come on, let's get out of here."

They ran back to the street and found a cab to take them home.

Double-locking the cottage door behind them, Lily pulled Wes into the kitchen and sat him down. "Let me see your wound."

"It's nothing, just a nick."

Gently, she removed his shirt and slipped it off. His nothing was an inch-long furrow that had dug away a centimeter depth of flesh. From a goddamn bullet! But he was right, nothing major was damaged.

He scrutinized his arm. "Won't even need stitches."

She disinfected the wound, then applied antibiotic ointment and a gauze dressing.

"You're well stocked," he said, eyeing the bulky first aid kit.

"My mom. She likes being prepared. Heat rash, snake bites, and bullet wounds," Lily said, wrapping the last layer of gauze around his arm. Then she lost her cool and started sobbing.

He stood up, pulled her against his chest. "Hey, hey. It's all right."

"It's not all right. Someone was shooting at us! You could have been killed! It must be that creep, Billy Lim. They never caught him. We're unsafe here."

"Let me call the bureau." Wes put in a call to Langley and let them know what had transpired.

While he was reporting the incident, Lily spoke to her own commander. The order was to get out of there.

"I'm to return with you to New York," Wes said.

"Just as a bodyguard?" Lily asked.

"No. As your lover. Would you mind that?"

"Not at all."

10

Wes and Lily arrived at LaGuardia Airport just in time for early morning rush hour. Somehow returning to a city with one of the highest crime rates in the world made Lily feel safer. Could it be that it was her home? Where she walked her beat, and knew every street and avenue by heart?

The cab ride from the airport to her apartment in Manhattan took longer than the flight back from the Keys. New York traffic. What a bitch.

How nice it was to have Wes at her side, opening the cab door, helping her out, and paying for the cab—his insistence. And how right it felt bringing him to her home.

But the feeling of comfort and safety was premature, Lily realized as soon as she opened the door and turned on the lights of the foyer in her apartment.

"Shut the door." The steely voice came from the dim living room. It was Billy Lim. He was holding Lily's mother from behind, a sharp, gleaming knife to her throat.

"Mama!" Lily cried.

"I'm okay," Anna said.

"Get inside and shut the door," Billy snapped. "Hands up in the air now or . . ." He jabbed the knife tip and Anna Huang gave a painful cry. Red blood trickled.

"Easy, Billy," Wes said. "The door's shut. My hands are up."

"Please release my mother," Lily said. "She has nothing to do with this."

"You know better than that, little girl. Only not so little, are you?"

"Was that your man who tried to shoot us?" Wes asked.

"Good help is so hard to find, but just as well he didn't kill you on the beach. Now I get that pleasure. You two have ruined my life. I lost a highly profitable business that I spent a lifetime building. You got all my men, who I groomed and trained for years. My massage parlors are all shut down and my bank accounts frozen. Quite disrupting, really. Your gun, Special Agent Wesley Penzatti, with your left hand. Toss it to me now."

Slowly Wes took out his gun and slid it on the floor. It came to a halt a few feet from Billy.

"Now, my dear Lily, slide your hands slowly down your lover's body to see if he's hiding anything else. I'm sure you've had plenty of practice by now."

Lily patted Wes down along the sides.

"The inner thighs," Billy ordered.

Lily did as she was told. "He's clean."

"Now you check her, lover boy. Enjoy it."

Wes frisked Lily down from head to toe. "Nothing, as you can see."

"Good," Billy said. "Let's get the party started." He flicked his knife quickly, lightly. Anna and Lily both screamed. A thin line of blood welled and overflowed down Anna's throat.

"Quiet, girls. It's only a little cut. I haven't even started yet."

"You are an evil man," Anna spat. "And you will pay for your actions."

"Pay for my actions? Like this?" He made another slice.

"You can have me!" Lily cried. "Just let my mother go."

"What a good daughter you are. Come here, Lily," Billy said.

"I'll come," Wes said hoarsely, stepping forward.

"No, I don't think so," Billy said, pressing the sharp blade warningly against his captive. "Just Lily for now."

"Don't go, Lily," Wes said in a low voice. His body was coiled in readiness but he was too far away to jump Billy.

"I have to. She's my mother," Lily said quietly and started walking toward Billy.

Then something happened that none of them could have predicted. Tiny, genteel Dr. Anna Huang, wide-eyed and deathly pale, suddenly slammed her fist back into Billy Lim's groin. Then she dropped and rolled on the floor.

In that split second, Lily took one big step and leaped into the air, flying her right foot high and smashing it into Billy's ugly face. Using the momentum, Lily spun around, just enough to deliver a snapping back kick into the same nasty face. Billy's head snapped back, his nose spewing blood, his lips flapping, and his tongue dripping with blood. Broken teeth flew in the air. Slowly he fell, his arms flailing. With a big thud, he landed backward on the hardwood floor. In a final move, Lily jumped on him, flipped the asshole over, and locked his arms behind him.

Wes cocked the gun he had retrieved and aimed it at Billy's temple. "Doesn't look like I need to use this. Too bad."

But it didn't look like Billy's pain was over just yet. Anna Huang rose to her dainty, Italian-shoed feet and stormed over to Billy like an enraged lioness gone mad. She drew back her pointy toes and kicked and kicked and kicked her former assailant, screaming, "No one hurts my daughter!" She bent down low so Billy could see her eyes, narrowed and mean. "No one," she spat into his face.

11

The police, officers from Lily's own precinct, took Billy away, handcuffs nice and tight and uncomfortable behind him. He shuffled away, his broken nose swollen and puffed to the size of a plum, bent over slightly from his bashed balls or perhaps from Dr. Huang's pointy-shoed kicks.

"You ladies seem to have worked him over nice and right," Lieutenant Ken Kumura said, walking to the door after having taken their statements. "I'd be real careful, Agent Penzatti. Wouldn't want to piss off the little mom again." He winked at Wes and left.

"Not bad advice," Anna Huang said to Wes.

"Can I take you to the hospital, Dr. Huang?" Wes offered.

"What's the point? I'm a doctor and I can tell you I'm fine. All I need is some Band-Aids. Lily, dear, go get me some."

Lily got out the first aid kit and fumbled through it. Carefully, she cleaned her mother's cuts and covered them with butterfly Band-Aids, stark strips of white against her delicate skin.

"Mama, that was very impressive. How did you know to hit him like that?" Lily asked.

"The self-defense classes I took with you when you were a little girl. Talking about my little girl," Anna said, turning to Wes. "Agent Penzatti, what are your intentions toward my daughter?"

"Mother!"

Anna held up a hand. Long habit and deeply ingrained respect was all that kept Lily silent.

"My intentions?" Wes asked.

"Yes. What do you plan to do with her now that you found her?"

"I . . . um . . . love your daughter, ma'am."

Wes's words were the greatest shock of all tonight. But, oh, what a lovely shock. A warm, giddy feeling that felt something like happiness welled within Lily.

"I know that. I could see it in your eyes the first time I met you," Anna said kindly, patiently. "But you didn't answer my question. What do you plan to do with her now?"

He cleared his throat. "Um . . . with your permission, I would like to continue . . . uh, seeing your daughter for as long as she wants me."

Some of Lily's giddiness started to fade. "Mama . . ." Lily gripped her mother's shoulder.

"Not good enough, young man. I'm an old-fashioned mother, Mr. Penzatti, who raised an old-fashioned daughter. You are going to marry her."

Lily gasped. The lovely shock had become an embarrassing nightmare. "Mama, stop it! I'm sorry, Wes. I don't know what's gotten into her."

"I am not a wealthy man," Wes told Anna quietly.

Anna snorted. "Lily doesn't need a wealthy man. What she needs is you, someone who loves her. Someone who will cherish her. Someone who will risk his life for her. She's a treasure

fallen into your hands, young man. Do not let her get away."
She sighed. "You might not know it but it is what your heart
desires, both of you. Bye-bye."

She kissed Lily on the cheek, nodded to Wes, and gently
closed the door behind her.

They were alone now, sitting awkwardly on the couch. Lily
broke the silence first. "I'm sorry, Wes, that my mother put you
through that. It's not called for."

Wes turned to face her and grabbed her shoulders, his eyes
gentle with love. "Is she right?"

"About what?"

"Is that what your heart desires?" he asked.

She spoke carefully. "There have been no promises. My
mother had no right to try and pressure you."

"Lily," Wes said, looking touchingly unsure of himself. "I
come from a simple background. My mother is a nurse and my
father is a butcher. I only make fifty thousand dollars a year."

"It matters little to me how much you make. My mother
was right. I'm not looking for a wealthy man."

"Was your mother right about the other thing?"

"What other thing?"

"Do you want to marry me?"

Lily caught her breath. "Are you, by chance, proposing to
me?"

Wes inhaled. Exhaled. "Yes. Yes, I am." He got down on his
knees. "Lily." He took her hands in his. "I promise I will always love and cherish you until the day I die. I will be faithful
to you. Your name will be last word on my lips. You are my
life. Lily Huang, will you do me the honor and make me the
happiest man in the world by marrying me?"

Tears trickled down her cheek. Lily had dreamed of this moment since she had met Wes and it was more powerful than
anything she could ever have imagined. She was lost for a moment as joy filled her and spilled over. "Oh, Wes. You are the

beating of my heart, the very air I breathe. My life would be so empty without you. Yes, I will marry you. I want to grow old and toothless with you, surrounded by our children and our children's children."

"Oh baby." He swung her into his arms and took her into the bedroom. Gently he set her down on the high tester bed, his chest tightening as he gazed down at her. How beautiful she was, his treasure. She lay there with her eyes dark and mysterious, her skin white like new-fallen snow. She was his.

Tenderness stirred. He wanted to love her sweetly, softly. He wanted to cherish and protect her as he had just promised. He wanted Lily to never fear his strength but to depend upon it as if it was her own. And it was.

Tenderly he undressed her, and then himself. The mattress dipped as he crawled onto the bed and leaned over her. She was so tiny, so little, so delicately made. He could encircle both of her wrists with one hand.

She raised one hand and laid her slim fingers against him, cool against his hot chest. They moved in a too-brief caress that made him want to moan, flicking to life an instinctive desire to fall upon her and claim her in the most primitive way, in the most primitive manner. He breathed in deeply, reining in the wayward urge. Another time, another moment. This time, now, he wanted to show her how much he loved her. He wanted to love her sweetly, tenderly.

But it seemed as if she had other plans. Those slender fingers pushed against him, the lightest pressure, and he toppled onto his side, felled by her delicate strength. Those hands ran down his hands. Those slender fingers intertwined with his and spread his arms out. She lay on top of him and captured his eyes. "Do you remember when we did this before?" she asked.

As if he could ever forget. "Yes."

Her lashes swept down like gossamer veils. "Did you like it?" she asked shyly.

Memories of it shot a quiver through his muscles. "You know I did."

She pressed his hands into the bed in silent command—*Stay*—and ran her fingers up his sensitive underarms, making him shiver under her delicate touch.

She bit her lower lip. "Would you mind if we did something . . . similar?"

He hesitated. He'd just asked her to marry him and she'd just accepted and told him that she loved him. They were supposed to make sweet, tender love now, weren't they? "Um . . . What did you have in mind?"

She climbed down off the bed, opened a drawer, and to his complete and utter surprise, returned with two scarves in her hand, one brilliant scarlet, the other indigo blue.

Oh shit. Sweat dampened his brow. "You, uh, want to tie me up?"

She nodded shyly. "Only if you want to."

He closed his eyes, lost. As a temptress, she was devastating, but it was her shyness, her uncertainly that he could not say no to.

He swallowed hard. "Go ahead. Do with me what you will."

12

What had he just agreed to? Wes wondered. It had been torturous enough last time. This . . . this was . . .

The sensuous feel of cool silk wrapped around his wrists, binding each of his arms to the corner post. He tugged testingly. They were tight and secure and the silk felt surprisingly strong. He could free himself, but only if he broke the bedposts. It wouldn't come to that, he told himself. Lily would free him with one word. But she wanted this and he wanted to please her. He was bound more by that desire than the ties. He was . . . no other term for it . . . tied up and about to be royally screwed.

But however his mind might be conflicted, Wes's body wasn't. His dick lengthened and swelled to full mast as the last knot was secured.

"I'm beginning to really enjoy making love to you slow and easy," Lily murmured, running kisses over his chest, making him wish he'd never said those words to her. Slow and easy. More like slow and hellish. She nibbled his collarbone, tested her teeth against a taut tendon in his neck. His mast nodded and bobbed.

"I love making you hot," she whispered, blowing her warm breath into the shell of his ear. Apallingly, he couldn't prevent himself from squirming. Jesus H. Christ, he was squirming.

Her hands, those devastating, soft hands, ran over his angled face in light butterfly caresses. She traced the outline of his tense lips. She looked down at him, her eyes welling with excitement, spilling over with the feminine power growing within her. "I love making you wait."

He felt like cursing, crying. Begging for mercy. She was going to kill him. His hands involuntarily tightened, pulled. The blasted bindings held.

She looked at the scarves, looked at him, and smiled. Her nipples peaked and hardened.

He closed his eyes, shutting out her growing excitement, but that only seemed to make it worse. Now his other senses were brought more sharply into play. He could hear her breathing, light and fast. He could smell her arousal seeping into the air, surrounding him like the most enticing of fragrances, beckoning. He could feel her lightest touch—around his nipples, down his pectoral valley, up the muscled ridge, close, so damn close but not touching his sensitive flat brown discs.

"I love how you smell," she said, and his eyes flew open to find her nose close to his armpit. She inhaled deeply. "Like musk, like man."

He laughed to cover his embarrassment, fought not to squirm. Before he could say anything, her tongue flicked out and licked him there, lapping like a cat at cream. Unbelievably, the unexpected sensation shot straight to his groin and his dick swelled even more. God, her tongue was so soft, so hot, so pink, almost the same color as her sheath. He groaned and twisted and the knots tightened around him—*captive*—reminding him of his self-imposed helplessness and making his dick grow even thicker so that it poled straight up against his belly.

The cool tickle of her hair swept his chest, his stomach. His abdomen locked into ridges, his thighs tensed.

"You're crying down here," she murmured, her nose next to the tip of his cock, "weeping with desire." She blew, right into the little hole.

"Oh God," he cried and jerked and wanted to weep for real.

Her small hand wrapped around his pole, holding him squeezingly tight. The pressure was both relief and torment, making him want more. More friction, more pressure, making him want to move. His buttocks clenched, his thigh muscles tightened. She licked him. Yes! Sweet sensation, sharp pleasure focused just there, there, where she was lapping him with that soft, devastating tongue, delicately, then roughly, like he was a melting ice-cream cone.

"Fluid is oozing out of you," she crooned. "And your slit is opening more, as if it wants me to penetrate it there." The pointy tip of her tongue pushed slightly into him and he uttered a single, sharp curse.

Lily looked up and their gazes locked for a heated moment. "You can't come yet," she said, making him almost spill then and there. She lowered her head and took him into her mouth. Hot, wet. A soft, soft cavern. A wicked tongue. She sucked a groan out of him, nibbled down his shaft, squeezing hard with her hand, almost brutally hard, the way he'd shown her he liked it, one finger tightening and compressing at a time. He felt her lips press against his balls. Then she opened her mouth and sucked the entire sac into her mouth, closing around him, her teeth cushioned by her lips. She opened up, let him pop out and rubbed his balls with her hand. She squeezed them.

"Your balls are drawn up so tight, so hard. You want to

come," she said softly, her eyes like two dark burning coals. "But you can't."

Shit!

"Not yet."

"Lily..."

She released his scrotum and he felt a finger slide down even farther, touching the thick line of perineal tissue behind it. She traced it all the way back to his anus, ran her finger around the puckered skin, making him lift up, trying to escape, and returned halfway back down. Then she stopped and pressed down right there with firm, hard pressure. It was the oddest sensation. A little jolt. Her lips curved in an almost feline smile that made fear flutter in Wes's chest.

The pressure lifted. Her finger ran back up to his balls. "We'll save that for later, when you really need it."

Holy shit.

She pounced on him like a wicked kitten, straddling his thighs, kneading his chest with her fingers, digging her beautiful claws into his flesh. She raked a fingernail over his brown areola and it beaded to immediate attention. She gave a husky, delighted laugh, and then proceeded to torture him with that delicate tongue and devious mouth, nipping, sucking, taking the attentive brown soldier between her teeth and pulling back, stretching the little nub. He moaned. She groaned, her slit hot and damp, flowing like heated honey. She shifted so that she straddled only one of his thighs and rocked against it, wetting him as she continued to play with first one and then the other nipple, lavishing equal and ardent attention on both, her soft belly brushing against his dick in a soft body caress with each undulation of her pelvis against his thigh. Her pearl was hardened, swollen enough to feel, a distinct round point. His hands flexed, wanting to touch it and unable to. The silk bound him as surely as ropes.

"Lily, please," he said, his chest moving up and down in rapid puffs.

She lifted her head. "Do you want me to take you in?"

"Yes," he gritted. "God, more than anything in the world."

She smiled and scooted up and pulled his thick pole back from his belly. She swirled the head of his cock in her cream, lavishly coating the tip, then sank down the tiniest bit over his mushroom-shaped dome. "Like this?" she purred.

"Yes," he cried, just breaching her gate, feeling her hot, burning juice running over him in the sweetest of caresses.

"Or like this?" Without warning, she impaled herself on his thick pole with reckless force, slamming down in one rough lunge. He surged all the way home into her honeyed depths to the very hilt with a wrenching cry. Without even a moment's pause, she began riding him, vigorously, at full gallop, lunging up and down with full abandon. "Don't come yet," she gasped.

Fuck, fuck, fuck. Don't come, don't come, he chanted. He counted backwards, tried to name the capitals of each state. His balls became so tight they passed blue and went straight to violet. His legs locked, his toes squirmed. "Oh God! Lily . . ." he warned.

She took him straight up to the edge, both of them, and then stopped. "Shit. Lily!"

She caressed his face with soothing hands, kissed his lips. Her tongue swept across his seam, asking permission, and swept gently in when he opened his mouth. He sucked in her tongue, then let her suck his into hers, tangling them in a wet, lazy duel. When he had calmed enough, she sat back up and began moving again, swiveling her hips.

"Yes . . . that feels good," he muttered.

She gave another delicious twirl. "*You* feel good, inside me." She began moving in pleasurable gyrations, her breath coming in soft puffs, around and around, twisting and turning, leaning back with her hands braced on his knees, and then leaning forward, her breasts dangling in his face. He took a nipple into his mouth and feasted. She sighed. He laved the hard nub with his rough tongue. She purred, rotated her pelvis a little harder against him, and he felt another surge of wetness anoint him. He sucked and pulled on her nipple, elongating the tip. Her breathing grew raspier and she began to move up and down, riding him with harder, sharper thrusts.

He set his teeth gently around her hard tip and pulled, lengthening it even more and she cried out. Hearing his name on her lips was unbearably arousing. He tugged on her nipple, thrust slightly with his hips. When she didn't object, he tugged harder, thrust harder. They fell into an escalating rhythm. With his hands bound, his focus became concentrated solely on where his flesh touched her, on the feel of her, the sweet, musky smell of her. Tug, thrust. With hands restrained, he worked less, enjoyed more. Nip, pull. Short, fierce stab. His balls lifted. The end was nearing.

Her nipple slid out of his mouth with a wet pop. "Lily . . ." His voice cracked. "I can't hold on much longer."

She leaned back. Her hand reached down past his tightly drawn-up balls. Blindly, her finger found that spot that she had pressed before. She pushed down hard with her fingertip, sending a jolting sensation through him. "Yes," she said huskily. "Come now."

Oh, how he wanted to but she wasn't with him. And he couldn't move his hands. He couldn't reach down and pluck and squeeze her juicy magic button. He couldn't even suck on her nipple anymore. All he could do was thrust and thrust and hang on desperately, slipping and sliding down that mental control slope with each passing, sweating second. Please, please, please, please, please. He didn't want to go without her. And the witch knew what he was going through. Their eyes held and clung, their desire, their excitement, his desperation plainly evident.

"Come for me," she whispered, a siren's call whispering down his back and shooting straight to his leaking, weeping, ready-for-bursting dick.

"Not without you." The words were so gravely, so deep, they were barely comprehendible. He stared into her witchy eyes, let her see everything he was feeling. "I'm going to fuck you hard," he promised. Threatened.

Her eyes dilated even more until they were completely black. And with that statement of intent, he relaxed back into the bed and plunged into her, hip action only, stabbing, shoving, spearing into her, relentlessly, with full force. He closed his eyes, searching by sense alone for her G-spot, that plump, swollen mound of tissue within. That sensitive, sensitive spot just behind her pubis. She cried out. His turn to smile, or rather grimace. Ah, yes, right there. He changed the angle of his hips and poled into her hard. Right. There. She cried and shivered, began to shudder. He rotated his hips as he withdrew. "Do you like it?" he rumbled. Plunged back into her, angling so that he hit her relentlessly again. "Me fucking you . . . right"—grunt—"there"—thrust—"*hard*." Another stabbing stroke.

She apparently did. Her fluttering muscles relaxed for that infinitesimal preorgasmic second, swallowing him in, sucking his entire length even deeper into her, and then tightened around his cock like a powerful, squeezing fist, pulsing and clenching, spasming around him. His balls lifted even higher, plastering themselves right up against his dick, and then he was coming. Or trying to. He felt Lily's finger pressing hard in that spot halfway down between his anus and his balls. She didn't let up the pressure, not even during her racking orgasm.

He began to spurt within her. Or tried to. He felt one little hot jet of fluid leave him, but then no more, even though he was coming. God, was he coming. He couldn't stop coming. One minute. Two. Pulsing and jerking, waves and waves of shocking pleasure that tried to wring him dry. Only there was no more ejaculate. It was like sticking your hand in a socket and having the electric current flowing through your body, refusing to release you from its tenacious grip. Three minutes. Four. And he knew for the first time in his life what it felt like to almost faint. White dots floated across his vision. One last wringing, gasping shudder and breathless curse. Then he was done.

The mattress swayed as Lily left him. And then his hands were free. Wes felt her soft kisses against his fingers as she massaged his wrists and arms. He managed somehow to summon enough energy into his shaking limbs to pull her on top of him. Her light weight sprawled out over him, a soft bundle fitting him perfectly.

"Jesus, Lily," he said when he had enough breath. "What did you do?"

She nuzzled his chin. "That was your Jen-Mo spot, an acupressure point. I can halt your ejaculation by pressing there and draw out your orgasm much longer."

Much longer indeed. He stroked her silky, soft hair. "Did you learn that from the high school girls?"

"No. That I picked up in China." He felt her smile against his neck. "Along with some other interesting bits of information."

An involuntary shudder ran through his poor muscles. "I don't know whether to be happy or afraid." He started to chuckle. "One thing for certain. It's going to be very interesting being married to you."

He turned and cuddled her, spooning her from behind, and asked lazily, "Where do you want to start our lives together? Virginia or New York?"

Lily caressed the back of his hand. "I can either work for the FBI or be a Virginia suburban soccer mom."

Each word was a drip of honey sweetening Wes's heart. And life with her was going to be even sweeter. "God, Lily, I love you."

Take a supernatural, super*sexy* walk on the wild side . . .
with WOLF TALES by Kate Douglas.
Available now . . .

Warmth. The most wonderful sense of warmth, of content- ment. Sighing, Xandi snuggled deeper into the blankets, aware of a slight tingling in her toes and fingers, a sense of heat radiat- ing all around her, of weight and comfort and safety.

And something very large, very long, very solid, wedged tightly between her bare buttocks, following the crease of her labia and resting hot and hard against her clit. She blinked, opened her eyes wide, saw only darkness.

Awake now, she felt soft breath tickling the back of her neck, warm arms encircling her, a hard, muscular body enfold- ing hers. She held herself very still, forcing her fuzzy mind into a clarity it really wasn't ready for. Okay . . . she remembered being been lost in a snowstorm, remembered thinking about building a shelter, remembered . . . nothing. Nothing beyond the sense that it was too late, she was too cold . . . then nothing.

The body behind her shifted. The huge cock—at least that much she recognized—slipped against her clit as the person holding her thrust his hips just a bit closer to hers.

Xandi cleared her throat. Whoever held her had obviously saved her life. Everyone knew more heat was given off by naked bodies, but she'd never really thought of the concept of awakening in the dark, wrapped securely together with a totally unknown naked body. No, that really hadn't entered her mind . . . at least until now.

She fought the need to giggle. Nerves. Had to be nerves. But she felt her labia softening, engorging, knew her clit was beginning to peek out from its little hood of flesh, searching for closer contact with that hot cock. The arms holding her tightened just a bit. One of the hands moved to cover her breast.

Neither one of them spoke. He knew what she looked like. She had no idea who held her. What age he was, what race, what anything.

He saved your life.

There was that. She arched her back, forcing her breast into the huge hand that palmed it. In response, thick fingers compressed the nipple. She bit back a moan. Jared hated it when she made noises during sex.

This isn't Jared, you idiot.

The fingers pinched harder, rolled the turgid flesh between them. *Screw it.* She moaned, at the same time parting her legs just a bit so that she could settle herself on the huge cock that seemed to be growing even larger. Then she tightened her thighs around it, sliding her butt back against his rock-hard belly.

She felt the thick curl of pubic hair tickling her butt, rested against the hard root of his penis where it sprung solidly from his groin and clenched her thighs once again, holding on to him. She felt the air go out of his lungs, then the lightest touch of warm lips against her ear, the soft, exploring tip of his tongue as he circled just the outside, the soft puff of his breath.

Shivers raced along her spine. She wrapped her fingers around his wrists, anchoring herself while at the same time holding both of his hands tightly against her breasts. The hair on his arms was soft, almost silky. She tried to picture her hidden lover, but before an image came to mind, he hmmm'd against her ear, then ran his tongue along the side of her throat.

She felt the sizzle all the way to her pussy, felt his lips exploring her throat, his mobile tongue teasing the wispy little hairs at the back of her neck. His hands massaged her breasts, squeezed her nipples, then rubbed away the pain. His hips pressed against her, forcing his cock to slide very slowly back and forth between her swollen labia.

She moaned again, the sound working its way up and out of her throat before she even recognized it as her own voice. The heat surrounding her intensified. Whoever he was, whoever held her . . . she sighed. He literally radiated fire and warmth and pure carnal lust. One of his big hands slipped down to her belly, cupped her mons and pressed her against him. Still gripping his forearm tightly in her left hand, she felt his finger slide down between her legs.

His fingertip paused at her swollen clit, applying the merest bit of pressure. She held perfectly still, afraid he'd stop if she moved, afraid of her own reaction to this most intimate touch by an absolute stranger. She kept a death grip on the wrist near her breast. The fingers of her right hand dug into the corded tendons on the underside of his forearm, and everything in her cried out to thrust her hips forward, to beg him to stroke her, to bury more than just his finger in the moist heat between her legs.

Instead, as her body trembled with the fierce need to move, she held her hips immobile. After a moment that might have lasted forever, he gently rubbed his fingertip around her clit, dipping inside her wet pussy for some of her moisture, then bringing it back to stroke her once more.

She bit back a scream as his roughened fingertip touched her again, the circular motion so light as to hardly register. Her trembling increased, her desire, her barely controllable need to tilt and force her hips against him, to make him enter her.

She didn't care if he used his cock, his tongue, his finger . . . hell, at this point, he could use his whole fucking hand and it wouldn't be enough. She choked back a whimper as he changed the direction of his massage, moving his fingertip slowly up and down over the small hooded organ. Each stroke took him closer to her pussy. Closer, but not nearly close enough.

Her breath caught in her throat when he dipped inside her, swirled his thick finger around the streaming walls of her pussy, then returned to caress her clit once more. A small part of Xandi's mind reminded her she was being beautifully fucked by a total stranger, that her fingers were clutching thick, muscular arms, that she was clasping her thighs around the biggest cock she'd ever felt in her life—and that they still hadn't exchanged a single word.

It came to her then, in an almost blinding flash of insight, a personal epiphany of pure, carnal need and unmitigated lust, that she'd never, even in her most imaginative fantasy, been this turned on in her entire life. Never felt so tightly linked—mentally, physically, sexually—to anyone. She moaned aloud as his finger once more slipped back between her legs. His thumb stroked her clit now, and that one, thick finger plunged carefully in and out of her weeping flesh.

Suddenly, the hot tip of his tongue traced the whorl of her ear, then dipped inside. Shocked, she thrust her hips forward, forcing his fingers deep. His breath tickled the top of her ear, his tongue swirled the interior, leaving it all hot and damp, filled with lush promise.

She thrust harder against his fingers, still holding one of his hands against her breast, forcing the other deep between her legs. She felt the thick rush of fluid, the hot coil of her climax building, building with each slick thrust of his cock between her thighs, each dip of his fingers, each . . .

Without warning, he rolled her to her stomach, breaking her grip on his forearms as if it were nothing. He grabbed her hips and lifted her. Xandi moaned, spreading her legs wide, welcoming him, begging with her body. Eyes wide open, she saw nothing but darkness, felt no sense of space, lost all concept of time. She quivered, hanging at the precipice of a frightening, endless fall.

His big hands clasped her hips, held her tightly. He massaged her buttocks for a moment with both his thumbs, spreading her cheeks wide. She felt her slick moisture on his fingertip, almost preternaturally aware of each tiny spot on her body where she made contact with his.

She wondered how much he could see, if his night vision was better than hers. It was as dark as the inside of a cave, wherever they were. No matter how hard she tried, she couldn't see the soft bed beneath her, couldn't see her own hands.

Couldn't see his.

Yet the link persisted, the sense of connection, of need, of desire so gut deep it was suddenly part of her existence, of her entire world. A link she knew would be forged forever when he finally entered her, filled her with heat and pulsing need.

He lifted her higher, his hands slipping down to grab her thighs, raising her up so that her knees no longer touched the mattress, so that her weight was on her forearms, her face pressed tightly to the pillow.

She expected his thick cock to fill her pussy. Wanted his cock, now. *Please, now!* Her breath caught in short, wild gasps for air, her legs quivered, and she hung there in his grasp, waiting . . . waiting. Hovering there, held aloft, the cool air drifting across her hot, needy flesh. Waiting for him to fill her.

Instead, she felt him pull away, felt the mattress dip as he shifted his weight . . . felt the fiery wet slide of his tongue between her legs.

"Ahhh . . ." Her cry ended on a whimper. He looped his

arms through her thighs and lifted her even higher, his tongue finding entry into her gushing pussy, his lips grabbing at her engorged labia, suckling each fleshy lip into his hot mouth. He nibbled and sucked, spearing her with his tongue, nipping at her with sharp teeth, then laving her with soft, warm strokes. Suddenly his lips encircled her clit, and he suckled, hard, pressing down on the sensitive little organ with his tongue.

The scream exploded out of her. She clamped her legs against the sides of his head, peripherally aware of scratchy whiskers, strong jaw. His tongue lapped and twisted, filling her streaming pussy, as she bucked against him. He was strong, stronger than any man she'd ever known, holding her aloft, eating her out like a hungry beast, his mouth all lips and tongue and hard-edged teeth.

He dragged his tongue across her clit once more, suckled her labia between his lips and brought her to another clenching, screaming climax. Once more, licking her now, long, slow sweeps from clit to anus, each stroke taking her higher, farther. His tongue snaked across her flesh, dipping inside to lap at her moist center, tickling her sensitive clit, ringing the tight sphincter in her ass. Gasping, shivering, her legs trembling, Xandi struggled for breath, reached for yet another climax.

He left her there, once more on the edge. Cool air brushed across her damp flesh, raising goose bumps across her thighs and belly.

He lowered her until her knees once more rested on the bed. She felt his hot thighs pressing against her own, his big hands clasping her hips, the broad, velvety soft tip of his cock resting at the mouth of her vagina.

Slowly, with great care and control, he pushed into her. Damn, he was huge. She shifted her legs, relaxed her spasming muscles as best she could. Still, her flesh stretched, the lubrication from her orgasms easing the way as he slowly, inexorably, seated himself within her.

She felt him press up against the mouth of her womb at the same time his balls nestled against her clit and pubic mound. He waited a moment, giving her time to adjust to his huge girth and length, then he started to move.

Slowly at first, easing his way in, then out, stretching her, filling her. Xandi fisted the pillow in her hands as she caught his rhythm. In, out, in again, his balls tickling her clit with each careful thrust. She pressed back against him, forcing him deeper, inviting him.

He groaned, then slammed into her harder. She took him, reveled in the power and strength of her mystery lover, felt another climax beginning to build, knew she would not go alone this time.

She reached back between her legs, grasping his lightly furred sac between her fingers just as he thrust hard against her cervix. His strangled cry encouraged her. Grinning, feeling empowered—feminine and so very strong—she squeezed him gently in the palm of her hand, felt his balls contract, tighten, draw up close to his body.

She slipped one finger behind his sac, pressed the sensitive area, then ran her sharp fingernail lightly back to his testicles. He slammed into her, his body rigid with a fierce power. Shouting a warrior's cry of victory, he pounded into her harder, stronger. She kept a tight but careful hold on his balls, until the hot gush of his seed filled her.

Overwhelmed, overstimulated, she screamed and thrust her hips hard against his groin. Her vaginal muscles clamped down, wrapping around his cock, trapping and holding him close. Suddenly, he filled her even more, his cock swelling to fit tightly against the clenching muscles of her pussy, locking his body close against hers.

Linking the two of them together. A binding deeper than the act itself, more powerful than anything she'd ever known.

He slumped across her back, then rolled to his side, taking

Xandi with him. She felt the hot burst of his gasping breath, the rhythmic pulsing of his cock, the pounding of her own heart. Suddenly, inexplicably exhausted, her pussy rippling against the heat of his still amazingly engorged penis, Xandi snuggled close to his rock-hard body and allowed her eyes to drift slowly shut.

Tomorrow. She'd learn who he was tomorrow.

Elegant. Decadent. And very, very sexy.
That's THREE, by Noelle Mack.
Available now . . .

"I want to make you wait, love. Does it excite you to watch in this way?"

"Yes," Fiona whispered.

The woman in the window turned from the mirror and went back to the bed, rummaging through the drawers of the night-stand. She took out a huge penis of ivory, with attached balls made of softer stuff, round and heavy, which swayed in the air when she gave them a playful slap.

"Ah. Now for some devilish good play." Thomas's voice roughened with male lust.

Then the woman settled back on the bed and spread her legs more widely than before, touching each bottom bedpost with an elegantly arched foot. Fiona and Thomas had an excellent view, despite the flickering of the candles next to the bed.

They watched her slide the ivory rod in and out, vigorously thrusting it into her snug pussy, obviously enjoying the bounce of the stuffed leather balls against her arse cheeks. Then, with-out further ado, she twisted up and around, turning her bum to them and holding the false penis. The sudden screwing motion seemed to excite her even more.

The woman crouched on her knees, reaching back between her thighs to slide the thing in even deeper, but the last inch or so of the thick ivory rod, gleaming white, stuck out from her swollen nether lips.

"I would love nothing more than to see you push that dildo in for her," Thomas said into Fiona's ear.

"We must be content to watch," Fiona replied. She heard Thomas gasp when the woman began to rock on all fours, making the dangling balls swing and slap hard upon her cunny.

He could stand it no longer. He rammed his cock into Fiona, all the way. She thrust back against him, matching his strokes, employing the same rhythm as the woman they watched, to give him even more stimulation.

Then . . . they both stopped when a door opened in the room of the house a cross the street and a tall, well-built man entered, quite naked.

"Perhaps he was watching her as well from the closet or the next room," Thomas said softly, holding Fiona still once more but growing even larger inside her.

Fiona nodded. The woman, half-crazy with pleasure, didn't even notice that she was no longer alone. Her face, when they could glimpse it, was wet with sweat, close to the ultimate satisfaction she craved, giving herself deep, repeated thrusts of the dildo and harder slaps from the attached balls, her mouth open in a moan.

Fiona could see that the woman's eyes were closed, until she felt the man who had entered her room caress her cheek. She raised her head, eyes wide to see his enormous erection was only an inch away from her panting lips.

Thomas began to slide in and out of Fiona's pussy again, with tantalizing slowness but he speeded up when he saw the woman take the other man's cock into her mouth and begin to suck greedily, as if it were the most delicious thing on earth.

Unattended, the ivory penis fell out, pulled down by the heavy balls. The man took his cock from her mouth, withdrawing slowly as the woman tightened her full lips around him, reluctant to let him go. Her lover or master or whoever he was grabbed the ivory one to replace his, putting it in her mouth and making her taste her own juices. The woman licked the long dildo clean, looking up at the man with lascivious affection, eager to arouse him even more.

She succeeded. The man took the dildo away and stroked her tangled hair, her back, her haunches, as if soothing her . . . or preparing her for what he wanted to do next.

Then he turned around, spreading her buttocks wide open and resting his big hands upon them while Fiona and Thomas watched, transfixed. They strained to see, joined and moving in a way that made Thomas bite his lower lip to keep from ejaculating straightaway. "What next?"

"I think I know," Fiona said softly.

The woman kept her arse up but buried her face in the pillows.

"Yes," Fiona breathed. "She loves to play the wanton. And she loves extreme stimulation. He will give her what she craves, Thomas. Just you wait."

"I cannot restrain myself much longer," he growled. "Do keep still!" He clasped Fiona's hips even more tightly. "But do keep talking . . . the sound of your voice is as erotic as the show . . ." He ended with a low moan.

"A man's firm hand upon her soft flesh is what she wants," Fiona went on in a whisper calculated to arouse. "A man who will discipline her but with such gentleness that her resistance melts not from fear but from opening her soul to the one who thus commands her."

As if the man in the opposite room had heard, he curved a strong arm around the waiting woman's hips and gave her a long, sensual, and very thorough spanking with his free hand while she cried out her pleasure and her gratitude for his skill. Then he got on his knees behind her, plunging his very real and thickly satisfying cock into the woman, stroking her sensitized buttocks with especial tenderness to take her to climax at last. The lovers reached the moment at the same second, rocking so closely together that they seemed to be one being, not two, and collapsed upon the bed, twined around each other, lost in erotic bliss.

Men this hot are irresistible! Take a sneak peek at
GOTTA HAVE IT, by Renée Alexis.
Available now . . .

Marc moved in next to her, lacing his hand up and down the silkiness of her skirt. "Please, Caroline. I really want to be with you now that you're not in my imagination." He slid his hand under her skirt and stroked her smooth upper thighs just above her garter. "You're right here with me, and you smell so damn good." He kissed her earlobe. "Come home with me. I won't force anything on you. We can do whatever you want to do."

The way he was making her feel, she'd have clearly jumped into a pool of stingrays with him. "What . . . what about my ticket?"

He placed the credit card in her hand. "Let's get it changed, and if nothing's available, I'll let you go, or drive you there myself. Please! I want to make love to you so badly that I can taste you. I can still feel your breasts in my hands, your tongue winding around mine. Your flavor is still on my fingers and I'm just shy of sucking them to regain that sensuous aroma."

"Marc . . ." No one alive or dead ever said that to her and in the way he said it. Marc had a way with words and sex, and if his tactics developed the way his body had over the years, she'd never leave Lake Shore Drive. Her life would be spent within his world.

She didn't know if it was her mind playing games with her or if Marc's fingers really found her spot. Without thinking, her hand lowered, landing on top of his and from that point on her hand guided his movements. Her thick moisture saturated both her hand and his as his fingers swirled around her clit, stroking it with smooth, precise caresses. He inched deeper inside filling her. She could hear her own moisture mixing with his movements and the sound alone made her quiver and constrict around him. "Marc, Marc . . . please . . ."

His voice tickled her ears. "Come home with me, Caroline. Take me out of this misery."

The protrusion busting his pants apart beckoned her, and her hand gripped the clothed swollen gland, working it, manipulating it until he could barely stand the pressure. Their mouths met with steam and passion, nibbling on lips separated from each other for way too long. His mouth temporarily broke free from hers, trailing across to her earlobe, then down her neck. His breathy voice pursued. "Let's buy your ticket because that late plane will not be seeing you today."

Without any hesitation, Caroline followed her captor through the bar, leaving a half devoured Blue Crush on the table. Hand in hand, they approached the Delta Airlines ticket agent and made the exchange with ease.

With a new departure date the following morning, Caroline happily skipped out of Midway Airport with Marc Brown by her side. They reached his Porsche and she stared in wonder. "You see, this is what money does for you."

"Anytime you want it, it's yours."

She smoothed her hand along the jet-black auto. "No, what I really want is the man driving it. That's all I've ever wanted, Marc."

"Then your life is made because there's no way in fucking hell you're getting rid of me." He unlocked the door and helped her inside. Her skirt slid up her leg as she entered the vehicle and Marc's tongue practically wagged out of control. *Lord, get me and that girl him fast before I explode!*

The tour along Lake Shore Drive was amazing. She'd seen it many times, but never from Marc's window. It was a beautiful, sunny day, a more perfect day hadn't been created, and what made it absolutely perfect was that she was spending it in Marc's arms. The minute they entered his mansion, she knew she'd wrap herself around him so tightly that they'd make the first human rubberband. She could actually feel Marc sliding that hulking thick meat into her and shattering what was left of her sanity. That was what she needed. No man in her past left an impression upon her the way he did with one evening in a shower. From that point on in her life, wherever she moved to, she made sure the shower was on jam!

Marc took her mind from her bathroom orgasm. "Hey, pretty girl. Whatcha thinkin' about?"

The side of her dainty little mouth perked up. "I don't think you want to know that."

"Now I really want to know."

Her hand stroked his inner tight. "Well, I was thinking about showers." She faced him bluntly. "And I don't mean rain showers."

"Girl, I like the sound of that. So tell me, what were we doing in the shower?"

"I didn't get into it that deeply, but there's something about showers that turns me out!" Her hand moved from his leg, to his groin, on to his stomach and caressed his chest. He was still so soft, baby flesh, like she remembered from years ago. "You still feel so good."

"I think it's that aftershave I advertise."

"I have seen that commercial. Sexy, sexy as can be."

"So, finish that shower thing you went off on."

"I was just wondering how it would be making love to you in your shower. I'm sure you have many."

"I have four, and I plan to christen you in all of them."

Her hand moved back to his erection, stroking it, making the linen pants material cause friction against it. She loved the way his eyes glowed from her affection; how his muscles tensed, the degree of heat emitting from those pants. Heat wasn't exactly the only thing she wanted from those pants; she wanted fire, steam, white-hot lava and she wanted it dripping slowly and thickly down his shaft. She tugged at his zipper, then eyed him. "May I?"

"God! Yes."

There was no one on the tree-lined street but them and his Porsche, so he pulled to the side of road. "Why wait for the shower when we can get wet right here?"

"Ummm, I like how you talk, Mr. Marc Brown, king of the Sox bullpen."

"I want to be your king, your every-damn-thing, pretty girl!"

With his hand covering hers, they slid his zipper down. Before the zipper was at half-mast, his tight, seething erection was trying to bust apart all that was in its way. To tease Marc into exquisite hardness, her tongue darted at the clothed tip, rubbing wetly against the roughness of the Hanes briefs. Marc was ready to go into spasms just from the friction of underwear and her mouth. The feast d' resistance came when she totally took the covered shaft into her mouth, sucking the damp material, making it cling against his rod.

Watching Caroline dine on him made his breathing quicken, his stomach heaved in and out. Her other hand raised his shirt, stroked soft thick flesh and muscles—taming his breathing. His words worked on her as she worked on him. "Damn, this is so fucking good, Caroline. Don't stop . . . don't stop." He reached down and delivered his shaft from the wet material while reclining the bucket seat.

Exposed to her hungry eyes was a shaft so beautiful and cinnamon brown that she almost came. Her fingers glided up and down the thick, rigid erection as it continued to pulsate. The sight of it took her breath away. It'd been so long since her beloved Marc was in her arms; just knowing she'd never mix with him again, never feel any real love from him. But as she stroked his molten flesh, she knew it was real, Marc was real, and her dreams were about to come true again.

He beckoned her. "Take it, darling."

More than just words, it was action. Caroline's mouth started at his tip, feasting on it, tenderizing it before she dove in for the rest. Marc stroked it up and down for her satisfaction, and his, as her mouth sank deeper and deeper in it. His thick veins tickled her inner cheeks and throat and she smiled over the fact that he was still way different from what she remembered in her dad's medical book. He was an awakening, then and now.

Marc's hips pumped to her rhythm, forcing the shaft deep within her mouth. She was taking it, taking it all but found her comfort zone at the plump, rounded tip. She sipped him, as though he were a fine wine and watched as he erupted from her hand action. He slumped in the seat, staring at his glorious princess. "You are so incredible, Caroline. How'd you learn to do that?"

"I had a good teacher—you. You made me want to be good at it."

"But we only did it once."

"Good teachers need only teach a lesson once."

He kissed her in a long, sucking motion, getting his fill of her before pulling away. "Sit on me. Let me feel what it's like again to be with you. You were so good."

"I was a virgin."

"That meant you were a natural. Come on, sit on me."